# THE RECIPIENT

by
Shail Rajan

Name: Shail Rajan, author
Title: The Recipient/Shail Rajan
Identifiers: ISBN-13: 978-0-578-37167-2 (paperback)
Subjects: BISAC | FICTION / Romance / Suspense |
FICTION / Romance / Contemporary


Printed in the United States of America.

*For my readers...you have made chasing this dream more incredible than I ever expected.*

*For my family...the best travel companions I could have hoped for on this journey.*

*And always for mom.*

# CONTENTS

# PROLOGUE

"Hey, babe."

"Hi. Are you on your way home?"

"Yup, I should be there in another ten minutes."

"Any ideas on what to have for dinner?"

"Want to grill something? Eat out on the back patio, enjoy a glass of wine?"

"Mmmm, that sounds perfect."

"Great, I'll see you in a few. I love you, Katherine Claire."

"I love you, Robert Patrick."

Robert disconnected the speaker phone and waited for the traffic light. Thinking about the relaxing evening ahead with his new wife made him smile.

The light turned green, and he started to ease through the intersection. An unexpected flash of movement on his left made him turn his head quickly. His mind barely registered the large pickup truck with no headlights on barreling towards him. His heart, however, knew he would never see the love of his life again.

# PART 1

*Six Years Later*

# CHAPTER 1

## The House on Willow Avenue

As the rock ballad came to an end, the DJ chimed in, "I don't know about you, but that song gets me every time I hear it. It was off the first album by Mirrors, one of my all-time favorite bands. The newest album has been panned by critics but has still gone multi-platinum. Too bad Jett Vanders, the lead singer, seems to be focused more on partying than making music. Looks like the band may be cancelling the rest of their world tour dates so that he can 'rest.' Anyway, enough with me letting the real world infringe on our idyllic little bubble. Okay, let's see, it's just a few minutes before eight, which means it's time for a quick word on the weather and an update on your commute. First, the weather: sunny and cold. And now, the commute: there is no traffic anywhere. Just another one of the reasons I love living in Sycamore Ridge! All right, folks, back to the music. Here's another great tune you can sing along with. Enjoy!"

Kacie turned up the radio and started singing along rather loudly and, truth be told, rather badly. Fortunately, no one was around to hear her. As her mother was fond of teasing, "You can't hold a tune to save your life, but I love that you sing with gusto!"

As she turned right onto Willow Avenue, Kacie tapped

her hands on the steering wheel in time with the music, in no rush to get to work. This portion of her fifteen-minute "commute" along the beautiful tree-lined street was her favorite. The stately homes ran the gamut of architectural styles, from classic bungalows and Craftsman to the grander Tudors and Colonials and were set far back from the road with broad sweeping lawns and flower beds that were patiently waiting for warmer weather. A light dusting of morning frost was still visible on the lawns, and everything shone in the sunlight.

As she rounded a slight curve, Kacie looked forward to seeing her favorite home, a sprawling light gray Colonial with black shutters. The curving driveway led up a gentle incline to a three-car garage and intersected with a walkway leading to the welcoming white front door.

It had been several years since the original owners had lived there. Kacie had never met them, but she had heard through the town grapevine that the elderly couple, married for over 60 years, had passed away within a few short months of each other. The house had been left to their only child, a hot-shot entertainment lawyer on the West Coast, who had made a couple of feeble attempts at bringing his family to the house for short vacations. Unfortunately, his teenaged children had not been interested in spending their breaks in a rural town, and frankly, neither had he. He had stopped pushing the issue, and eventually, they had stopped coming to the house altogether. Oddly, though, he seemed in no rush to sell it, either.

Kacie sighed. Not that she could afford a house like that, and she certainly didn't need all that space for only herself and Cooper. It just made her feel sad that such a beautiful house couldn't become home to a nice family.

"Oh, what have we here?" Kacie asked aloud to no one. A nondescript four-door sedan, a rental from the looks of it, was parked on the street in front of the house and a couple was standing nearby it on the front lawn looking up towards the beautiful home.

Despite numerous admonitions about curiosity and the cat, Kacie couldn't help herself and pulled up behind the car to see if she could be of assistance.

"Hi there, can I help you?" she asked, stepping out of her car.

The woman, dressed in intimidating stiletto heeled boots, managed to walk gracefully across the lawn towards Kacie and asked in a snide and impatient tone, "Are you Walter?"

Kacie, not one to take things lying down, cocked her eyebrow at the woman as she appraised her. In addition to the stylish yet impractical boots, she was dressed well in a beautifully tailored off-white, long winter coat that was unbuttoned to reveal a slim figure clad in skintight jeans and a black turtleneck sweater. Her makeup was impeccable, the kind that looked natural but in reality took a long time to apply. Her long blonde hair was tied up in a harsh ponytail and straightened and sprayed in such a way that not one single hair dared pop out of place.

"Cut it out, Lindsay," the gentleman said as he walked over to join the two women. At just that moment, Lindsay's phone rang, and she immediately answered it. The only words Kacie heard her say as she was walking away were, "Did you do it exactly the way I told you? Because I expect nothing less than perfection."

"Sorry about that. Our flight got in really late last night, and we had to get an early start this morning. I'm Robert Wilkens." He held out his hand, and Kacie took it with some relief that he seemed to be a normal person.

"Kacie Nolan, nice to meet you."

"Pleasure," Robert smiled. Like Lindsay, he was also well dressed. But unlike Lindsay, his smile appeared genuine. It reached his grey eyes and made a few crow lines appear. Based on the smattering of grey hair at his temples, Kacie guessed his age to be late forties, maybe early fifties. He was tall and seemed to have managed to avoid developing the paunch that so many men his age sported.

"I'm pretty sure the owners aren't home," Kacie said gesturing towards the house. "They hardly ever come here anymore."

"Actually, I'm hoping to become the new owner."

"Oh? I didn't know the house was on the market. Are you sure you have the right address?"

"Yup. The owner, Stephan, is a friend of a friend. Somehow word got around that I was looking to purchase a vacation home that was relatively off the grid, and he called me last week saying he might be interested in selling if the offer was right. I guess he contacted someone named," here he paused to look at his phone, "let's see... here it is. A real estate agent named Walter Reid. He was supposed to meet us here at 8:15."

"I know Walter. If he says he's going to be somewhere, he'll definitely show up." Kacie checked her watch, "It's only 8:08 right now."

"True," Robert chuckled, "and very precise. Do you live around here?"

"I've only lived in Sycamore Ridge for the past few years, but I consider it my home. My family lives a short drive from here."

"Nice. I grew up about two hours away from here, and we have a lot of emotional ties to this area. It's funny, I hadn't even heard about Sycamore Ridge until last week. This street reminds me so much of the neighborhood my family lived in when we were kids. I'd love to give my own family a chance to experience this lifestyle."

"It's a great place to live. I wouldn't want to be anywhere else."

"Would you mind if I ask you some questions about the town? I didn't have much time to research the house or the surrounding area before coming out here."

Kacie smiled. "Absolutely. You'll find that most people around here always have at least a few minutes to chat. Walter did some work on the house a few years back, so he'll be able to tell you all about the home and the property, but I can answer just about any question you have about the town. What would you like to know?"

"Anything you can tell me, really. How about a quick sales pitch? Pretend you're trying to convince me to move here."

"I can certainly try." Kacie took a moment to collect her thoughts and then launched into a topic on which she was knowledgeable and of which she was extremely proud.

"As you know, we're about a two-hour drive from the city and the international airport and about an hour from two well-known universities. For a lot of people, those distances are detractors. But for the folks who choose to live here, they're one of the huge pluses. In the grand scheme of things, two hours isn't a lot if you really need to get somewhere. And for staff and professors at the university, it puts just enough distance between them and their students. Our location makes a huge difference in the type of people who make Sycamore Ridge their home."

Kacie paused for a moment to gauge Robert's reaction.

He appeared to be listening intently to what she was saying, so she continued. "When the trend towards working remotely first took off, everyone was looking at homes within a 30-minute drive of the city. Then property prices started spiking, so people pushed out to within an hour of the city. But they weren't willing to go past that, even when the traffic started getting bad, prices increased, and space decreased. We cater to people who really want to be 'off the grid' but with access to a lot of great amenities like restaurants, spas, outdoor space, hiking trails. Here, we have managed to find a great balance: little to no traffic, decent property values, plenty of open space, and, most importantly a small-town feel."

Robert was duly impressed at how smoothly Kacie's "impromptu" pitch seemed to roll off her tongue, and he told her as much. "Wow...I almost feel like you've practiced that."

Now it was Kacie's turn to chuckle. "How'd I do?"

Just as Robert was saying "great," they heard a car approaching and both turned to see a dark green, vintage pickup truck turning into the driveway. The word Sally had been elaborately painted in white on the passenger side door.

"8:12. Early, as I expected."

"All right, that's my cue." Smiling, Robert reached out his hand and took Kacie's once again. "It really was great meeting you. And thanks for the sales pitch!"

He started to walk away and then turned back. "One more question...you mentioned there's a small-town feel. How does that translate into respecting people's privacy? That's a really important reason for why I'm looking at more rural locations."

"I think you'll find people are generally helpful and

friendly, like in many small towns. But most of our residents live here because they also value their own privacy. I believe they are largely respectful of others' privacy, as well."

"Fair enough." Robert smiled at her one more time and then nodded his head in the direction of Walter's car. "I'd better head on over there before Lindsay bites Walter's head off, too."

Unfortunately for Walter, Robert didn't head over quickly enough.

∞∞∞

Walter got out of his truck and attempted to straighten out his outdated suit. It was already a bit snug and now it was wrinkled, too. He wondered for the hundredth time that morning whether the suit made him look like his grandpa. Maybe he should have just dressed in his favorite pair of jeans and his worn denim shirt. *Oh well,* he thought. *Too late now. Anyway, they're here to see the house, not me.*

Turning towards the street, he saw a woman confidently striding towards him in high heeled boots while snapping orders at some unfortunate soul on the other end of her cell phone. There were some sharp dressers in Sycamore Ridge, but this woman put them to shame. Her elegant clothes and impeccable appearance made Walter think she had probably never seen a wrinkle in her life. Women like her tended to make Walter nervous. Walter almost chuckled out loud as he admitted to himself that truth be told, most women made him nervous. He could feel himself starting to sweat, and as she got closer, he realized that not only was she perfectly dressed, but she was also quite beautiful. His sweat glands immediately jumped into overdrive mode. Worried that she would hold out her hand to shake his, Walter made a feeble attempt at wiping his palms on his crinkled-up suit jacket without her noticing.

He was off to a very shaky start. Walter reminded himself to take a deep calming breath in and out as she closed the distance between them. *Calm down, Walter,* he thought. *You need this sale and the commission. For Sally.*

The woman stopped in front of him but continued with her phone call.

"Did you get the list I sent you? It's all clearly laid out there, and none of it is up for negotiation," she snapped. "If you can't do it, I can find someone in a heartbeat to replace you. Someone who understands how important my clients are." She angrily tapped the end call button without saying goodbye.

"Walter Reid?" she asked. The way she said his name made him feel almost ashamed. Like he had something slimy hanging out of his nose. She held her perfectly manicured hand out, and Walter stared at it for a moment.

"Yes," he said hesitantly, resisting the urge to wipe his nose before taking her hand in his. Her skin was soft and cool, and again, Walter found himself resisting another urge: the urge to raise her hand to his lips and kiss the back of it ever so softly.

"I'm Lindsay Waller." They shook hands briefly, and Walter got the distinct impression that she was contemplating whether to wipe her hand on her coat. He could feel beads of sweat starting to form at his hairline and was suddenly grateful that he had on his wrinkly suit jacket to hide the unseemly sweat stains that were undoubtedly forming on his shirt.

"Why don't we wait for my partner to join us before starting the house tour?" Lindsay turned her attention away from Walter and back towards the end of the driveway where Robert was standing, still apparently deep in conversation with the woman who had stopped to "help" them. Not a fan of small towns in general, Lindsay wondered to herself what kind of person would randomly stop on the street when they were on their way somewhere just to talk to two complete strangers. And she wondered, not for the first time, how Robert could manage to be lured into conversations with just about anyone he met. Sighing, she turned back towards Walter and almost laughed aloud at his obvious discomfort.

Walter was not a bad looking man, she thought. He had eager, bright blue eyes and wavy blonde hair that was rather unfashionably styled and desperately in need of a cut. His wrinkled suit jacket was unbuttoned and worn over a traditional white collared shirt that hosted a small smudge of what looked like strawberry jelly just between the top two buttons. His belt was on one notch too tight, as if that would help hold in his slight paunch. And his shoes, well, his shoes made Lindsay cringe.

Despite all of that, Lindsay could tell that with some well-tailored clothes, a little exercise, and a new haircut, Walter would be quite good looking. She had a knack for style and a penchant for before-and-afters. Her makeover fantasy was interrupted when her phone started ringing again. She glanced at the screen to see who was calling and excused herself to take the call. "I need to take this. Get started without me."

Walter breathed a sigh of relief and hoped that Lindsay's partner, who was finally making his way up the driveway, was nicer than she was.

∞∞∞

"Hi, Walter?" The man had a confidence and elegance about him similar to Lindsay's, but there was something kind about his face which put Walter immediately at ease.

"Yes, you must be Robert. Good to meet you." The two men shook hands. "I see you've already met our mayor."

Confused, Robert asked, "How's that?"

"Kacie. The woman you were just talking to. She's the mayor of Sycamore Ridge."

"Well, that explains it," Robert mumbled almost to himself. "She didn't mention it."

"I'm not surprised. Let me guess, she was driving by and saw your car? Got out to see if you needed any help?"

Robert nodded.

"That's Kacie for you. Always trying to be helpful. She's a big reason Sycamore Ridge is such a great place to live." Switching gears and feeling his confidence returning, Walter asked, "Shall we get started?"

And without waiting for an answer, he led Robert towards the front door and began describing the property with almost as much knowledge and pride as Kacie had described Sycamore Ridge.

∞∞∞

Kacie was stripping faded olive green paint off an antique, five-drawer dresser she was refurbishing when the bell on her workshop door chimed. She looked up to see Walter balancing two cups of coffee and a light blue pastry box. The sight made her mouth water.

"Rebekah's? Wow, what's the occasion?" Kacie asked.

Walter smiled at his friend, who was almost unrecognizable hidden behind her layers of safety gear. "Take off

14

your equipment and come on over," he said. "I'll tell you all about it."

Kacie was dying to get her hands on the contents of the blue box. She quickly took off her safety goggles, respiratory mask, and heavy-duty rubber gloves. As she walked over to the small seating area where Walter was waiting, the heavenly smell of coffee and freshly baked pastries wafted to her nose.

Walter handed her one of the coffee cups. "Lots of cream and two sugars, just the way you like it."

Kacie removed the lid from her cup, blew on the piping hot beverage and gingerly took a sip, waiting with almost childlike anticipation as she watched Walter open the box. He reached inside and handed Kacie her favorite pastry, a golden, flaky, buttery, cinnamon-y morning bun delicately seasoned with just a hint of yuzu peel. "You are not going to believe it."

Kacie, not being able to control her craving any longer, took a bite of the bun and asked through her full mouth covered in sugar and cinnamon, "You sold the house?"

"I didn't just sell it, I sold it for fifteen percent over the appraised value. But honestly, I can't really take any credit for it. I guess that was the agreement that Robert and Stephan had struck before Robert even came out to see the house. Stephan basically gave him right of first refusal. If he didn't like the house, he could walk away. But if he did, he'd have to pay a premium to keep Stephan from putting the house on the market. I almost felt bad for Robert, seems like a good guy. But he did not hesitate at the price and made a full cash offer with a quick close. Apparently, they want to get a bunch of renovations done inside of six weeks."

"That's fantastic! Congratulations!" Kacie smiled

through another mouthful. If anyone deserved a little happiness, she thought, it was Walter. He and Sally had been through so much the past couple of years. Kacie was thrilled for his success.

"And get this, when Robert found out that I used to be a general contractor, he convinced me to handle the renovations. I hesitated at first because I really want to focus on building up my real estate business, but when he told me how much work they wanted to get done, I figured it was worth it. Besides, I don't have any other listings right now."

Kacie sighed as she took another big bite of her morning bun. "I'm so happy for you. For both you and Sally." Licking her fingers, she asked, "Is it just me or do these get better every time Rebekah makes them? Delicious."

Walter smiled. Kacie was one of his dearest friends in the world, and even though he knew she was genuinely happy for him, he also knew she was even happier with a morning bun in her hand.

"What kind of work does he want you to do on the house?" Kacie asked, between another bite and a sip of the steaming hot coffee.

"Tear out the entire kitchen. Cabinets, countertops, appliances. The works."

"Didn't Stephan do a renovation a few years back to persuade his family to come out to the house? Seems like a waste."

"He did, but he didn't get around to touching the kitchen. I tried to convince him that a full kitchen renovation would add to the value of his house, but he said no one ever cooked, so why should he waste his money on renovating a room no one would use."

Kacie rolled her eyes and took another bite. She tried to

pace herself, but it was useless.

"The floors and bathrooms are in great shape. They spent a lot of money on the master bathroom and the finished basement."

"I remember you telling me something about that. So, what else is there for you to do besides the kitchen?"

"Oh, not much," Walter said nonchalantly. "Just tearing down the pool house and building a new guest house." His comment had the effect he was expecting.

Kacie almost choked on her last bite as she exclaimed with her mouth full, "A guest house? You mean with a kitchen, bathroom, bedroom, everything?"

"Everything."

"In six weeks?"

It wasn't until then that the reality of how much work he had to do really sunk in. Walter stuffed the last of his morning bun into his mouth, mumbled a hasty goodbye and practically ran out of Kacie's shop to get things started.

# CHAPTER 2

## *Fountain Walk*

As Robert turned onto Willow Avenue, he couldn't help but smile at the heartwarming nostalgia the wide, tree-lined street elicited. It was so much like the streets in the neighborhood where he had grown up. The large, stately homes and even larger yards reminded him of all the time he had spent playing outdoors with his siblings and the other neighborhood children. There was something peaceful and safe about the memory. And both of those things had been at the very top of his list of priorities for finding a new home.

Robert couldn't believe it had already been two weeks since he had bought the house. He had been looking forward to making this quick overnight trip to Sycamore Ridge ever since then so that he could get to know the neighborhood and its residents a bit more. He was also very eager to see how the renovations were coming along. A longer stay would have been ideal, but his schedule just didn't allow for it.

For a brief moment, Robert wondered if he would remember which house he had bought. The decision had been so spontaneous, and he had hoped it had also been the right one. As he drove slowly down the street, a driveway up ahead lined with pickup trucks, including a dark green vintage one with the word Sally painted on it, was as good as a signal marker pointing to his new home.

Now that the house was before him, Robert was certain he had made the right decision. It was also quite obvious he had made the right decision in hiring Walter, based solely on the number of trucks in the driveway.

Robert realized he was actually looking quite forward to meeting with Walter again. He had made a strong first impression on Robert when he was showing the house. And while he had been a bit awkward when Lindsay was around, he certainly seemed to be very knowledgeable about the house and somehow gave Robert the sense that he was both honest and hardworking.

As soon as the terms of the sale were finalized, Robert had decided to go with his gut and asked Walter to oversee all the renovations. Despite some initial hesitation, Walter had agreed, and Robert couldn't have been happier with his decision. While he had never really believed that Walter would be able to complete all of the renovations within the agreed upon six-week window, all his preconceptions about things moving at a slow pace in small towns went out the window thanks in large part to Walter's aggressive renovation timeline and extensive connections in Sycamore Ridge. He seemed to know everyone and anyone who could help move things along.

Within a week after buying the house, Robert had entered into a contract with a local architecture and design firm recommended by Walter. Technically, Robert thought, it hadn't exactly been a recommendation. More like a directive. According to Walter, this firm was the best in the business, there was no one else who could do the job right, and there was no one else who he would work with. He hadn't really left Robert much choice in the matter. Within a surprisingly short time, blueprints and plans had been drafted, revised, and approved, and demolition had already begun.

As he pulled into the driveway, Robert was pleased by the general buzz of activity as people unloaded trucks and moved busily about the property.

"Can I help you?" an older man with a large toolbelt around his waist and work gloves on asked suspiciously as Robert stepped out of his car.

"I'm looking for Walter."

"You the new owner?"

"Something like that," Robert replied.

The man looked him over and apparently decided he wasn't from the IRS or the mob and gestured towards the back of the house with his head. "He's out back overseeing demo on the pool house."

"Thanks."

"You may want to be careful back there. Wouldn't want you to ruin those fancy shoes."

Robert smiled and walked in the direction the man had pointed, thinking maybe there was a bit of small town about Sycamore Ridge after all.

ooo000

"You've made a lot of progress, Walter. I've been through a couple of major home remodels, and I'm impressed with how smoothly things are going." The two men were standing in the backyard watching half a dozen subcontractors going about their projects.

A steady, low buzzing sound began and one of the workers called out from the side of the house, "Sorry about the noise, Walter." He was wearing a bright yellow cap and matching bright yellow t shirt which were both emblazoned with the words Pool Guy.

"We have to get the pool drained so we can get the repairs done on time. You may want to talk inside the main house."

Walter gave the Pool Guy a thumbs up and started walking towards the house. Raising his voice in order to be heard over the din, he said, "Your...uhhh...partner, Ms. Waller? She's been clear about the importance of staying on time whenever I talk to her." Then he quietly added under his breath, "Which seems to be every five minutes." The comment wasn't meant for Robert's ears, but Robert's hearing was good enough that he caught the gist of what Walter had mumbled.

Walter didn't bother to mention that he broke out in a sweat each time Lindsay's number popped up on his phone screen. While he had plenty of experience dealing with demanding and often unreasonable clients before, dealing with Lindsay was a different story altogether. She was never rude per se, but she was exacting, thorough, precise. She expected him to know the answer to every question the moment she asked it, and she did not like to be surprised by any unexpected or unforeseen circumstances. Fortunately for Walter, he was very good at his job and that seemed to be mollifying her. At least for now.

Robert could see both the quality and quantity of work Walter was doing, and although he wanted to tell him not to worry too much about Lindsay, he knew that would be a mistake. Lindsay's strength lay in her ability to keep people on their toes, and Robert was not about to take that away from her. He needed this renovation completed on time. And if making Walter sweat a little was what it took, then so be it. "Lindsay is very good at her job."

She might be good at her job, Walter thought, but Robert was the one writing the checks and he was much more pleasant to deal with. "How long are you in town?"

"Just for the day. I have a meeting with the designer later this afternoon, and I thought I'd take some time to check out downtown."

"You should stop by Kacie's office. She loves to give new residents tours of Sycamore Ridge."

∞∞∞

Following Walter's clear and simple directions, Robert drove the short distance to a sprawling red brick building which, according to the sign outside, housed the town library, mayor's office, town court, and police station.

He parked his rental car and entered a set of double doors located next to the lot which led him straight into the library. It was much larger than he expected and appeared to be very well funded. Rows and rows of shelves were filled to overflowing with books, computer stations were scattered throughout the expansive room, along with tables and comfortable looking chairs. Dozens of patrons were milling about and quietly talking, yet somehow, the gentle, familiar hush that seemed to pervade all libraries was being maintained.

The quiet was suddenly broken by the faux whisper of a young child telling her mommy that she needed to go potty. Robert turned towards the sound which had come from a large alcove with an arched opening capped with a colorful sign above which welcomed visitors to enter Storyland.

Not seeing any apparent signs for the mayor's office, Robert walked up to the circulation desk where two young women were chatting amiably. They simultaneously looked up at his approach.

"Hi, I'm Shelby. Can I help you?" asked one.

Shelby's slightly frizzy brown hair appeared to be fighting against some sort of band which was meant to keep it at bay, and Robert almost felt sorry for her. Until she smiled at him. Two deep dimples accentuated her perfect, white smile and she practically glowed with good nature.

Unable to help himself, Robert beamed back at her, "Good afternoon, yes, can you point me to the mayor's office?"

"I'm not sure she's in right now. Let me call over and see where she is." Picking up the phone, she efficiently punched in a three-digit extension, "Hi Suzanne, it's Shelby. I have a gentleman here to see the mayor. Is she in her office?"

After a brief pause, Shelby continued. "Mmm hmmm, okay, yup. Got it. Thanks. I'll let him know." She put down the phone and smiled up at Robert. "Kacie's at her workshop today. She should be back around two. Or, if you'd like, you can head on over there. It's only a two-minute drive."

"Are you sure that would be okay? I don't want to intrude."

"Oh, no. It would be fine. She holds meetings there sometimes. She won't mind. Asha, can you hand me the town map?"

Robert turned towards Asha and caught his breath for a moment. The two women couldn't have been more different. Asha had long black hair that hung in loose waves around her exquisite face. Her dark almond shaped eyes were framed by thick eyelashes. Knowing the effect she often had on the opposite sex, Asha slowly smiled and practically batted her eyelashes at Robert. She opened a drawer in her desk, dug around until she found what she was looking for, and handed a map over to Shelby.

Shelby pointed at the map, "We're here at the library building. If you go about a quarter mile this way, you'll come to a roundabout with a fountain at the center. You can't miss it. Our downtown doesn't have any parking. The main street, Fountain Walk, is closed off to everything but pedestrian traffic, so you'll have to take the first right off the traffic circle. You'll find plenty of street parking and a public parking lot. Just park and head back to the fountain and walk towards the cobblestone street. Kacie's shop is two blocks down on the left."

Robert took the map, pleasantly surprised by the layout of the downtown area. "Thank you, ladies. Have a great day."

As he walked away, Asha leaned towards Shelby and whispered, "I don't generally go for older men. But he is...," and she waved her hand at her face as if trying to cool herself off.

"He certainly is," Shelby agreed.

ooooo

Robert managed to find a parking spot quickly enough and put on his coat for the short walk to Kacie's shop. Although it was cool outside, the sun was shining brightly, and a recent rain made everything look fresh and clean. He was quite looking forward to discovering the downtown area. And, if truth be told, he was looking forward to seeing Kacie again. There was something about her friendly, open nature that had left an impression on him.

As he approached the roundabout, Robert noticed just how beautiful and inviting the area was. The large, carved fountain at the center had three tiers of gently cascading water and a decidedly European flair to it. The sound of the water was somehow both lively and soothing. Perfectly trimmed shrubs encircled the fountain. Four curving flower beds radiated out from the center, and Robert could see the start of some early spring blooms getting ready to showcase their colors. The remaining area was covered in grass and several trees were planted so that their canopies provided shade to the nearby garden benches. He could imagine whiling away a couple of hours sitting there watching people go about their day.

Turning towards the cobblestone path known as Fountain Walk confirmed Robert's initial pleasure at having chosen Sycamore Ridge as the perfect place to purchase a home. The wide avenue before him was reminiscent of streets he had seen throughout many of the quaint European towns he had visited in the past. This street was flanked by a variety of one- and two-story buildings, most of which were fronted in brick which had patinaed beautifully. A variety of colorful awnings and signs enlivened the street and roused his curiosity. Lampposts with hanging baskets lined the sidewalks and were sure to be filled with abundant flowers over the coming weeks. Scattered bistro tables in front of several of the buildings signaled an ample selection of restaurants and cafes.

As he started walking towards Kacie's shop, he forced himself to slow down from his usual brisk pace and learn the names of some of the businesses for future reference. He passed a bakery called Rebekah's, the law offices of Destiny Jones, the Bookstack bookstore, and a florist called It's About Blooming Time, among others. The distinct smell of Indian food coming from an unassuming restaurant called Mumbai Kitchen made his mouth water. Maybe he'd order take-out from there. A nice steaming hot bowl of fragrant basmati rice smothered in saag paneer sounded perfect for his first overnight stay in Sycamore Ridge.

The ringing sound of a small bell drew his attention to a shop door up ahead on his left. A harried looking woman carrying a brown paper wrapped canvas almost as tall as she was stepped out and went on her way. The simple wooden sign above the glass door said, "The Workshop." Assuming that was his destination, he walked over and opened the door. The bell chimed again, and he heard a voice call out, "I'll be right there."

Robert took the time to look around the space that was much larger than it appeared from the front. The main entrance and a window overlooked the street and opened onto a modest entryway. By the window, there was a small café table with two worn but comfortable looking chairs. One was upholstered in a faded floral pattern and the other in stripes. It was a strange combination, and yet it worked together to make a comfortable and inviting looking spot for two people to talk.

A little further into the entryway, there was a cluttered desk with a laptop computer on it and numerous piles of papers. The kind of piles that made it appear disorganized to anyone but the person who had created the piles. Robert walked towards the desk and took a closer look at it. From the uneven edges, he guessed he was looking at a unique table. He ran his hands over a small section that was not covered with papers and was surprised at how smooth the finish on it was. It had been expertly sanded down, but still showed all the irregularities and natural knots in the wood grain. It was quite a beautiful effect. A few steps to his right, heading away from the front window, the shop opened into an expansive workspace. Several large machines – he had no idea what they were – were scattered throughout. And there was wood everywhere he looked. A stack of doors in assorted sizes that looked like they were rotting, piles of window frames with no glass in them, broken pieces of wooden furniture, and more stacks of what could only be described as lumber. It was a mess. But the earthy smell of wood that had been recently worked was oddly pleasing.

A head popped up from behind one of the machines, "Sorry, give me one more second." When Kacie recognized who was in her shop, she stood up. "Robert?"

Robert smiled, "You remember me. I'm flattered."

"Of course! How are you? Are you here to check on the renovations?"

"I am. And I wanted to explore the town a little more."

"Ahh, well, what do you think so far?" She wiped her hands on a towel laying close by and walked towards him.

"I haven't gotten far yet. I stopped by your other office to meet you before they sent me over here. You never mentioned you were the mayor. Now I know why you had that pitch ready to go."

Kacie smiled. "Guilty."

She was standing a few feet away from Robert, and the light from the front window fell on her face. Robert recalled thinking she was a nice-looking woman during their brief initial meeting, but now that he had a chance to study her face a bit more closely, he realized he had been wrong. She was not just a nice-looking woman. She was quite lovely. Kacie had beautiful light brown eyes that were framed by thick, dark, and long eyelashes. Her dark brown hair was tied back in a ponytail, and her skin which was clear and bright, had a certain rosiness to it that looked like it came from a healthy and active life-

27

style. When she smiled at him, he noticed her teeth were straight and white, except for the two front teeth which slightly overlapped one another. This gave her an endearing quality that made him instinctively smile back at her. She was taller than he remembered, with long legs that were accentuated by well-fitting yet slightly worn jeans. She had on a grey plaid flannel shirt with the sleeves rolled up. Her overall style could only be described as casual, and yet somehow, she looked a lot sexier than women who were dressed and made-up a whole lot better. Not that he was interested. But he was a man after all.

"How are the renovations coming along?"

"Pretty good. They've ripped out the old kitchen and demolished the pool house. We got the final plans from the architect and designer and Walter got all the permits in place, so we're ready to move on to the rebuilding phase."

"I heard you went with Jerome Randall and his daughter Erica for the design work?"

Robert nodded.

"I'm so happy you're keeping things local. You'll find their work to be impeccable."

"I have a meeting with them later this afternoon to finalize all the appliances, fixtures, lighting, and other finishings."

"Wow...not to gender stereotype, but I'm impressed your wife lets you make all those decisions without her. She didn't strike me as the type to give up decision making power." Kacie hadn't intended to be rude, but the words had just escaped her. She hoped Robert wouldn't take offense.

It took a moment for Robert to realize who Kacie was talking about. "You mean Lindsay?" Robert asked while laughing out loud. "She's not my wife. No. She's our personal assistant, and about as good as they come. We literally couldn't function without her. Let's just say that Lindsay is an acquired taste."

Kacie smiled. "I'm relieved to hear that." Walter had been sharing stories about his conversations with Lindsay on an almost daily basis, and Kacie had enough experience with demanding clients to hope she never had to deal with Lindsay in a professional capacity.

"My wife's name is Lorraine," Robert added. "She's a cardiovascular surgeon and mom to our three kids. In other words, Lindsay's polar opposite. But somehow, they're close friends. Go figure."

Robert hoped he had dodged Kacie's curiosity about why his wife gave him the decision-making power. He felt bad lying to her, but he wasn't ready to tell a relative stranger the truth just yet.

"Walter tells me you're a great tour guide. What are the chances I can get a tour of downtown guided by the mayor?"

"If you're buying my mid-morning coffee, I'd say they were excellent."

∞∞∞∞

Kacie's idea of mid-morning coffee turned out to be an almost two-hour culinary tour of Sycamore Ridge, which basically meant meandering down one side of the cobblestone street and up the other. It had been a wonderful, and surprisingly educational, experience. Kacie seemed to know just about everything there was to know about each of the shops and restaurants, and almost everyone they met seemed to know Kacie personally. She was clearly an extremely popular and well-liked mayor, and it was easy to see why. She was friendly and approachable, quick to laugh, and remembered small details about her constituents that made her seem more like a family friend than the town mayor.

Several of the restaurant owners had given them small plates of their daily specials to try. They had been treated to grilled potato tacos loaded with guacamole, a mini vegan bahn mi sandwich, minestrone soup, a leek and potato gratin, and his favorite, saag paneer from Mumbai Kitchen. A couple of the chefs also handed small packets to Kacie to take home for Cooper to enjoy. As if that wasn't enough, they had also managed to pick up free, freshly baked chocolate chip cookies from one of the bakeries. By the time he was supposed to head over to meet the designers, he was completely full without even having stopped anywhere for a proper lunch. He was also fully in the know about almost every single retailer and restaurant in downtown. He had met several of the chefs, and he even had a handful of takeout menus and a few coupons to take home with him.

"You know, for a small town, you have a lot of amenities and a huge variety of fantastic restaurants."

Kacie beamed with pride. "Most of our growth has happened in the past few years. But we're fortunate because it's been at a slow and manageable pace. It's usually from word of mouth, and, for whatever reason, a lot of people at the top of their games seem to hit a wall and need to slow down. A couple of those restaurants you ate at, they're owned by Michelin-rated chefs. That's no joke. Especially for a small town like Sycamore Ridge."

Kacie stopped in front of a building on the opposite side of the street from her workshop. "Here we are," she pointed. "Just go in this door and head on upstairs. Jerome and Erica have the entire second floor. And remember, be sure to stop into Rebekah's before you head home. Tell her I sent you!"

"Will do. Thanks so much Kacie. This has been an education in overeating."

Kacie laughed, and Robert realized how much he enjoyed the sound of her laughter and her company.

"When do you leave?"

"I have a flight out tomorrow, so I'll need to head out first thing in the morning."

"Be sure to stop by when you're back in town! I had a great time eating my way through Sycamore Ridge with you."

As she walked away, Robert was certain he'd be visiting her again.

# CHAPTER 3

## *Little Secrets*

"Oooo weee did it pour last night!" Suzanne said in her usual boisterous, louder than necessary voice.

"You know what I love the most about a heavy rain at night? The clean, fresh smell of earth in the morning. The air was so crisp when I left the house," Kacie said, putting on her bright yellow raincoat.

"Sun's out. I don't think you'll need that monstrosity right now."

"I don't know what you have against my raincoat."

"Someone needs to take it out back and put an end to its misery."

"It's not that bad!"

"If you say so."

Kacie laughed at the running joke she and Suzanne shared. Every spring, when the rainy weather started, Kacie brought out her favorite raincoat. And every spring, Suzanne mercilessly poked fun at it.

"I think I'm going to walk over to the workshop. I'll be there for the next few hours if anyone is looking for me."

"When you're wearing that thing, anyone who is looking for you, will find you. I guarantee." Suzanne laughed at her own joke as her "boss" left the office. She'd been working for Kacie for over three years now, but she considered her more of a friend than an employer. Suzanne knew just about everything there was to know about Kacie, except why she felt the need to keep her one very peculiar obsession a secret. How could one of the nicest, smartest women she knew be so silly and think that everyone around her didn't see the bulge in her raincoat pocket?

∞∞∞

Inordinately pleased with her decision to walk, Kacie breathed in the mild spring air. There was still a coolness to it which hinted at the possibility of more rain and made her signature rain jacket an absolute necessity. As she strolled along the sidewalk towards Fountain Walk, Kacie had to resist the urge to start skipping like a young child.

Even at her leisurely pace, the walk to the rotunda, one of her favorite places in Sycamore Ridge, took less than ten minutes. The park benches there, spread out under the trees, were usually the perfect place for people watching or to enjoy a quick lunch. But after a rain like last night, they were empty. Kacie briefly considered trying to wipe one down and sit for a few moments to appreciate the large planting beds that were bursting with early spring blooms. Deciding it would be futile to wipe down a bench under a tree canopy whose leaves were laden with rain drops, Kacie reluctantly kept going.

All up and down the wide cobblestone street ahead, flower baskets were showing off their own riotous color. People had shed their winter coats in favor of light jackets and sweaters and were gathered in small groups in front of the cafes and restaurants. The patio umbrellas were not set out yet so that patrons could keep warm in the sunlight. But Kacie knew that as soon as summer came around, those umbrellas would add their own bright hues to the beautiful scene. She took a deep breath in and exhaled slowly. This was just one of the many reasons she loved Sycamore Ridge.

"Hello Kacie!" The sound of her name in a familiar, slightly raspy voice brought a smile to her face.

"Mr. Randall! How are you, sir?" Despite having been admonished numerous times to call him Jerome, Kacie couldn't bring herself to call the older man by his first name. He was one of the most distinguished, elegant gentlemen she knew. An award-winning architect and accomplished piano player, she was always in awe of him. As a young architect, he had broken racial barriers to quickly become a partner at a successful firm in Chicago before giving up big city life and moving to Sycamore Ridge in search of a less stressful and slower paced lifestyle. Recently semi-retired, he was helping his daughter Erica establish her interior design business and only taking on occasional architecture projects that appealed to him.

"I'm doing okay. On my way to a meeting with the toughest boss I've ever had."

Kacie laughed, "Erica?"

"Who knew my daughter would be so hard on me? Meetings, deadlines, and more meetings! It's like I never left the pressure cooker of Chicago."

"What are you working on right now?"

"She's got some big renovation up by the university that I'm helping out with. Plus, that pool house and kitchen renovation for Robert. I've enjoyed working on that a lot more than the other project. Robert has very good taste."

"I can't wait to see it."

"Should be done in another couple of weeks. You know, Robert's coming out tomorrow to check on the progress. I'm hoping he'll spare some time for a round of chess with me."

"Brave man."

"I have a feeling he'll be able to hold his own. By the way, he speaks very highly of you, Kacie. I think he's quite happy with his decision to purchase a home here, partly because you're the mayor."

"I think it's been a team effort, Mr. Randall. But thank you for your kind words."

"You're welcome." A buzzing sound from his pocket interrupted their conversation. "How is it I always lose track of time when I stop to chat, especially with you? I was on my way to a meeting and now I'm running late. Have a good day."

"You, too," Kacie said as he walked away. "And let me know how that chess match goes!"

Kacie sighed with relief. It was a good thing she had decided against sitting on that park bench for a few moments to indulge in her habit. She would have been absolutely mortified if Mr. Randall had seen her. She was certain it would somehow lower his impression of her. But she had to have her fix. She couldn't, wouldn't deny herself this one thing that she loved beyond reason.

Desperate to satisfy her craving, Kacie hurried the rest of the way to her workshop and sat down behind her desk. She had set aside exactly a half an hour each workday to appease her compulsion. At night, she was free to spend as much time as she wanted on it.

Taking a deep breath and enjoying the heady rush of anticipation, Kacie slowly pulled her favorite tabloid magazine out of her jacket pocket and spread it across her opened laptop. Eager to get her fill of the latest celebrity dirt, she started reading from the very beginning and didn't stop until she reached the very last page.

She had installed the small bell on her workshop door specifically to protect her privacy during this daily ritual. And while Kacie knew that being obsessed with tabloid gossip wasn't exactly the worst habit in the world, she preferred to keep her obsession with celebrities private. Which was rather ironic. She wanted to know all about celebrities who were complete strangers, but she didn't want her neighbors to know that she wanted to know about it.

In case anyone stopped by the workshop, Kacie was prepared with a proven method to hide what she was doing. The moment she heard that bell chime, she closed the magazine, tucked it inside her laptop and lowered the screen. This accomplished two things. First, she could keep what she was reading a secret. And second, the person coming in would believe they were more important than whatever she had been reading. It was really a win-win situation for everyone.

The front cover of the magazine that had come in the mail the day before once again featured the sad decline of one of the most popular musicians of the last few years: the lead singer of one of her favorite bands, Mirrors. Jett Vanders did not look good in the full-page cover photo. He had dark circles under his eyes, his hair looked limp and dirty, and he appeared downright gaunt. His cheeks were hollow, and his skin cast an unhealthy pallor. As usual, he was clutching a small black flask in his hand while his other hand was covering his eyes as if he could hide himself from the dozens of paparazzi that always followed him around.

Kacie sighed, feeling sad for the once beautiful and accomplished singer. She wondered if he had any close family or friends and why they didn't step in to help him. It was bad enough his career was suffering, but from the looks of his recent photos, his health was starting to suffer, too.

∞∞∞

"I can't take this anymore," Jett said through gritted teeth. "I'm exhausted. I need to stop."

"Just a few more weeks and then you can take a well-deserved break." His brother nodded at the doctor, giving him the go ahead to administer the clear liquid in the syringe. "This will help you. Try to rest now. It's almost over. You have to finish up this tour for the rest of the band. Do you understand?"

Jett sighed, defeatedly. "Yes, yes. Of course. I just really need a break after this."

"I know, buddy. And you'll get it."

"What about the other thing?"

"We haven't gotten anything else from her. I think the close call last time must have given her a good scare. I don't think we need to worry about her anymore."

"Good. She was unhinged."

"Yeah. But put her out of your mind. Go take a hot bath. I'll get your food ordered, and then you can go straight to bed."

"What would I do without you?"

"I ask myself that every day!"

Jett smiled and, as always, did what his older brother said.

∞∞∞

"He doesn't look good, Francois."

"He's just tired. I've been keeping a close eye on his blood work and other labs. There's nothing else wrong with him. Trust me, my old friend." The doctor's words, spoken in a hush, were somehow made more calming by his French accent.

"He has to finish out this tour. The band is counting on him. So much money and so many jobs are at stake here."

"He knows that. He could have thrown in the towel a long time ago. He won't let you or the band down."

The man knew Francois was right. His younger brother always did the right thing, and he almost felt guilty for keeping secrets from Jett. But telling him about the latest letter, which was discreetly tucked into the inside pocket of his suit jacket, would do nothing but cause him stress and anxiety.

Thankfully, this letter had come through the regular mail delivery at the hotel. At least he had been honest with his brother about the fact that the close call seemed to have scared her. But it hadn't stopped her or her deranged fantasizing. His frustration mounted with each new letter. They were no closer to finding the stalker than they had been before. Postmarked from a different European city each time, this latest letter happened to be postmarked from Paris, the city Jett was in for another two days. Written with glued together letters cut out from a variety of magazines, the message was clear: *I won't let anyone come between us, my love. We'll be together. I promise.*

ooooo

It was another mild, sunny day in Sycamore Ridge, and Kacie was working at the back of her shop with the double garage doors, used for loading and unloading large pieces, wide open. Cooper was stretched out near the door, lounging as always. She was humming to herself while putting the finishing touches on a set of antique French paneled oak doors. A client of hers, who flipped houses for a living, had rescued them from an old home built in the early 1900s. Kacie had lovingly repaired, sanded, and polished the doors to their natural beauty. She would never understand why people felt the need to paint over wood this beautiful. The original brass hardware had also been polished and looked lovely against the natural wood grain. She couldn't wait to see photos of how they looked back in their original home.

The bell on her front door chimed, and Kacie looked up to see one of her favorite people pop her head in. Min-seo owned a ceramics studio just across the street. While she tended to lean towards utilitarian items like platters, serving bowls, and dishware in earth tones and crackled finishes, it was her craftsmanship and eye for subtle detail that commanded a high price for her pieces. Fortunately, Min-seo reciprocated Kacie's appreciation for quality work, and so the two friends often bartered with each other.

"Hey Kacie, do you know what's going on outside of Rebekah's?"

"No, why?"

"There's a small crowd gathered there."

"Oh my gosh, are you kidding me? Is she giving away morning buns?" Kacie asked, a little too excitedly.

Min-seo rolled her eyes and laughed. "Breathe. I'm sure you're not going to be too late if that is what she's doing. Come on, let's go check it out."

Wiping her hands on one of her ever-present towels,

Kacie joined her friend and they walked across the street to Rebekah's to see what was going on.

Several people greeted them, and they managed to move around the crowd to get a good view. Much to Kacie's disappointment, there were no morning buns to be had. But she quickly overcame that feeling when she realized what everyone was doing. Jerome and Robert were facing off against one another over a chess board.

"Who's winning?" she whispered to the onlooker closest to her.

"Shhhhhh," was the only response she got.

At that moment, she heard the familiar, raspy voice say, "checkmate." The crowd, many of whom knew Jerome but few who knew Robert, began clapping and then slowly dispersed to go about their business.

"That's one for team Sycamore Ridge!" Kacie exclaimed.

The two opponents turned towards her, and both beamed. Jerome because he had beaten a worthy opponent, and Robert because he was genuinely happy to see Kacie.

"Kacie! It's good to see you. I was going to head over to your shop when I was done beating Jerome. Little did I know...."

Jerome laughed good naturedly and shook hands with Robert. "Another match the next time you're in town? Best of three?"

"You're on. I need to recoup my dignity after that beating you just gave me."

"I would hardly call that a beating." The two men smiled at one another. "Good to see you, Mayor. Robert, I need to go check on a couple of things. Reservations are at one. I'll meet you at the restaurant?"

"Sounds good. It'll give me a chance to catch up with Kacie." Jerome went on his way, and Kacie took the opportunity to introduce Min-seo to Robert as the threesome headed back towards her workshop.

"I heard you're doing some renovations on the old Russell home?" Min-seo asked.

"I am." Robert prepared himself for more questions but was pleasantly surprised when Min-seo just smiled at him.

"It's a beautiful house, one of my favorites on Willow. You have good taste. Let me know if you need any dishware. I better get back to my studio and check on the kiln. Nice to meet you!" she waved as she left the two of them standing in front of Kacie's shop.

"When did you get to town?"

"Would you believe this morning? Jerome practically ambushed me at the house, said he'd be waiting for me outside of Rebekah's at eleven and not to be late."

"Yikes. He doesn't mess around when it comes to chess."

"I learned that the hard way. I'm glad to see you. Jerome tells me you're working on some stuff for the main house and the guest house."

"If you have a few minutes, I can show you."

"Absolutely." Robert had been looking forward to spending some time with Kacie. She looked just as pretty as he remembered. A few strands of her hair had fallen free of her ponytail and framed her face beautifully. Robert almost cringed when he realized she was wearing overalls under the denim shirt she had left unbuttoned. He was not a fan of overalls, but she even managed to make those look good. And her obvious enthusiasm and love for the work she did as she showed him into the shop quickly diverted his mind from her wardrobe.

"Cooper is here, by the way. I'm excited for you two to meet."

"How long have you two been together?"

Kacie gave him an odd look. "More than five years."

Robert was surprised. Not that he was old fashioned, but he hadn't expected Kacie to stay with a man for that long without getting married. He didn't know how old she was, but he'd guess she was at the age when a lot of women – especially ones in long term relationships – would want to settle down and start a family.

"That's a long time."

"Yup, I got him when he was just a baby."

Now it was Robert's turn to give Kacie an odd look. "Are we talking about the same thing here?"

"I don't know...I'm talking about Cooper."

At the sound of his name, Cooper roused himself from his lounging and slowly padded over to the front of her shop. As soon as he saw Robert, his tail started wagging and he began running around in happy little circles.

Kacie rolled her eyes, "Robert, meet Cooper. My guard dog," she added sarcastically.

Robert laughed. "I don't know about guard dog, but he sure is beautiful. What kind of dog is he?"

"Part border collie, part German shepherd, part who knows what."

Robert let the dog sniff him and petted him. A beautiful dog for a beautiful girl, he thought.

With Cooper following her, Kacie walked further into the shop. "I found this old dresser on the side of the road a couple of years back. Someone was renovating a house and just left it out on the road. Like a piece of trash. Can you imagine?" Kacie handed him a photo of an old, beat-up dresser with a couple of drawers askew and missing drawer pulls.

"Actually, no I can't imagine." Robert looked from the photo to the bathroom vanity that Kacie was lovingly running her hands across. "It's unrecognizable and just beautiful. I bet it took a lot of work to get it to look like this."

Kacie nodded. "I had to clean it, sand it, strip it, repair it, and then stain and seal it. Then I had a custom countertop made and installed the sinks and faucets." Thinking for a moment, Kacie added, "And I added legs to it to make it the right height for a bathroom vanity."

Robert stared at Kacie, feeling rather unaccomplished in the face of this skilled woman. "Almost looks like a piece of furniture for the bathroom."

Kacie beamed at the compliment. "As soon as I saw it, I knew I had to have it. But it took some doing to get it here. It's quite heavy." Kacie sighed. "They don't make them like they used to. Just look at this construction. All the drawers are solid wood, with tongue and groove design. This is high quality craftsmanship. I mean, think about it. When it was first purchased, it was someone's treasure. Then the next person came along and tossed it out like trash."

"But you've made it a treasure again."

"Well, that is my official motto, you know. 'One man's treasure is another man's trash is another woman's treasure'."

"That's your official motto?" Robert almost laughed until he realized Kacie was being serious. He bit his lip to keep from chuckling and mumbled under his breath, "Quite a mouthful."

But Kacie heard him and laughed, putting him back

at ease. "I Googled 'trash to treasure,' but it was already being used by so many other shops. I thought something a little more original would be clever. Until I realized how much it would cost to have a sign made with all those words on it! So now no one knows my official motto but me. And you."

Robert smiled. The more he talked to her, the more he was drawn to her good nature.

Kacie started walking towards another large but surprisingly different looking table. While the dresser looked almost new, this other table looked unfinished. But not in an unappealing way.

"What do you think?" Kacie asked.

Robert took a closer look and realized the table was similar to the desk in Kacie's reception area. The natural grain of the wood flowed across the top of the table, almost like a river. The patch along the center was a rich, dark brown and faded into a lighter shade towards the outer edges. The table was mounted on rectangular, black metal legs. The incongruity between the materials and the shapes produced a spectacular effect.

Kacie waited patiently as Robert walked around the table, looking at it from different angles. She knew it was one of her best pieces, and she knew that a man like Robert would appreciate beauty when he saw it.

"I'm not even sure what to say. It's just...it's incredible. It looks like it belongs in an art gallery."

Kacie radiated pride.

"You made this? For my house?"

"Yup. Erica was looking for something to put in the front entryway that would make a statement."

"This is more than a statement, Kacie. This is an exclamation! I absolutely love it."

"I can't wait to see it in the space. Just waiting until the painters are done and then I'll deliver it. Would it be okay if I take a look around the rest of the house with Erica when I go out there?"

Hearing Erica's name again reminded Robert that he was supposed to meet Jerome for lunch.

"Yes, definitely. Feel free to look around and let me know if there's anything we've missed or we should do differently. I could stand here and appreciate your work for hours, but I have to go meet Jerome for lunch. Apparently, he had to pull some strings to get us a table at Remy's."

"I bet he did. It's usually packed during lunch. I'd recommend trying the shiitake mushroom and asparagus risotto. It's divine."

"I'll do that. I'm meeting with a home security company tomorrow morning and then heading out immediately after, so I probably won't get a chance to see you until I get back for the move. In a few weeks, I think. I'll be sure to stop in and say hello."

As Robert left, Kacie's stomach growled thinking about Remy's luscious risotto. Not one to fight her cravings, Kacie called Remy's to place a takeout order.

# CHAPTER 4

## *A Home on Willow*

Kacie's windshield wipers were going at full speed. It was a complete downpour and visibility was low enough that she didn't even feel comfortable turning on her radio.

As she turned her delivery truck onto Willow, she slowed to a crawl to make sure she didn't drive right past Robert's house. A short lull in the rain shower helped her get her bearings, and she turned into the driveway and backed the truck into the garage. Unfortunately, the front of the truck didn't make it all the way in which meant Kacie was going to get a little wet, whether she liked it or not.

Looking through the sideview mirror, she saw the door leading to the house open. Erica stood waiting for her. Pulling the hood of her yellow raincoat over her baseball cap, Kacie stepped out of the truck and ran inside. Her old-school duck boots made a splashing sound and dripped water onto the garage floor.

Erica, having to shout over the pounding rain to be heard, asked, "Is it me, or is the rain getting heavier each year?"

"It's definitely not you." Kacie shouted back. "Don't get me wrong, I love a good thunderstorm, but it's been raining non-stop for almost a week now." Kacie opened the back of the truck and lowered the ramp.

"Let me grab a couple of the guys to help you get that furniture out."

Erica returned a moment later with two of the men working on the house and they made quick business of unloading the furniture.

"Want the unofficial tour?" Erica asked.

"I'd love it. I had mentioned it to Robert when he was here last time, and he said it would be okay."

"Yup, he told me. Come on in. You won't believe the difference. I wish Walter was here to show you around, too. He's very proud of the work he's done."

"I think he's spending the day with Sally."

"Glad to hear it."

Erica led Kacie through a short hallway from the garage into a spacious mudroom that held the washer and dryer, plenty of storage cabinets, and a deep utility sink. Attached to this room was a full bathroom with a shower which could also be accessed from the pool area out back. Both rooms were staged to perfection and made even the garage entrance to the house feel like an inviting space.

"The previous owner had already renovated this area, so we didn't do much here. Just basic touch-ups. And staging, obviously. But wait until you see the kitchen."

"Lead the way." Kacie was surprised to feel anticipation in seeing a room that didn't even belong to her. But she had a feeling that between Robert's refined taste, Erica's eye for design, and Walter's craftmanship, the room would be a treat.

She wasn't disappointed.

The far wall had upper and lower cabinets with a white shaker style door, while the lower cabinets in the island were painted a dark, almost midnight, blue. It was all offset beautifully by white countertops with grey veining and unexpected, but surprisingly sexy rose gold colored hardware. The windows above the sink, which overlooked the backyard, were surrounded by open wooden shelves that added warmth and more color to the space. The stainless-steel appliances were state of the art and included a built-in side-by-side refrigerator, a six-burner stove, and dual wall ovens. The countertops and shelves were staged with an assortment of dishes, wooden cutting boards, dish towels, and a spectacular arrangement of peonies. If she hadn't known differently, Kacie would have thought she was looking at a lived-in and well-loved home.

Next to the kitchen area was a bay window with an upholstered window seat and a large, round dining table which Kacie recognized from the previous owner's renovation.

"You kept my table." Kacie ran her hand over the top of the table. It still looked beautiful.

"Are you kidding me? That was the only nice thing in this kitchen. Walter gutted everything else. I just can't imagine why someone would spend all that money on a renovation and leave the kitchen untouched."

"Most people are a mystery to me."

"I hear that."

The two friends continued past the dining table into the living space. Two distinct seating areas lent a coziness to the expansive room. Immediately in front of Kacie was a light grey sectional sofa that could easily seat ten people comfortably, even with the plethora of boldly colored throw pillows scattered on it. An oversized ottoman and media center with a wall mounted television rounded out the first seating area. It would be the perfect place to watch a game on tv or just sit around with friends and family. But it was the second seating area that Kacie was drawn to. At the far end of the room, there was a brick fireplace with two cream colored wingback chairs nestled across from it. She could just imagine spending a quiet evening there with Cooper, a cup of hot chocolate, and a good book.

"Like it?"

"I love it."

"I had a feeling you would."

"But there's something different. It looks a lot brighter in here. Oh, it stopped raining." Kacie looked around and realized there was still something different and then she noticed what it was. The windows that faced the backyard had been replaced with three sets of French doors. But as she looked more closely, she noticed they weren't regular French doors.

"Wait a second, there's something different about these."

"I knew you'd notice. I've been wanting to find a client who had the vision and the wallet to let me install these. And I found him in Robert. Check this out."

Erica walked over to the traditional looking doors, the kind that normally open out from the center. But when she opened them, they actually folded onto each other like an accordion until the center four doors were completely tucked up against the two on either end. It made the transition from indoors to outdoors almost seamless.

Kacie expelled her breath. "This looks amazing, Erica."

"I know," Erica smiled confidently, pleased by her friend's compliment. "Come on, let's finish ogling the rest of the main house and then I'll show you the guest house."

They walked towards the front of the house and passed the central staircase leading upstairs. The entryway was made bright by the windows on either side of the front door. Against the wall to the right of the door, proudly stood Kacie's wood and metal table. Erica had picked the perfect location for it.

"Oh, Erica...it looks just incredible."

"You've really outdone yourself with this piece. Once people see it, they're going to want something similar."

Kacie sighed and forced herself to redirect her attention to the house. "What's down that way?" she asked gesturing to the long hallway on the left.

"That leads to the master bedroom suite. We didn't do much in there. Just swapped out the furniture and a put in a new coat of paint. This," Erica pointed towards the room on the right, "is probably the one room I don't understand."

Kacie knew the room used to be a formal dining room, but now it was transformed into a beautiful music room with a set of barn doors on either side of the opening, which could be pulled shut for privacy. An antique walnut desk and masculine leather chair were in the center of the room facing the large front window. The walls behind the desk were lined with bookshelves and several empty guitar stands were scattered throughout.

"What's with all the empty guitar stands? Does Robert play?"

"I have no idea. That man is a study in contradictions. He is so friendly and open that I feel like I know him when, in fact, I barely know anything about him. Anyway, to each his own, I guess. There's not much to see upstairs. Just the four bedrooms and bathrooms. Pretty much unchanged except for new furniture and paint."

Kacie looked at Erica who was easing her way towards the back doors. "You're dying to show me the guest house, aren't you?"

"Yup, let's go! We'll go through the mudroom and grab the umbrellas in case it starts raining again."

"Hey, what's this panel here?"

"High-tech home security system. You wouldn't know it, but every single window and door is wired and there are cameras everywhere."

"Really? Robert doesn't strike me as the paranoid type."

"To each his own, I guess," Erica repeated and shrugged.

As they stepped out of the mudroom, they breathed in the incomparable fresh smell of earth after a good rain. The sun was starting to peak out from behind a few lingering clouds and glistened off some small puddles that had formed in the flower beds that lined the paved walkway. The path ended at the main patio that ran almost the entire length of the indoor living space. Once outdoor furniture was placed there, it would be a welcoming place to enjoy the beautiful backyard. The swimming pool and surrounding area had been renovated and all that was needed was a few lounge chairs to achieve perfection. From the main patio, another paved walkway led to the guest house.

Kacie stopped for a moment to take it all in. What used to be the old pool house had been replaced with a single-story home that mirrored the architectural style of the main house. And although it was newly constructed from the ground up, they had somehow managed to make it look as if it had always been there, as if it *should* have been there from the very beginning.

Erica opened the front door and stepped inside. "You're going to love it."

She was right.

As Kacie stepped inside, she was awed by how spacious the home looked. The outside had been deceiving. "How many square feet?"

"Just under 900."

Kacie widened her eyes, impressed.

To the right of the entrance was an L-shaped kitchen. The far wall had plenty of cabinet space, the refrigerator and range-oven combo. The wall along the front of the house held only lower cabinets, the sink, and open shelving above, much like the main house. The window over the sink looked out onto the pool area. Instead of a traditional island with barstool seating, which is what Kacie would have expected in a 900-square-foot house, Erica had chosen a built-in upholstered banquette that mirrored the L-shape of the kitchen with a round dining table.

On the left of the front door was the living room with a light grey sofa, two matching chairs, and a small coffee table. Another large window overlooking the pool and a side window facing the extensive backyard let light pour into the room. Fluffy, colorful throw pillows in a variety of patterns added a feminine touch to the room. Once again, despite the size of the house, clever furniture placement and use of materials made the space look open and welcoming.

"It's incredible. If you really stop to think about it, unless you have a bunch of kids running around, this is the perfect house for most single or married people."

"Shhhh, let's keep that to ourselves. You don't want to put me, my dad and Walter out of business, do you?"

Kacie laughed, "Show me the rest."

Erica walked past the front rooms to a short hallway and pointed out a powder room on the right and a laundry room on the left with a stackable washer and dryer. Although both rooms were small, they fulfilled their purpose with style.

"Where are the doors?"

"We decided to do pocket doors for these two rooms. Helps keep every square foot available for its intended purpose."

"Smart."

At the end of the hallway was another pocket door. Erica pushed it aside and led Kacie into the bedroom suite. A king-sized bed and two floating shelves that served as nightstands took up most of the room, but again, it didn't feel tight or constricted. The light grey paint, multiple windows, and a bed covered with pillows in contrasting patterns and fabrics made the room look bright and inviting. Across from the bed was the bathroom which featured a shower and the double vanity that Kacie had made. A well-appointed walk-in closet finished out the room.

"Robert also wanted to add a private outdoor area for whoever stays in this house, so we added a set of French doors and a small patio area."

"Nice. So, when is he planning to come out for his next visit?"

"Another couple of weeks. He's given us a hard deadline for the end of the month, and I think we'll be done with some time to spare."

"Doesn't look like you have too much more to do."

"Just some finishing touches."

"Is he going to finally bring his family with him?"

"Your guess is as good as mine. He seems like such a good guy, but I always feel like there's something he's not telling me."

"Oh?" Kacie's tone invited Erica to expound.

"I don't know how to explain it. He's been involved with high-level design, but Lindsay makes all the final decisions when it comes to specific choices for each room. I basically have carte-blanche to suggest whatever I want to purchase. I send her links to products I like, usually things made by local artisans and sold in locally owned stores. These are brands she would be completely unfamiliar with. And yet she reviews them almost immediately and almost always approves. I don't think Robert, or his wife, ever even see most of what I send over. I mean, come on, really? His wife is so busy she doesn't care how her husband is spending all this money?"

"That's what I thought! He tried to dodge the question when I asked him once. And I didn't push the issue because privacy seems so important to him."

"Maybe they're really loaded. I don't know what he does, but she's a surgeon so...."

Kacie's curiosity piqued. "You don't know what he does either? What about your dad? Does he know?"

"You know how my dad feels about privacy and gossip."

A shiver of guilt ran through Kacie. What, she wondered again, would Jerome think of her tabloid obsession?

Erica, not noticing Kacie's expression, continued, "If he did know, he wouldn't tell me. And unless Robert told him of his own accord, my dad would never even ask."

"They seem to spend quite a bit of time together. I wonder what they talk about."

"Who knows. Old men stuff."

"You're kidding me, right? They're not that old. I've seen women our age checking them out when they're out and about."

"Robert, maybe. But not my dad."

"Trust me. Your dad, too."

Now it was Erica's turn to shiver. "Stop it. This conversation is over."

# CHAPTER 5

## *The Final Show*

"I'm so glad this is almost over," Jett sighed. "I can't wait for some time away from the spotlight."

"You've earned it. Especially after tonight's performance. That was a master class in how to put on a rock concert. Even the critics were singing along."

Smiling at the compliment, particularly because it came from someone he respected, Jett agreed. "It was. I mean, we killed it. Did you hear Lola's solo on that bass guitar? And Derek on the drums? It was unbelievable. I feel like things have gone so well the past week since we changed the line-up and mixed things up a bit. Playing our old music has seemed to rev up the crowd and silence some of the critics. Plus, the band seem a lot happier."

"Maybe it's because everyone is seeing the light at the end of the tunnel. One more show and it's a wrap."

Jett pumped his fist in the air.

"And don't sell yourself short. Your vocals have been incredible."

"Yeah, that's because I've been able to focus on music instead of some crazy lady stalking me."

"Let's not worry about her," his brother replied, grateful he had intercepted the latest letter without Jett finding out about it. "Two more nights in a hotel and then the final show. That's all you need to focus on."

And all he needed to focus on was stopping these letters. They were no closer to learning anything about Jett's stalker than before. The letters were all postmarked from different European capitals, Munich being the most recent one. Thankfully it was intercepted by Jett's personal security. The message had been subtle but was somehow more threatening than the last: *Not much longer now.*

∞∞∞

"Great show, man," Mike, one of the stage crew members, said as he walked by and gave Jett a high five. He had been on Jett's crew for the past three years, and he was one of Jett's favorites. An older guy who'd been around the block a few times and partied too hard too many times. Several years earlier, Mike had finally reached the point where he made the decision to clean up his act and get his life together. Jett was glad he did and happy to have him on his crew. He was capable, knowledgeable, and hard working. As usual, he was dressed in an old pair of jeans and a faded concert tour t-shirt from a bygone era. Tattoos covered both of his arms, and his long hair hung in a loose ponytail down his back.

"You were incredible. No denying that. You're one of the best rock bands around today."

Jett beamed. Coming from a guy who'd toured with some of the best, that was a high compliment.

"Thanks, Mike. Means a lot coming from you."

"Mike, they need your help loading up the gear," another crew member said as he came over to hand Jett a towel and a bottle of water. "You need anything else, Jett?"

Jett shook his head and took the towel, using it to wipe

the sweat off his face and wrapping it around his neck.

"Oh, and the boss lady asked me to give you your phone, said your brother would be calling." Reaching into his back pocket, he handed Jett his cell phone.

Jett took the phone and stared at it blankly for a moment. He almost never answered his own calls, and he was surprised that he was being asked to do so. Tossing the phone on an old sofa, Jett sat down next to it. The backstage lounge he was in wasn't exactly luxurious, but his team always made sure there were a couple of decent sofas where the band could stretch out after the show. Wondering where the rest of his bandmates were, Jett unscrewed the cap on his water bottle and was taking a long drink when his cell phone rang.

"Hey big brother," he said answering the phone after seeing his brother's name in the caller ID.

"You're answering your own phone?"

"Yeah, trust me, I'm as surprised as you are. Apparently boss lady is having a 'discussion' with some poor soul. She had the phone brought over to me a few minutes ago, said you'd be calling."

"Makes sense." Abruptly switching gears, Jett's brother gushed, "Little brother, you really do know how to save the best for last! That was an exceptional way to end the tour."

"Wow, news travels fast."

"Texts and videos travel even faster. I've been getting clips all night long from people at the concert. I'm just sorry I had to miss it."

"I wish you could have been here, but I totally understand. Those pesky nephews of mine need some of your time, too."

"There was no way they were going to let me miss their

tournament."

"How'd they play?"

"They were great, but it's late and I know you have a big day tomorrow. Let's talk again after your press conference."

"Sounds good," Jett hung up the phone, feeling guilty at how much his brother did for him. Besides taking care of almost every aspect of Jett's career, his brother also had his own large family to care for. Once this tour was wrapped up, they could all enjoy some down time together.

Including his personal assistant, aka boss lady, Jett thought. She was always wound up so tight and, at present, was in a very heated discussion with the venue manager.

The rest of the band were finally making their way towards where Jett was sitting when his phone rang again. Assuming it was his brother with some last-minute advice on how to handle the final press conference, Jett answered without looking at the caller ID.

"Hello?"

"Oh, sweetheart, I'm so glad you answered. I was getting sick of hearing your assistant's voice every time I called." The voice on the other end wasn't particularly distinctive, but it made Jett's skin prickle with warning.

"Who is this?" Jett asked even as he slowly realized that he knew exactly who it was.

"We'll be together soon enough. They won't scare me off. I won't let them. You and I are meant to be together. I'm going to make you so...."

Jett hung up without waiting for her to finish. He had the strangest feeling of déjà vu. He'd heard that voice before, but he couldn't place it. And there was something about it that absolutely terrified him. His whole body was trembling now with a combination of fear and anger. No one had told him his stalker was still around. And now, it seemed, she had upped her game from sending letters and strange drawings to making phone calls to his personal cell phone.

"Hey, Jett. Ready to head back to the hotel? You'll have plenty of time for a good night's sleep because we're not meeting the press until noon tomorrow."

Despite her exhaustion and the annoying run-in with the venue manager, Jett's assistant was almost giddy with happiness over how well the concert had gone. The press was going to be eating out of the band's hands. The final leg of the tour was getting rave reviews from fans and critics alike. But when she saw Jett's face, the smile quickly faded from hers.

"What's the matter? Are you okay?"

"Cancel it," Jett snapped.

"What?"

"Cancel. It." Jett commanded through gritted teeth. "I'm not meeting the press. I'm done with this. Get me on a flight out of here. Tonight. Do you understand me?"

In all the years she'd been working for him, she had never seen Jett like this. He was seething.

"Jett, please try to be reasonable. We cannot just cancel the press conference. It took weeks to coordinate. All the major press outlets will be there, the entire band will be there. How will it look if you're the only one missing?"

"Tell them I'm sick."

"You know we can't do that. They'll eat you alive. Tell me what happened."

"Why didn't you tell me she was back?"

"Who?" It only took a moment before she realized who

he was talking about.

"She called your cell phone?"

Jett gave a terse nod.

"Give me the phone. Do not answer any more phone calls yourself. Do you understand me?" She grabbed the phone out of Jett's hand, shoved it into her bag, and used her own phone to call his personal security team, barking orders at whichever unlucky person who happened to answer her call.

"Who is she yelling at now? Why the long face, Jett?" Derek asked as he plopped himself down on the sofa next to Jett. Without waiting for an answer, he continued, "I don't know about everyone else, but I am pumped. Man, that was an amazing performance. And you? You my friend," here he paused to point one of the drumsticks he was perpetually carrying around and twirling with his fingers at Jett to emphasize his point. Smiling from ear to ear, he practically screamed, "You were on fire tonight!"

Despite the unsettling phone call, Jett couldn't help but return Derek's infectious smile. "*We*," he corrected his friend. "We were on fire tonight."

"I think what you both mean to say is that *I* was on fire tonight," Lola, the undeniable diva of their band, walked up to them and stood with her hands on her hips. "Well?" she asked, seeking affirmation.

"Well what? You were okay." Derek, who wouldn't dare miss a chance to tease his younger sister, decided to throw in another jab for good measure. "I'm pretty sure you missed a few notes in that flashy, long-winded solo you made us all sit through. I thought I saw some yawns from the audience."

"No one was yawning. I've never missed a note in my life. And you know it." Running her fingers through her long, wild, fire-engine red hair, Lola asked, "Well, are you two fools just going to sit there staring at me all night? Don't you know it's not polite to stay seated when a lady enters a room?"

Jett groaned. Lola was making it too easy, and Derek was only too willing to oblige. "Lady? I don't see a lady."

Laughing, Lola wedged herself onto the sofa between two of her favorite people in the world. Jett had practically grown up alongside the sibling duo, and they'd been making music together for almost a decade. She loved both of them more than she would ever admit. She put her arms around both men and declared, "I can't believe the tour is finally over! I'm looking forward to not having to see you two losers every day."

As the other members of the band and some of the crew sat down around the threesome, their infectious excitement and camaraderie slowly melted away what remained of Jett's anger. He reminded himself that he just had to get through another twenty-four hours in the public eye. After that, he'd disappear. And while he would miss his music family, he was looking forward to the time when no one would be able to find him.

# CHAPTER 6

## *True Identity*

The rainy days had finally drawn to an end, and Sycamore Ridge was once again bustling with activity. Residents came out from under their umbrellas to go about their business and Fountain Walk was practically humming with the sound of all the conversations taking place in front of the restaurants and shops. Kacie was looking forward to resuming her daily walks from the town hall building to her workshop once again. She was looking even more forward to all the friendly people she'd bump into on her short walk. What usually took less than ten minutes would end up taking over thirty. But that was just one of the many reasons she loved Sycamore Ridge.

"You have your lunch today?" Suzanne called out from her desk.

"Yup. He'll be here at twelve sharp. Like clockwork."

"Great, that means you have, let's see," Suzanne looked at her smart watch, "exactly seven minutes to keep banging away at your keyboard pretending to be doing something important."

"For your information, I happen to be working on the agenda for the city council meeting."

"Mmmm hmmmm," Suzanne replied dubiously.

Kacie felt a moment of guilt wondering what her colleagues would think if they knew what she had really been doing. Or at least thinking about doing. It had been just over a week since her tour of Robert's house and her conversation with Erica, and Kacie sat at her desk staring at the search bar on her internet browser. For what felt like the hundredth time, she typed in Robert's name and then, just as quickly, deleted it again. She was doing everything she could to curb her curiosity, but sometimes it felt like a losing battle. On the one hand, if the information was online, it was available to just about anyone willing to do a Google search. But, on the other, Robert wasn't a celebrity. She should respect his privacy. Especially now that he was one of her constituents.

This respect for privacy didn't exactly jive with her addiction to tabloid fodder, but, Kacie reminded herself, no one is perfect.

Even though she had been expecting it, she was startled by the brusque double tap on her door. "Ready for lunch?"

Kacie looked up and smiled, trying not to look guilty. "Yup, let's go."

The older gentleman returned her smile and held the door open for her. His lips got lost under his old-fashioned handlebar mustache, the color of which matched his grey hair. He was dressed as usual in his perfectly ironed khaki colored Sheriff's uniform with his gleaming badge and sidearm. Seeing his paunch, his slight limp, and his grey hair, people often mistook him for feeble. But they couldn't be more wrong. Frank, a former New York detective who had worked homicide cases for over twenty years, was as tough as they came. A gunshot wound to his right thigh had almost taken his life, but he had fought his way back. If it had been left up to him, he would have gone back to his job as a detective, but his wife had been too terrified by the close call to even entertain that thought.

As an ICU nurse, Emma had known only too well how close she had come to losing her husband, and she felt she had no choice but to put her foot down. Under her gentle care and not-so-gentle pressure, he had relented and retired from the force. Once that decision had been made, it had taken them no time to decide to relocate to the only place they had family.

Emma's unmarried older sister had been living in Sycamore Ridge for years, and they had visited her often, always enjoying their time in the slow-paced, friendly town. When a position in the Sheriff's office had serendipitously opened up, the decision had become even easier.

Frank and Emma had quickly established themselves in the community. And when Kacie moved to Sycamore Ridge, into a house just down the street from theirs, they had taken her under their protective wing almost immediately, treating her like a part of their family. She had dinner with them at least once a week, and every Wednesday, she had a standing lunch date with Frank to discuss anything of importance going on in their peaceful town.

"What are you working on?" Frank gestured at the open laptop on Kacie's desk.

For a brief moment, Kacie considered asking Frank to look into Robert's background but quickly decided against it. "Oh, just the agenda for the next city council meeting. We have to go over the fiscal...."

Frank held up his hand, "Stop right there. I'm already bored. Where to today?"

Kacie laughed. "How about Slice of Pi?"

"Pizza? Now, you're talking!"

ooooo

Two slices of deep-dish pizza filled with spinach, mushrooms, and gooey mozzarella cheese and smothered in the most incredible marinara sauce had hit the spot perfectly.

Kacie sat back and watched as Frank polished off his fourth slice. "Aren't New Yorkers supposed to only like thin crust pizza?"

"I like to keep an open mind." Frank wiped his mouth and asked, "Couple slices left. You want to take them home for dinner?"

"I'd love to."

"Great. So, shall we talk some business?"

"You go first."

"Not much to tell really. Had a couple of small shoplifting incidents, mostly kids being kids. Sometimes I can't believe the things they decide to take. Couple of days ago, down at the Mercantile, they caught some kid with fifteen pencils in his pocket. Not one or two. Fifteen. What was he planning to do with fifteen pencils? Sell them and retire on the profits?" Frank shook his head and chuckled. "There was a fender bender yesterday because the roads are so slippery from the rain. Other than that, not much. Just your basic small-town disturbances."

"Don't sound too disappointed. That's how we want to keep things here. I was on a call with other mayors from across the state last week, and the crime problems they're facing are intense. Drugs, gangs, gun violence. The works."

"It's been almost a decade since I was in the NYPD, and

can you believe I still miss the adrenaline rush?" Frank sighed. "Don't get me wrong, I love it here, and I wouldn't go back to that life, but I'd be okay with a little excitement every now and then."

"You know what I think?"

"Enlighten me."

"I think you need a hobby."

Frank fixed his piercing glare on her for what felt like an eternity. At first, Kacie tried to give him an innocent smile. But when his expression didn't change, her smile faded, and she found herself squirming in her seat and fidgeting with her utensils. This, she thought, is what it must have felt like to be on the receiving end of an interrogation by Frank.

Slowly and carefully placing his napkin in his plate, Frank signaled to their server for the check. Then he turned his attention back on Kacie, and she gulped.

"You've been talking to Emma." It was statement more than a question.

Before Kacie could suggest any of the hobbies on the list she and Emma had made earlier that day, Frank pushed his chair away from the table and stood up. He took cash from his wallet, laid it on the table, and started walking towards the door. And with that, Kacie realized their conversation was decidedly over before it had even really started.

"So much for keeping an open mind," Kacie mumbled as she followed him out like a child who had just been told to mind her manners.

∞∞∞∞

"How was your lunch?"

Kacie sat down in the chair across from the small receptionist's desk outside her office. "Fine."

"Did you bring up the hobby?"

"I tried."

"That bad, huh?"

"Yup. How have things been here?"

"I would say quiet except that Shelby stopped by to drop off a message for you. That girl can talk."

"That she can. What was the message?"

Suzanne lifted her latest crossword puzzle book up and found the note. "Here you go. Looks like Asha actually took the message."

Kacie walked into her office reading the note written in Asha's distinctive and beautiful handwriting. It said Linda Walker had called to schedule an "official" meeting with her. Glancing at the time written on the note, Kacie realized the call must have been automatically forwarded to the library while both she and Suzanne had been out to lunch.

Not recognizing the name on the note, Kacie picked up her phone and dialed the library extension. "Hey Shelby, is Asha there?"

"Hi Kacie, yup hold on a second." Kacie heard some shuffling sounds, a little girl's voice singing loudly in the background, and an adult admonishing her to "shhhhh."

"Hello?"

"Hi Asha, I just got your note about a Linda Walker. Did she say anything about what this was regarding?"

"No, she said something about being in town and wanting to meet. She said you'd know who she was and why she was calling."

"Hmmmm, the name doesn't ring a bell. She wants to meet with me?"

"No, no. Sorry about that. She called to schedule a

meeting between you and Robert."

"Oh, you mean Lindsay Waller called?"

"Maybe that was her name. It was hard to understand her because she was talking down to me from a very high pedestal."

Kacie laughed at Asha's perfect portrayal of Lindsay.

"Did she say what it was for?"

"I asked her a couple of times, but she wouldn't tell me. She just said Robert needed to talk to you, it was important, and he had a tight schedule. She wasn't exactly friendly and forthcoming."

"Oh, you have no idea. I met her when they first came to see the house. She was cold."

"Robert, on the other hand, is ho…."

Before Asha could finish her thought, Kacie cut her off with a chuckle. "He is indeed," and disconnected the line to call someone she wasn't exactly as eager to talk to.

The phone was answered on the first ring with a curt, "Lindsay."

Determined to be polite and friendly, Kacie replied, "Hi Lindsay, this is Kacie from Sycamore Ridge returning your call."

"Are you free for a 30-minute meeting with Robert at your office tomorrow at ten?"

So much for being friendly. Kacie didn't have to check her schedule to know she had free time and replied immediately, "Yes."

"I'll put it on his calendar. Don't be late. He's only there for a short time and has a lot to get done."

Kacie rolled her eyes as the line was disconnected.

∞∞∞

Ten o'clock arrived faster than Kacie had expected it to.

She was sitting behind her desk reading a tabloid hidden inside a nature magazine when a gentle tap on her open door announced that Robert had arrived.

Kacie expertly closed the magazines so that the one on the inside was fully hidden by the one on the outside, stood, and walked around her desk.

"Robert, so good to see you. Please have a seat." She pointed to one of two chairs in front of her desk and sat down in the other one.

"Kacie, I must apologize for all the formality of this meeting. Is it okay if I close the door?"

"Of course." Kacie's voice didn't betray her continually piquing curiosity, which was now mixed with a hint of worry over some bad news Robert seemed to be preparing her for.

As Robert closed the door, sat down, and crossed his legs, Kacie had a brief moment to study him. With the warmer weather, he was dressed in fewer layers. Well-tailored khaki trousers and a crisp white button-down shirt opened at the top looked even better on him with his tall, trim physique. Asha was right. He really was....

Robert cleared his throat, rousing Kacie from her improper thoughts. He seemed surprisingly nervous.

"Is everything okay?"

"Kacie...I haven't been exactly forthcoming with you."

Here it comes, Kacie thought. The bad news. She waited for him to continue.

"I'm not sure how to tell you this, so I'll just be as direct as I can be." Robert fidgeted with the cuff of his shirt as if trying to buy one extra minute. "Have you heard of a band called Mirrors? The lead singer is named Jett Vanders?"

Kacie wasn't sure what she had been expecting, but it certainly wasn't a discussion of rock bands. Unsure of the direction this was heading, Kacie hesitantly nodded her head.

"Good. Good." Robert fumbled around looking for the best way to say what he knew he needed to tell her. What she deserved to know. After a few seconds of awkward silence which Kacie refused to break, Robert knew he had no choice but to say what he had come to tell her. "Jett's my younger brother. The house on Willow was bought and renovated for him to come live in for the next few months. After that, we'll see."

To say that Kacie was dumbstruck would have been a huge understatement. She had literally just been reading yet another article about the struggling musician.

"The lead singer of Mirrors is your brother? Jett Vanders is your brother?" Kacie repeated rather stupidly.

"Yes." Robert waited patiently for the news to sink in.

"I'm sorry, let me get this straight. You bought the house for him? He's coming to live in Sycamore Ridge? Jett Vanders, your younger brother, is coming to live here? In the house on Willow?"

"Yes, that is correct." Robert knew there was nothing Kacie could do to stop him, but he also believed it was crucial for her to know the truth. To help protect Jett's privacy in any way she could.

Kacie took a deep, quivering breath. Robert's initial evasiveness began to make sense now. Combined with what she had read in the tabloids, she quickly concluded that Jett was moving to Sycamore Ridge to go through some sort of rehabilitation program at a house that was renovated specifically for that purpose.

She knew she had to tread carefully with Robert at this point. He had every right to expect his own privacy, and perhaps more accurately, his brother's. Over the past several weeks, they had funneled a great deal of money into the local economy. Not that the residents of Sycamore Ridge were struggling financially, but she was pleased that most of the work and items purchased for the house was done by local craftsmen. It was important to her that all her constituents be well-employed.

But on the other hand, it was also her responsibility, her duty, to protect the residents of her town. She wasn't about to let some wild rock star upset their harmonious lifestyle without getting some guarantees from Robert.

Despite feeling personally deceived, Kacie knew she had to play a neutral role and do the right thing for her residents, old *and* new.

"Wow, I'm not sure I know what to say. I have to admit that I thought you were keeping something from us. But never something like this." Kacie paused as the gravity of the news sunk in further. "Is there anything more you feel comfortable sharing with me?"

"Why don't you tell me what you'd like to know, and I'll do my best to answer your questions."

Almost immediately, Kacie knew what she wanted the answer to first. "Why Sycamore Ridge?"

"Few reasons, really. If you remember when we first met, I mentioned to you that we grew up a couple of hours away from here. It was a great place to live, and I would have loved to get a place there, but too many people would have recognized Jett. We have some other emotional and financial connections to this area, but I don't want to go into that at the moment. Look, the one thing Jett needs right now, more than anything else, is to disappear from the public eye. He needs time and space to rest. To not feel the pressure of the paparazzi misconstruing his every move."

Kacie wasn't sure what Robert meant about 'misconstruing,' but she didn't think this was the right time to get into Jett's recent behavior and appearance.

"So he's looking to keep a low profile? No parties? No press?"

Robert nodded, "Correct. To be honest, I doubt he'll even leave the house."

Kacie wanted to believe Robert, but in the end, it didn't really matter what he said. It only mattered what Jett decided to do.

"Look, Kacie, it isn't our intention to disrupt your small-town lifestyle. I just want my brother to be happy and have the space he needs. I like Sycamore Ridge, and I think it's the perfect place for him right now."

"I guess it's settled then. As far as I'm concerned, he's just another new homeowner. And as a resident of Sycamore Ridge, he's entitled to the same privacy as everyone else who lives here. As long as your brother keeps a low profile, you'll find that no one will disturb him or pry into his personal life. I think it's fair to say that you've experienced this, too, on your multiple visits here?"

"I have. There is one other thing though."

"Oh?"

"We thought it would be better if he used his real name while he's here. Jack Wilkens."

"Jack Wilkens," Kacie repeated, trying to picture this new name for the man she had always referred to as Jett Vanders. "Got it. You know, Robert, you've unloaded a pretty heavy burden on my mayoral shoulders today."

Robert thought, hoped, that he heard a hint of Kacie's general affability returning.

"I have. And you've handled it with enviable aplomb."

"Thank you. You know, there is one other thing on

my end, too," Kacie said, wanting desperately to ease the tension with this man whose company she had come to enjoy so much.

"I see," Robert smiled. He sensed what was coming, but he played along anyway, "And what's that?"

"I didn't have time to grab breakfast this morning."

"Oh, well, we need to fix that right away. If you have time, I'd love to buy you some coffee."

"Coffee?" Kacie repeated, trying to keep the disappointment from her voice.

"And maybe I can throw in a morning bun from Rebekah's?"

Kacie was halfway out the door before Robert even had a chance to stand up from his chair.

∞∞∞∞

Jack fell asleep before the private plane that would whisk him away from the spotlight even left the runway. Thankfully, he had managed to give one last great performance at the press conference, and no one had suspected a thing. He had even convincingly told his cover story about spending the next few weeks visiting a secret location with a 'special' friend. That calculated lie was sure to send the paparazzi rumor mill into a frenzy.

Jack had hated having to lie to his bandmates though, especially Lola and Derek, but Robert had convinced him otherwise. The less everyone knew, the more likely it was that his privacy could be protected. Besides, Robert had promised that he could call them once he was settled in whatever hick town his new house was in.

While Jack slept soundly, Lindsay took the time to speak to Robert at length about how they should handle the latest stalker phone call. Two previous hang-ups from an unknown caller earlier in the week which Lindsay had answered had put them on edge.

"I should never have let him answer the phone. I don't know what I was thinking."

"You were thinking that the only person who was going to call him was me," Robert said gently, trying to reassure Lindsay. "There's no way you could have known she was going to call at that exact moment."

"That's the whole point, isn't it? There's no way to know anything that will happen. That's why we're always supposed to be on our guard."

"Look, Lindsay, stop beating yourself up over this. No one blames you." Robert's tone was more firm this time. He needed Lindsay to focus on next steps. "I'm glad you destroyed the phone. All that data is backed up anyway. I think maybe we should just be upfront with Jack. Let him know we made a mistake, but we've fixed it now. There's no way she'll ever be able to get to him in Sycamore Ridge. And as for his cell phone, he doesn't need his own line anyway. Especially since he seems committed to disconnecting and getting some downtime. Besides, he's always got a couple of our people with him so if we ever need to reach him, we can call them."

"Agreed."

"How is he?"

"Sleeping right now, but I have never seen him that angry. He yelled at me, Robert. I've worked for him for years, and I've never heard him raise his voice."

"I wish I could have been there, but I couldn't miss the kids' tournaments."

"And he wouldn't have wanted you to. When are you planning on coming to see him?"

"In about a week. Make sure he's settled before you

leave Sycamore Ridge."

"You know I will."

"Yup, that's why we can't live without you, Lindsay."

Lindsay smiled and put down her phone.

The rest of the flight and drive to the new house were thankfully uneventful. As soon as he walked through the front door, Jack asked where his room was and promptly walked towards the door Lindsay was pointing at. He left her standing in the hall, without saying a word about the house.

# CHAPTER 7

## *A Misguided Walk*

"It's not even nine yet, and it's already starting to get hot. A little early in the season, I think."

"Yeah, it is. Hopefully, it's just a fluke."

"Let me grab a couple of the guys, and we'll get the pickup unloaded for you."

Bill started to walk towards the house when a low growl from Cooper made him stop.

Kacie looked at Bill, surprised to hear her normally friendly dog growling. She turned towards the cab of the pickup where Cooper had been lounging the moment before. Now, he was standing on the front seat looking out the window at a stranger walking towards them.

"Easy, Cooper. Come on out." Kacie opened the door and let her dog, who was finally behaving like a guard dog, out.

She held on to his collar as his growling became deeper. Bill came over to stand next to her as the stranger kept walking towards them. As he got closer to the end of the driveway where they were standing, Bill called out to him.

"Can I help you?" Bill tried to keep his voice friendly. He did not like the look of this man who was wearing a baseball cap pulled low over long, limp, blonde hair. Dark circles under his eyes, an unshaven face with a scruffy beard and mustache, and dingy looking clothes that were too big on his gaunt figure made Bill think of drug addicts he had seen in the city.

The man slowed but didn't stop. He put his hands into his jean pockets and mumbled just loud enough for them to hear, "No, I'm just out for a walk."

"Do you live around here?" Bill asked with a slight edge to his voice, not willing to let it go. He was protective of his community and did not want to see this element start making its way in.

Cooper started barking.

The stranger picked up on the warning tone in Bill's voice and decided it would be better to stop.

"Yeah, I do."

"Easy Cooper," Kacie said as she struggled to hold on to the dog's collar. He was becoming increasingly agitated.

"Great, where?"

"Where what?"

"Where do you live?"

"Look, man, I was just out for a walk, and I got lost."

"That's not what I asked you. I asked where you live."

The stranger shrugged his shoulders and looked as though he was considering walking away.

"Do you really think you can outrun this dog if we let go of his collar?"

Clearly frustrated, the man raised his voice. "I don't know the address, okay? I just moved here a few days ago. It's a grey house up on a hill. They just did a bunch of renovations on it." He felt so foolish not even knowing his own address. And being disconnected from a cell phone was not helping him right now.

Hearing the man's response, Kacie commanded Cooper

to be quiet and the dog finally acquiesced. "Are you Robert's younger brother?"

Kacie could tell that the stranger was looking right at her, but with his cap pulled down so low over his eyes, it was difficult to make out his expression. If she had to guess, she would say it was a mixture of surprise and trepidation. He seemed to hesitate before answering. If he said yes, and she recognized who he was, he worried she would make a scene. If he said no, he worried that the man standing next to her would give him a hard time. After a moment of studying her earnest expression, he decided to be honest.

"I am."

Kacie, still holding on tightly to Cooper's collar, turned to Bill. "It's okay, Bill. I know where he lives. You remember the old Russell place that Walter was working on? I think you did some work there, too?"

Bill nodded and she continued, gesturing towards the man. "His brother owns it."

"The guy with the fancy shoes is this guy's brother?" Bill asked incredulously. Right at that moment, one of his workers yelled out from a second story window that was open, "Hey Bill, you better come check out this wiring. Doesn't look up to code."

Bill cursed under his breath and looked to Kacie to gauge her reaction.

"Go on, Bill. I'm fine. I'll just give him directions and be right in."

"You sure?"

"Yeah, besides, I have my trusty guard dog with me."

"Okay, just holler if you need anything." Bill went inside after shooting what he hoped was a stern warning glare at the man not to try any funny business.

Kacie walked to the end of the driveway, still holding on to Cooper's collar. He was straining against it and had begun growling again. "Cooper, cut it out."

When she was a few feet away from the man, a strange thing happened. Cooper suddenly stopped growling and began whimpering. He stopped straining against her hold and began wagging his tail furiously. Kacie looked down at him, and he looked up with an "I'll be a good boy" expression. She eased her grip on him to test things out, and he continued wagging his tail and assumed a very non-threatening posture.

"Looks like he's not scared of me now. Can I pet him?"

"Oh, ummm, sure," Kacie agreed.

"I'm Jack," he said as he bent to pet Cooper who now looked as happy as a kid in a candy store.

"I'm Kacie," she replied as she watched this world-famous celebrity playing with her dog. He certainly didn't look like a celebrity, though. His clothes looked disheveled and dirty, and he smelled like he could use a shower. He looked up at her almost as though he could hear her thoughts.

"Thanks for not telling him who I am." Without waiting for her reply, he continued, "I'm a bit of a mess. I got up and decided to go for a walk and then I got lost a while back, and I've just been wandering. I didn't plan to be out for so long and it's hotter than I expected. I don't have a phone, either." He looked embarrassed and surprisingly vulnerable.

"You're not far from home," Kacie said gently. She turned to her right and pointed, "If you walk about a quarter mile that way, you'll come to a path through that wooded area. Just follow that path for another half mile and it'll end in your backyard."

He appreciated that she didn't judge him or comment on his foolishness in leaving his house in a strange town, without knowing his own address or having his cell phone. "Thank you. I really appreciate it."

"Listen, I have cold water and some granola bars in the car. Would you like some?"

Jack wasn't sure what to say, but again, her kind expression guided him. "Yes, please."

"Can you watch Cooper for a sec? I'll just grab them for you."

Kacie ran to her truck and grabbed a bottle of water out of her little cooler and some granola bars she had made the day before. Walking back towards him, she smiled at how much both he and Cooper appeared to be enjoying each other's company. After handing everything over to him, she asked, "Will you be okay?"

Nodding his head, he took a long drink of water and immediately began feeling better.

"Do you want me to drive you?"

"No. I feel better already. Thank you so much for helping me. Robert's been raving about this place and how friendly everyone is. Now I know why. I'll be alright." He gave her a reassuring smile and started walking backwards in the direction she had pointed out. "Thanks again."

She smiled at him and waved.

"Bye Cooper," he called out as he turned his back and walked away.

So much for never leaving the house, Kacie thought to herself. She wondered what Robert would say if he knew that Jack was wandering around Sycamore Ridge on his own.

∞∞∞∞

Between the cold water and the delicious granola bars, which must have been homemade, Jack felt revived and enjoyed the rest of his walk along a beautiful trail that wound through a sun-dappled wooded area. The patches of shade also helped cool him. At the end of the trail, just as promised, was the far end of a backyard. His back-yard. At least he guessed it was his. Considering he hadn't stepped foot out the door since he'd arrived almost three days ago, he was basing his assumption on Kacie's direc-tions and a few things Robert had mentioned about the house, including that it had a pool and guest house. This house had both of those and was grey. Hoping he was right, he walked the length of the backyard with some unease. He didn't want to have another run-in like he had had with Bill. If that did happen, he knew there was no chance there'd be another person around like Kacie to help him.

As he got closer to the pool area, he noticed a side door that had a few moving boxes stacked up next to it. Just to the right of them was an empty guitar rack.

"Grey house, pool, guest house, moving boxes, and a guitar rack," he mumbled to himself. "What are the chances this isn't my place?" Concluding that it had to be his house and yard, Jack looked around. It really was just as nice as Robert had described it. Nicer, even. The yard felt expansive after all the congested cities he'd spent the last few months in. It was great to have private space to move around without worrying about running into someone trying to take his photo or get his autograph. The wooded area he had walked through appeared to ex-tend all around the back of his property, and he thought he saw another trail entrance a little further down. It looked inviting, and he decided at that moment that he would explore as much of the area as he could. With a little more preparation next time. Standing in the sun surveying his new home put a smile on his face. Maybe now, he hoped, he might finally get some time to unwind.

But first, he wanted to get out of his sweaty clothes. Maybe cool off by taking a dip in the beckoning pool. That's when he realized he didn't even have a key to the house. It looked like, in addition to relaxing and exploring, he was going to have to spend some time figuring out how to live like an adult in the real world. But for now, he didn't care. There was no one around. He felt free and relaxed for the first time in a long time. Throwing caution to the wind, he took off all his clothes and dove into the deep end of the pool. It had been ages since he'd swum a lap, but muscle memory took over and his clean strokes propelled him to the other end of the pool. Feeling invigorated by the cold water and the freedom, he swam a few more laps before getting the sensation that he was being watched. Pushing his hair out of his face, he wiped the water from his eyes and saw someone standing at the edge of the pool.

# CHAPTER 8

## *Transformation*

"Geez, Laura, you scared me."

"I scared you? How do you think I feel? I thought you were still sleeping in your room. Suddenly I hear a noise outside and look out the window to see a naked man in the pool! I've been in the kitchen for almost half an hour. There's no way you could have walked past me without me noticing." The leggy, lithe woman with short blonde hair put her hands on her hips in indignation. Dressed in yoga pants and a sports bra, she was a knockout.

"Some bodyguard you are," Jack teased good-naturedly. "I left the house almost three hours ago. I was sick of being in my room. I had to get out. So, I went for a walk."

"You went for a walk?" Laura asked incredulously. "Just like that? By yourself?"

"Yup."

Laura cocked her eyebrow at him. "You went for a walk in a new town that you know nothing about. By yourself."

"Don't forget that I have no sense of direction, I know no one here, and I don't have a cell phone."

Laura was surprised to see Jack looking so happy about these facts. "Right...there's that, too."

Jack just smiled in response.

"Okay then. How was it?"

"Great. I got completely lost, and then I almost got attacked by a dog. But then the dog decided he liked me, and his owner somehow figured out I was Robert's brother. So, she was kind enough to give me directions, a bottle of water, and some granola bars. I felt almost like a regular guy."

Laura couldn't help but laugh at Jack's obvious pleasure in how well his misguided walk had ended.

"Do we have any eggs, Laura?"

"Yes, why?"

"I'm starving. Can you make me an omelet?"

This request made Laura even happier. "I'd love to. How about some breakfast potatoes to go with it?"

"Perfect. But before you do that...," Jack began as he pulled himself out of the pool.

"Get you a towel?" Laura laughed and walked to the house without waiting for a response.

∞∞∞∞

Wrapped up in a plush towel, Jack stretched out on one of the pool chairs and put his arms behind his head. It was so peaceful and secluded in the yard that he didn't hear the sound of a car pulling into the driveway.

The front door opened, and a woman walked in carrying two bags of groceries.

"Laura? Are you cooking something? It smells amazing." She walked into the kitchen and put the bags down on the island.

"Hi babe," Laura turned from the stove and gave the love of her life a quick peck on the cheek. "You're not going to believe what happened while you were gone."

Laura filled Ellie in on everything, while she put away the groceries. When she got to the part about Jack having left the house on his own before they had even woken up, Ellie stopped her, clearly upset.

"He can't do things like that. He knows better."

"I don't know if I agree. I think maybe it was good for him. He needs to get some of his confidence back. And besides, no one knows we're here."

"That's what we thought last time. And the time before."

"This is different. Our tour dates and locations were public knowledge. Plus, there are so many rumors floating around right now about where he is – Lake Como, Bali, Paris. It'll take a long time for someone to figure out that none of those rumors has any merit."

Ellie could only hope that Laura was right.

∞∞∞

"I just can't get over how different he looks," Lindsay remarked as she poured herself a glass of wine from an open bottle on the patio table. She sat down and rested her head on the back of her chair to look up at the night sky. "You guys have no idea how awful he looked when we first got here."

"I can't believe he never even came out of his room those first few days. Even when we got here. And then he up and goes for a walk? By himself?" Ellie, still unsettled by the unnecessary risk Jack had taken, couldn't shake the feeling that she should have somehow been able to stop him.

Laura took a sip of her wine and cast a sideways glance at Ellie, knowing exactly what she was thinking. "Ellie, stop obsessing over it. I think that walk was a turning point for him. His whole demeanor has changed since he went on that walk. He's so much more like his old self. Re-

86

laxed, *happy*."

"And eating. I don't think I've ever seen him eat the way he's been eating the past few days," Lindsay laughed. "You've got your work cut out for you Laura."

"Don't I know it. But trust me, if he keeps swimming as much as he has been, he'll be fine. He needed to put on a few pounds anyway. I watched some video clips of him from that last concert, and he looked way too thin."

"Are you guys talking about me?" Jack asked as he joined three of his favorite women on the back porch. Freshly showered and wearing nothing but his pajama pants, Jack walked to the edge of the patio and breathed deeply. "Is it just me or is this place perfect?"

Turning towards his friends, who were technically his employees, but felt more like family, Jack asked. "So, tell me...and be honest. Am I as good looking as they say?" He flashed them a mischievous smile that would have sent his legions of fans swooning. But today, all he got in return were eye rolls and a "shut up, Jack."

∞∞∞∞

"Jackie! Look at you!" Robert exclaimed as he gave his younger brother a big hug. "You look fantastic!"

"I thought you weren't getting here until tomorrow! I'm so glad to see you!"

"I thought I'd surprise you! Besides, these three have been going on and on about how much you've changed, I had to come see for myself."

Robert walked over to the dining table where Lindsay, Laura, and Ellie were sitting and gave them all an emotional hug. He knew how much they did for Jack, and he wanted them to know how much he appreciated each of them.

"So, what do you think? Have you changed your mind about this place yet?"

"Absolutely. I'm so glad you bought this house. It's just perfect. I can't imagine how much extra work this created for you, but it means so much to me. You always take such good care of me," Jack said, fighting back his emotions.

"Maybe now that your brother is here, you'll feel compelled to wear clothes around the house and while you're in the pool?" Ellie teased to lighten the mood a little.

Robert laughed, "He had better!"

"I don't know why I would need to," Jack retorted with his signature grin. "I mean, there's no one else here. Just look around, it's only open space and privacy."

"There are people living in the houses on either side of yours, you do know that right?"

"Yeah, but with all this space between the houses and the big trees between the yards, they can't see us. I feel like we're in this perfect cocoon. I'm not sure I'm ever going to want to leave."

"What's for lunch? I'm starving." Robert asked, deftly changing the subject.

∞∞∞∞

"What's for breakfast? I'm starving?" Jack sauntered into the kitchen long after everyone else had finished eating.

"You're kidding me, right? We all ate over an hour ago."

Jack inhaled deeply and asked, "Let me guess, French toast casserole? And, because I know how much you love me, I bet you've kept some warming in the oven for me?"

Laura laughed. "Yes, but this isn't a restaurant, and I am not going to serve you, your highness. There's a plate on the table. Take the casserole out of the oven and grab the maple syrup and blueberries yourself."

"Yes ma'am."

Jack was contemplating licking the last of the syrup off his plate when Robert walked in.

"Look who's finally awake."

"Where have you been?"

"In the office taking care of some post-tour business. The numbers look good, Jackie. Really good."

"We should celebrate."

"What did you have in mind?" Robert asked cautiously.

"Maybe get the grill going and cook outside?"

Relieved, Robert agreed. "Sounds like a plan. I'll go into Sycamore Ridge later this afternoon and pick up whatever Laura needs." Almost as an afterthought, Robert added, "I should drop by and say hello to the mayor while I'm there."

"The mayor? Why? Is he a friend of yours?"

"Not he, she. And yes, I would definitely consider Kacie a friend."

"Wait a second, did you say Kacie?"

Robert nodded. Wondering if they were talking about the same person, Jack asked, "Dark haired girl with a dog named Cooper?"

"Yes...how could you possibly know that?"

"Know what?" Ellie asked as she joined them in the kitchen.

"Listen, Robert, I need to tell you something. Laura and Ellie already know about it, but I made them promise not to tell you."

"Is that right?" Robert asked looking at Ellie, who shrugged her shoulders.

"Don't look at me. I wanted to tell you, but he and his fan girl ganged up on me."

Robert turned his attention back on Jack and crossed his arms. "Go ahead, I'm listening."

"Look, I can tell that you're getting upset, but try to understand. You don't know what it was like when I first got here. I was miserable and exhausted and scared. All I wanted to do was hide in a corner and lick my wounds. And that's just what I did for the first...I don't even know how many...days. Just ask the girls."

"I don't have to ask them, Jack. I spoke with them every day, multiple times a day. We knew how much you needed time out of the public eye. We understood, and we gave you the space you deserved." Robert's tone had softened, and Jack took this as a sign of encouragement to continue.

"One morning, I woke up and just had to get out of the house. I couldn't stand being in that room anymore. It was early and everyone else was still sleeping, so I snuck out as quietly as I could. I thought I'd just go for a short walk up and down the street, but when I got outside... I just suddenly felt so free. There was no one there. Not a soul. No paparazzi, no fans, no entourage. Just me. So, I kept walking, and the next thing I knew, I got turned around on one of the streets and couldn't remember the name of our street or what the house looked like except that it was grey."

"Jack...."

"I know, I know. Trust me I get how stupid it was. But then I was walking down this one street where there were a bunch of people working on a house, and that's where I met Kacie." Intentionally leaving out the parts about Bill and Cooper almost attacking him, Jack went on, "I told her that I had just moved to town and described what I could about the house, which wasn't much, but she figured it out almost immediately. Once she knew that I was your younger brother, she was so kind to me. She gave me water and food and told me how to get home. She even offered to drive me home."

Robert sighed, grateful once again for Kacie and her kindness. He wondered how upset she was about Jack wandering around outside when Robert had given her his word that Jack would keep a low profile. Now he knew he absolutely had to go see her and try to explain.

"That was a pretty stupid thing you did, Jack. I had given Kacie my word that you would stay close to home and not draw attention to yourself."

"I haven't left the house or backyard since then. But if you're going to see Kacie, I'd like to go with you. She really did go out of her way to help me, and I'd like to thank her."

Ellie, who had been listening quietly, decided to weigh in. "I'm not sure that's such a good idea."

"Why not? What're the chances that anyone besides Kacie and the people in this house know that I'm living in Sycamore Ridge?"

"Don't be naïve, Jack. Someone could recognize you."

Without saying a word, Jack went to his room and returned with a magazine and turned to an earmarked page that had a close-up photo of his face from a few weeks earlier. He held it up next to his face and asked, "Really? You think that someone is going to see me in Sycamore Ridge and recognize me? Doubtful."

Laura had come back into the room mid-conversation and threw her support behind Jack. "I think Jack's right. No one is going to know who he is because no one would ever even consider that he'd be in Sycamore Ridge. That's his best cover if you ask me. If he moves around like a regular Joe, people will just think he's a regular Joe. Albeit a very good looking one."

Robert was quiet, weighing the likelihood and risk of someone recognizing Jack versus the benefits to his brother of being able to live a 'normal' life, even if just for a short time. Uncharacteristically going with his gut, he announced, "Okay, we'll head out after lunch."

∞∞∞

Kacie had to keep herself from laughing aloud while reading the latest tabloid speculation about Jett Vanders being holed up in a "majestic chateau" with a "pouty" French model. She was sitting at her desk with the magazine discreetly tucked inside her laptop and so engrossed in the story that she didn't see the two men walk up to her main door.

Thankfully, her little bell dutifully did its job and the ringing sound brought her back to reality just in time. She slammed her laptop shut and looked up to see Robert and an unfamiliar looking man walk in.

"Kacie! Hi! I hope we didn't startle you! You look like you just got caught with your hand in the cookie jar!" Robert laughed.

Kacie stood and walked around her desk to give him a quick hug. "Oh, no, sorry about that, I was just reading...ummmm...," hoping they didn't hear the sound of her heart pounding, she finished lamely, "an email from a client."

Robert was surprised by Kacie's obvious fib but didn't want to embarrass her further. Maybe, he thought, she had been reading an email from a gentleman friend. He was about to change the subject to more neutral territory when Cooper came bounding out of the back of the shop with his tail wagging wildly. Mistakenly thinking that Cooper was excited to see him, Robert bent down to pet the dog and was once again surprised when Cooper ran right past him and straight to Jack.

"Well then. I see where I stand," Robert laughed.

"Hey Cooper!" Jack kneeled and gave the ecstatic dog a good petting.

Robert stood back up and turned towards Kacie. "I had been planning on bringing Jack in to meet you, but I hear he already took care of that."

Kacie smiled at Robert and disbelievingly looked down at Jack. When he looked up and smiled back at her, her heart did an unexpected little flip. The man kneeling down petting her dog looked so different from the first time she had met him; he was almost unrecognizable. His shoulder length hair looked clean and a little darker than she had seen in the frequent photos of him. His usual goatee and five o'clock shadow had been shaved clean so that his chiseled jawline was visible. There were no dark circles under his eyes. His skin looked as though he had spent some time outdoors under the sun, and she thought he had gained a little weight. Most remarkably, though, was his expression. He seemed to have lost that scared little boy look. It was strange. He didn't look like the man in the tabloids, and he didn't look like the man she had helped earlier that week. He seemed relaxed and genuinely happy, and his almost too-perfect smile reached his eyes, making them sparkle.

"It's good to see you, Kacie."

"You're looking much better. I gather you found your way home without any trouble?"

"I did. That's actually why we're here. I wanted to tell you how much I appreciated your help that day."

"You're very welcome."

Jack smiled at her again, grateful for the simple and

honest conversation. She managed to pay him a straight-forward compliment and accepted his gratitude without pretense. He felt no judgement from her about his behavior. It was incredibly refreshing after all the time he had to spend around posers and hangers-on. He went back to petting Cooper while Robert added his words of thanks and caught up with Kacie as if they were the best of friends. It gave Jack a moment to get a better look at her.

Her hair was gathered up near the base of her neck in some sort of messy, side ponytail. Little whisps had come loose and curled around to frame her face. Her smooth, healthy skin was accentuated by bright eyes and full lips. When she smiled, he noticed that one of her front teeth slightly overlapped the one next to it. Although she wasn't painfully skinny like most of the women he had been with in the past, he appreciated her figure. She wore well-fitting jeans with a small hole at one knee, which, he thought, probably came from natural wear and tear as compared to the thousand-dollar jeans by designers like Balmain and Roberto Cavalli which he owned that were "professionally torn" before being sold. Her loose, open buttoned denim shirt draped over a fitted tank top which hugged her curves very nicely.

"Jack? Jack!" Robert's voice snapped him out of his reverie.

"Oh, sorry, what?" Jack stood up and realized that Kacie was taller than he remembered. Both he and Robert were tall men, over six feet, and he figured she must be almost 5'7" or 5'8" tall.

"I was just asking if you knew that your house is furnished with some of Kacie's work."

"Kacie's work? Wait a sec, I thought you said she's the mayor."

Kacie laughed aloud and Robert looked at his brother like he was not the brightest bulb in the bush.

"Then why would she be sitting at a desk in this work-shop looking at emails from..."

"A client," Kacie reiterated.

"I am so confused."

"Apparently," Robert smirked playfully at his brother.

"Don't be," Kacie added gently. "A lot of people, when they hear that I'm the mayor, assume that it's my full-time job. But in a relatively small town like Sycamore Ridge, it's not. I'm the mayor part-time. When I'm not performing the duties of that role, I'm here in my shop."

"Where 'one man's treasure is another man's trash is another woman's treasure,'" Robert added.

"You remembered my motto!"

"It's, how should I put it?" Robert paused to find the right words and settled on, "hard to forget."

Jack looked on at the easy banter between Kacie and Robert, who clearly enjoyed each other's company. His big brother had always had a knack for finding good people to connect with. Whenever they were at meetings, press events, endless parties, his brother always advised him on who he could rely on and trust. And Robert had never been wrong. In fact, without Robert, Jack wouldn't have Lindsay, Laura, or Ellie in his life. Robert had handpicked each of them to work for Jack years ago, and they were like family to him now.

"So, this whole store is yours?" Jack asked, forcing his focus to extend past Kacie to the rest of the space.

"I like to think of it as more of a workshop than a store," Kacie corrected. "If you have time, I can show you around."

Robert was about to reply that they had errands to run

but was surprised when Jack chimed in, "I'd like that."

∞∞∞

"That was fantastic. I had no idea she was so talented. I'm definitely going to take her up on her offer to teach me how to work some of those machines."

Robert raised his eyebrows, "Really? I never knew you were interested in woodworking."

"You're the one that's always telling me I should find some hobbies to get my mind off of music."

Chuckling at having his words of advice thrown back in his face, Robert nodded, "Fair enough."

"Where to now?"

"We'd better head to the grocery store since you were thoughtful enough to invite Kacie over for the 'cookout' we're having tonight."

"Yeah, about that...I just thought we should do something nice for her. After all, she practically saved my life."

"Indeed. You better let Laura know we're having company," Robert said as he handed Jack his phone.

While Jack talked to Laura about the evening's dinner menu, Robert had a few moments to reflect on things. He couldn't believe how much Jack seemed to have changed in the days since he'd arrived in Sycamore Ridge. Of course, he knew the first few days had been miserable, but it seemed things had begun turning around after Jack's initial run-in with Kacie. From that point on, there had been a slow transformation taking place in Jack – not just his physical improvement, but also in his emotional well-being. Jack was more engaged in conversations, had more confidence, and was much quicker to laugh. He just seemed relaxed and happier in general. Robert wasn't surprised that it had happened, but he was surprised at how quickly it had happened.

Kacie had been another revelation for Robert. Even though he believed her to be a well-balanced woman based on all his interactions with her, he had been worried at how she would react to meeting Jack. Robert had seen perfectly "normal" women, of all ages, completely lose their minds over meeting or even just seeing his brother on the street. There was no doubt about it that Jack was an exceptionally handsome man. He had hair that made women jealous and beautiful blue-grey eyes, which seemed to change colors depending on what he wore or the kind of light he was in. But it was his sexy, knockout smile that drove his fans crazy. And, today, he looked more handsome than usual in his casual, dark jeans and plain white t-shirt.

Although it was obvious Kacie had been flustered when they first walked into her shop, she had handled the rest of their visit with composure. She was her usual funny and kind self. Robert never saw her be obsequious towards Jack. She answered his questions with patience and knowledge, and she even teased him on a couple of occasions.

When they were getting ready to leave and Jack asked Kacie over for dinner, you could have knocked Robert over with a feather.

∞∞∞∞

Kacie wasn't sure what had just happened. One minute, she had been reading about Jack partying at a French chateau with some glamorous model and the next minute, she was giving him a tour of her workshop and being invited over for dinner. It was unsettling to say the least, but not in an unpleasant way. She found Jack to be attentive and inquisitive. He clearly respected and loved his older brother, and Robert doted on him in return. There was no sign of the "wild party boy" he was depicted as in the tabloids. And even though Robert had technically violated their informal agreement of keeping a low profile by bringing Jack to Fountain Walk instead of "never leaving the house," Kacie was happy that he had.

She wondered how the rest of Jack's day would go and whether anyone would recognize him. For his sake, she hoped not.

# CHAPTER 9

## *The Last of the Cobbler*

Robert was pacing back and forth on the driveway talking on the phone when Kacie pulled in. He waved at her and signaled for her to go around to the back of the house. Placing his hand over the phone, he whispered, "Jack is out on the patio. I'll join you in a few minutes."

Kacie made her way across the driveway and around to the back of the house. The faint sound of someone strumming a guitar made its way to her ears. She assumed it was Jack, but she had never heard him playing anything but rock on an electric guitar. This music was soothing and peaceful, almost like new age music. But not the kind that included nature sounds like birdsong and ocean waves crashing on the shore, which Kacie was not partial to. This was music that could make you relax and forget about your troubles for a while.

"That sounds beautiful."

Jack stopped playing and looked up at her. He smiled and tucked his hair behind his ear, and Kacie's heart did a cartwheel while her stomach filled with butterflies.

"Did you like it? It's something new I'm working on."

Not seeing any paper or recording device, Kacie asked, "Oh? How will you remember it? Don't you have to write it down or record it?"

Jack chuckled almost to himself. "Great question. No, I only write things down if I want to teach them to someone else. I have a very good ear, and I never forget a note that I like."

"That's incredible. Then there's me. I've never met a note that likes me."

Jack gave her a questioning look and she explained, "I literally have one of the worst voices in the world. I cannot hold a tune. At all."

Jack smiled at her again, "Good to know. What's in the dish? Smells delicious."

"So do you," Kacie mumbled under her breath.

"Sorry, what?" Jack asked.

"So do you...like apple and blueberry cobbler?" Kacie managed to blurt out as cover.

"If it tastes as good as it smells, I'm sure I will."

Fortunately, Kacie managed to keep her suggestive response to herself. She knew she needed to get herself away from him before she said anything she'd regret later.

"Where should I put this? It's kind of heavy."

"I'll take it. Come on into the kitchen, and I'll introduce you to Laura."

He put down his guitar, took the tray from her and went inside before she could ask who Laura was. The butterflies in her stomach had started turning to acid, but there was nothing to do except follow him inside. Maybe Laura was the pouty French model she'd read so much about. "Lucky me," Kacie thought. "I'll get to meet two celebrities inside of one week."

"Have I told you how gorgeous you look today?" Kacie overheard Laura asking Jack.

"Only about a dozen times."

"Fine, let's make it a baker's dozen." Turning towards

the open patio doors as Kacie entered, Laura smiled, "You must be Kacie. It's so nice to meet you. Your furniture is absolutely beautiful. I can't wait to come into your shop and see what else you're working on."

"I'd like that," Kacie was pleasantly surprised that Laura had heard about her. The leggy blonde was dressed in a tight, cropped white t-shirt that showed off her perfectly toned and tanned body. Paired with dark green joggers, she somehow managed to simultaneously look casual and like she'd just stepped out of a fashion shoot. Her short honey blonde hair accentuated her green eyes and perfect face.

"So, how does Jack look to you?"

Thankfully, before Kacie could figure out how to respond, another woman walked into the kitchen.

"Quit complimenting him, Laura. His ego is huge enough as it is." Kacie was surprised to hear Jack laugh aloud at what was apparently meant to be an insult.

"Why can't I compliment my own handiwork? He looks the way he does because I feed him well and make him exercise."

Noticing Kacie standing off to the side, the woman who looked to be closer in age to Robert, introduced herself. "You must be Kacie! I'm Ellie, it's nice to meet you."

Ellie was dressed more conservatively than Laura in a pair of jeans and a tank top. Despite her much looser fitting attire, there was no denying that Ellie was also in great shape. Her arms looked like she could inflict serious injury in a fight. She had dark brown hair pulled back in a tight ponytail. There was something almost harsh about her face, but it was saved by warm brown eyes and deep dimples when she smiled.

"Good to meet you."

"I want to talk to you about that table in the entryway. Laura and I would love something like that at our place."

More confused than before about who the two women were and how they were connected to Jack, Kacie asked, "If you live around here, you can come down to my shop. I'd be happy to show you around."

Now it was Ellie's turn to be confused. "You don't know where we live? Has Jack the Ego not told you anything about us?" She reached out, punched Jack in the arm before he could jump out of the way and explained. "Laura and I live in the guest house. She's his nutritionist and personal trainer. I'm his bodyguard. Together, we help him get through the daily grind of his incredibly hard life," she added jokingly.

Things were finally starting to fall into place for Kacie, except for one detail which became clear the very next moment.

"Quit picking on him, Ellie. If you weren't the love of my life, Jack would be."

Ellie rolled her eyes. "Are we going to stay in here talking or can we start grilling? I'm starving."

∞∞∞∞

"That was delicious," Jack sat back and smiled at Kacie. "The evil mistress of calorie counting here doesn't let me eat dessert very often." He shot Laura a mean glare, which she laughed off.

Kacie had thoroughly enjoyed her evening. There was an easy camaraderie to the interactions between the brothers and the two ladies, almost as if they had a close familial relationship rather than an employer-employee one. Robert, Ellie, and Laura doted on and teased Jack mercilessly like a baby brother, and he seemed to relish it.

"So, Kacie, I heard you've already met Lindsay? She had to fly back home yesterday. She's been gushing about how amazing you are and was disappointed to miss this chance to spend time with you. She asked me to say hello. She's hoping maybe the two of you can grab lunch together the next time she's in town."

"Oh…," unsettled by Jack's comment and dreading the thought of having to sit through a lunch with Lindsay, Kacie managed to mumble, "Say hi to her from me."

Jack laughed. "I'm just kidding. We know Lindsay's a tough pill to swallow, but she always has our best interest at heart."

Relieved, Kacie relaxed once again and took a sip of her lemonade. There was still no sign of the "wild party boy" in anything about Jack's behavior. He was intelligent, funny, and considering his fame, surprisingly relatable.

"I'll be right back," Robert said, going into the house. He returned a few seconds later with two bottles of wine, and Kacie realized she may have spoken too soon.

"We need to drink a toast to our new friend, Kacie."

"I'll grab the glasses."

"Not for me please," Kacie called out. "I don't drink."

Jack gave her a quizzical look. "You don't?"

Kacie shook her head in response, unsure of the direction things were going to go.

"Neither do I," he said softly.

She almost laughed out loud, but Robert interjected by saying only one word.

"Jack."

Kacie thought she heard a note of caution in his tone, and an odd silence fell across the table. What had once been a relaxed evening suddenly began to feel tense. Like an old fight that was starting up again.

"What? Who is she going to tell?"

Robert sighed, and Laura chimed in. "You know how I feel about this. I think it's okay for him to tell some people."

Kacie noticed Ellie looking over at Robert with an "I told you something like this would happen" expression.

"You told me this was a chance for me to relax and be myself. And look at me! When was the last time you saw me like this?" Without waiting for an answer, Jack continued. "Do you even know when the last time I *felt* like myself was? Do you know how exhausting it is to constantly be putting on a show? To be on display? To have people judging me based on a lie?"

Although Jack hadn't raised his voice, his hurt and frustration could be felt in every word he said. Kacie was beginning to feel like she should find an excuse to leave. She was about to stand up to start clearing the table when Robert started talking again.

"Take it easy, Jackie." Hoping the use of his brother's childhood nickname would ease some of the tension, Robert added, "We just want to do what's best for you."

"This is what's best for me. To be honest. To be myself. No one knows I'm here. And honestly, I don't think anyone around here would care. Kacie's not going to tell anyone. Are you?"

It was more of a statement than a question.

"That you don't drink?"

"That I can't drink. I'm not allowed to."

The strange turn of phrase gave Kacie pause, but Jack was looking at her with an expectant expression on his face, waiting for her response. She didn't really have to think about it. It was one thing to be a tabloid junkie, but it was another thing to sit across the table from someone, have them look you in the eye, and tell you a secret. She didn't quite understand *why* it was a secret, but she didn't think it was the right time or her place to ask. And it didn't really matter. A secret was a secret. And it was sacrosanct.

"That's entirely your business. I'm not sure why I'd have any reason to talk about that with anyone."

Jack beamed at her. "See," he said to the others without taking his eyes off hers. "Now, since you all are drinking your calories, I think it's only fair that Kacie and I get to finish off the last of the cobbler."

∞∞∞

When Kacie got home later that evening, she threw all her self-control out the window. Grabbing her laptop and a few tabloids that hadn't made their way into her recycling bin yet, she started doing some research. She felt guilty at first, but then immediately justified what she was doing by reminding herself that she was researching Jett Vanders, the public persona and not Jack Wilkens, the man she had just spent a lovely evening with.

All the stories written about him in the tabloids alluded to his spiraling out of control and often included photos of him looking drawn and often combative. In almost every photo, he was holding a black flask in his hand or drinking from it. Based on what Jack had revealed to her over dinner, Kacie couldn't help but wonder: what was in the flask?

Even if she did believe what Jack had said, and there was no real reason to doubt him, Kacie could explain away that question. It could be any one of many completely innocent drinks. For all she knew, it was just plain old water. Or better yet, for a singer, warm water with honey.

What she couldn't explain, though, is why he looked so unwell in all the photos.

The tabloids she had were all from the past couple of months and couldn't help her answer that question. But Kacie thought, maybe Google could. Thinking back, she recalled that the news about Jett's steady decline into "addiction" had really started picking up at the beginning of band's final world tour. Prior to that, most of the stories about the band focused on their growing legion of fans and their constant presence on the music awards circuit. In fact, apart from his status as an undeniable heartthrob, Jett had rarely been the sole focus of any article.

A sober, healthy musician apparently did not make for a good story or help with tabloid sales. Shutting down her laptop, Kacie got into bed and turned off the lights. She closed her eyes and images of the man from the tabloids flashed in her mind for a brief moment before being replaced by images of the healthy, incredibly good-looking man who had sat across from her eating her cobbler.

The thought of Jett Vanders taking second helpings of a dessert she had baked made her laugh out loud. And then, she thought about his smile when she had first arrived at his house, and all the butterflies it had sent swarming through her stomach came flying back.

The paparazzi may have gotten it all wrong about Jack's drinking problem. But they had definitely gotten one thing right. He was a bona fide heartthrob.

# CHAPTER 10

## Dolsot Bowls and Pie Safes

Kacie was putting the finishing touches on a small custom dining table she was building for a young couple who had recently moved to the area. They were part of what Kacie liked to call the "Great Migration" of tech workers who were leaving the crowded metropolitan cities in search of a better, slower lifestyle. Thankfully, not too many of them had heard of Sycamore Ridge, and she hoped to keep it that way. It was one thing to welcome a handful of new families to her town every year, but she had no interest in dealing with all the hassles that accompany a population boom.

Between the noise from her handheld sander and the music she had blaring from her small radio, Kacie didn't hear the bell on her front door. But Cooper did. When he stood up and started padding towards the front door wagging his tail, Kacie turned off the sander and turned down the volume on her radio.

"Kacie?"

"Hi Min-seo."

Following the sound of Kacie's voice, Min-seo made her way towards the back of the shop. "Guess what just came in the mail?" She was carrying a beat-up cardboard box covered with packing tape and looking like it had seen better days.

"A new car?"

"Ha-ha. Come on, I'm being serious. Guess."

"A dozen morning buns?"

Min-seo rolled her eyes. "You have a serious problem." She put the box down on the nearest surface and said, "Come on, let's open it together. I promise what's inside this box will make you almost as happy as your beloved morning buns."

Kacie put down her sander, and grabbing a pair of scissors off her desk, walked over to join her friend. After getting what seemed like an entire roll of packaging tape off the battered box, Min-seo stepped back. "Go ahead. It's all yours."

Surprised, Kacie asked, "Are you sure?"

"Yup, it's for you. My grandmother sent it."

"From Daegu?"

Min-seo smiled and nodded at her friend. Kacie always remembered the small things people told her. It was one of the reasons she was so well-liked. She actually *listened* when people talked to her.

The box was filled with bubble wrap and crumpled up newspapers. Having to dig through all of it just increased Kacie's anticipation of what she would find. She had absolutely no idea what to expect as she reached into the box. Her hands found two smaller boxes, and she pulled those out. They were not wrapped as obsessively as the outer box, and after a few seconds, she opened them and pulled out two stoneware bowls that were each about six inches in diameter.

"My own dolsot bowls!" Kacie exclaimed happily. "I still remember the first time your grandma made bibimbap for me when she was visiting last summer!"

"Yeah, and I remember how long it took me to convince her it wasn't illegal to make a vegetarian bibimbap," Min-seo laughed. "But after she saw how much you enjoyed it, she decided a vegetarian bibimbap didn't portend the end of the world."

"These are just beautiful. I can't wait to use them."

"And I can't wait to *not* have you over every other week for dinner."

Kacie was carefully placing the bowls back in the box when the bell rang again.

"Hello?" asked a now familiar voice that brought a smile to Kacie's face.

Min-seo, not recognizing the voice but clearly registering her friend's happiness on hearing it, mouthed "who's that?"

Kacie whispered back, "Robert's brother Jack. I'll be right back." Min-seo couldn't be certain, but she thought she noticed her friend blushing just a little before walking to the front of the store to welcome her new guest.

As it turned out, Jack wasn't alone. He was standing in the entryway with both Laura and Ellie. The unexpected pounding in Kacie's chest that had been triggered by the sound of Jack's voice eased just a little as she smiled at the threesome.

"Hi! What a nice surprise." It had only been a couple of days since their dinner together, and Kacie was pleased to see all of them again so soon.

"So, this is where the magic happens?" Laura asked.

"Yup, come on back. There's someone here I'd like you to meet."

"Maybe we should come back another time." Ellie didn't want to be rude, but it was her job to protect Jack, and Jack hadn't exactly been making her job any easier since their move to Sycamore Ridge. He was making impulsive decisions without asking for her advice or even thinking about the consequences. His ill-advised solo walk and impromptu dinner invitation to Kacie were things she would have never allowed.

"Why? You think Kacie's got a gaggle of paparazzi hiding out in her shop just waiting to ambush me? That would make great tabloid fodder. 'Washed Out Musician goes Furniture Shopping in Sycamore Ridge'. Lighten up, Ellie."

"He's got a point, babe."

Ellie sighed, acknowledging that what Jack was saying was perfectly logical.

To help set Ellie at ease, Kacie chimed in. "Min-seo has lived in Sycamore Ridge longer than I have and is one of my closest friends. And besides, she's more of a classical music fan."

"Fine. Outnumbered again. Lead the way, Kacie."

∞∞∞∞

It didn't take long for Ellie to let her guard down after meeting Min-seo, and Laura managed to drag her away from Jack to explore the shop.

As it turned out, Jack shared Min-seo's enjoyment of classical music, and they quickly fell into conversation. Kacie, however, did not. She liked a song she could sing along with, despite her lack of vocal ability. Thankfully, she was spared from having to listen to them discuss some composer or another's concerto when Laura called her over.

"Did you build this?" she asked pointing to a beautiful, antique pie safe.

"No, I found it at an estate sale and fixed it up."

"It's just perfect. We'll take it."

As a general rule, Kacie never said no to a sale. But she didn't think it was right for her to sell furniture to Laura which she knew would never fit in the small pool house. "Are you sure? It's a pretty big piece, and I'm not sure where you'd be able to put it. Unless you're planning on keeping it in the main house?"

"This is for our home on the West Coast. I've been looking for something like this for our kitchen."

"Our kitchen that we never cook in, and we never eat in."

Laura glared at Ellie and turned back to Kacie. "We'll take it. And you know what, I think we need to buy some new ceramics to display in our beautiful new pie safe."

∞∞∞

As Kacie lay in bed that night thinking about her day, a smile spread across her face. While the dolsot bowls, the visit from Jack, and the sale to Laura had been very pleasant surprises, it was what had happened just after that made her smile broaden a bit more.

True to her word, Laura was preparing to drag Ellie across the street to Min-seo's to buy ceramics when Jack announced that he would stay behind and work on something with Kacie. There had been an awkward pause before he added, "Go on. I won't melt or anything. Just swing back here when you're done." His gentle verbal nudge had the effect he wanted and sent the three ladies on their way.

Rubbing his hands together, he turned to Kacie, flashed her one of his butterfly-inducing smiles and said, "Okay, I'm all yours. Put me to work."

Kacie squinted her eyes at him, unsure of what he

meant. The first thought that went through her mind was decidedly inappropriate for a weekday afternoon in a workshop with a man she had only just met.

"I want to do something productive. Looks like you've got plenty of projects here you could use some help on. So, put me to work."

"Oh, right. Projects. Of course, I have lots of projects. Are you sure that's what you want to do?"

Jack nodded his head.

"Okay, well I need to finish sanding this table. Do you know how to use a sander?"

Cocking one eyebrow at her, he asked, "I think I may have used one during a woodshop class sophomore year in high school. Does that count?"

"Yikes. Come on, I'll show you."

They had spent almost an hour together, working side by side. Jack had been eager to learn and had an intense focus once he knew what he was doing. The noise from the sanders didn't afford them much opportunity to talk, but the silence had been companionable.

Kacie smiled at the thought of her newly developing friendship with a bona fide rock star as she began drifting off to sleep. It was too bad that his sexy smile suddenly popped into her mind and made sleep impossible until a little while later.

# CHAPTER 11

## At the End of the Trail

Kacie smiled to herself as she walked along the beautiful trail near her house. Cooper, who was off leash, was walking ahead of her on the sun dappled path. Very few people knew about this secluded trail that began near the end of her street or where it led. She hoped to always keep it that way. The canopy of trees overhead let in just enough sunlight to make the trail a cool and shady place to walk, while letting in enough sun to illuminate all the brilliant shades of green. A creek along her left ran in the opposite direction she was walking and made gentle babbling sounds as it ran over rocks and small branches. The water was cool and clear and reflected the sunlight with a sparkle that would make even the most hardened person smile.

Which is something Kacie seemed to be doing a lot these days. Sunday afternoons in the late spring and summer were something Kacie looked forward to all year. As soon as the weather got warm enough, she had a standing appointment to meet two of her favorite people at one of her favorite places.

About a half mile down, the trail gently curved to the left and then came to an abrupt end at a small meadow that was almost completely surrounded by woods. At the center of the green space was a pool of water bordered by large stones, and just beyond it was a slight rocky slope over which the creek poured playfully. The sound of water was louder here and provided the perfect backdrop.

"Cooper! Kacie!" A little girl's voice called out as they came into view. Cooper ran straight to the girl and immediately proceeded to knock her over in his exuberance.

"Careful, Cooper. We don't want to hurt Sally," Kacie added needlessly. Her dog loved Sally as much as he loved her, and she knew he would be gentle with the little girl.

"Hi Sally!" Kacie bent down and gave the rosy cheeked girl a big hug. "You look like a mermaid today," she added as she gently tugged on the girl's long, red hair that fell in tight ringlets to the middle of her back.

The compliment hit its mark as it was intended to, and Sally giggled with pleasure. "I'm getting better at swimming, too! Will you take me into the water today?"

"Hey, what about me?" Walter chimed in. He had been stretched out on a blanket next to Sally with his eyes closed, reveling in his sweet little daughter's joy.

"Hi, Walter."

"Hey, Kace."

Kacie laid out her blanket and put down her backpack. A handful of small groups of familiar people were spread out around the water. Kacie waved to a few of them and leaned back on the blanket. "It's the perfect day for a swim."

"Mmmmm," Walter agreed.

"You know, I was at the Russell house the other day."

"Yeah, Erica mentioned it. That was a few weeks ago, wasn't it?"

"I went out there again. For dinner."

Walter raised his arm off his face and looked hard at

Kacie. "Dinner, huh?"

"What's that supposed to mean?"

"Just a simple question. You do know that he's married right?"

"No, he's not."

"Yes, he is. He has a wife and three kids."

"You're talking about Robert, Walter."

"Isn't that who you're talking about?"

"No. I was talking about his brother."

"You went to the house to have dinner with his brother? Wow, that's moving pretty fast for you."

Kacie playfully slapped Walter's leg with the back of her hand. "I went over there because Robert was in town. And besides, there were two other women there, too."

"Great, thanks for clarifying. Now it's as clear as mud." Walter closed his eyes and just as quickly opened them back up again. "Wait a sec," he said with alarm, "Is that woman Lindsay back in town? Because if she is, I'm taking Sally up to my parents for a few days."

"Who's that, daddy?" Sally interrupted.

Walter propped himself up on his elbows and squinted at the three figures in the distance who Sally was pointing towards, "I don't know, baby. I've never seen them before. I wonder how they found this place."

Kacie looked towards the trio and said, "I know who that is! I'll be right back." She was walking over to join the new group as they were scouting out a place to lay their blankets, when one of them saw her and waved.

"You were right, Kacie, this place is beautiful," Laura said gesturing broadly with her arms to encompass the whole area.

"I'm glad you guys made it out. It's going to be a gorgeous day."

"Jack insisted on us coming, didn't give us a choice, really. But I will say the more we see of Sycamore Ridge, the more we like it," Ellie added.

"What's not to like?" Jack asked. "Look around you. No crowds. No cameras. No paparazzi. Just nature. Trees, meadow, the sound of water."

Laura and Ellie stared at him, mouths agape. Then they both burst into laughter.

"What's so funny?"

"Just nature. Trees, meadow, the sound of water," Ellie teased, lowering her voice and using a bad British accent to mimic Jack's words.

"Why are you talking in a British accent? I'm not British."

"Because you sound like that British guy who narrates all those nature shows."

"Laugh if you want. I like it here. It's good for me," Jack snapped back defensively.

Ellie held up her hands in a gesture of concession, "Fair enough, Jack."

"Kacie! Are you ready to take me swimming?" Sally called out at that moment. Walter had her on piggyback and was walking towards them with Cooper at his side. When the dog caught sight of Jack, he bounded towards him and was met with an equally enthusiastic petting.

"Who's that?" Ellie asked with concern.

"That's Walter and his daughter Sally. Walter did all the renovations on the house. I know he'd love to meet Jack. And unless Jack sings children's songs, there's no way Walter will recognize him."

"Robert spoke very highly of him." Short of grabbing Jack and running back into the woods, Ellie knew there wasn't much she could do to change things at this point.

"I guess it's okay."

"Hi Sally. Let me introduce your dad to everyone and then we can go play. Walter, meet Laura, Ellie, and Jack."

Walter perfunctorily shook everyone's hand. It took a moment for Kacie to realize from his guarded greeting that he had no idea exactly who these people were. "Walter," she nudged, "This is Robert's younger brother."

As realization dawned on Walter, he had a markedly warmer greeting towards Jack. Holding out his hand again, he shook Jack's hand warmly and rather vigorously. "Robert tells me that you're staying at the house right now? I can't thank your brother enough for giving me the work. It really helped me out of a tough spot."

"I'm the one who should be thanking you," Jack put his free hand on Walter's shoulder. "I love that house, man. It's so good to meet you."

Sally, who had been staring unabashedly at Jack, chimed in, "You're cute, and you have good hair."

Jack chuckled, "Yeah? Well, you're cuter and you have great hair. Like a mermaid."

Sally beamed from ear to ear. "Did Kacie tell you to say that?" Without waiting for an answer, she continued, "Mermaids love to swim. Someone take me swimming! Jack, you come with us."

"Kacie, can you take her? I want to talk to Jack for a minute."

"Sure. Come on, Sally, hop aboard."

Kacie went and stood next to Walter. In what looked like an often-practiced maneuver, Sally wrapped one arm around Kacie's neck without letting go of Walter with the other. With a slight grunting sound, she used the arm around Kacie to pull the rest of her body weight onto Kacie's back and quickly wrapped the other arm around her neck.

Jack, Laura, and Ellie looked on curiously, until Kacie turned her back to them to walk to the water. That's when they noticed that both of Sally's legs ended just above where her knees should have been.

After years of practice, Walter knew the best way to stifle people's stares and curiosity was to be honest and straightforward about the fact that his little girl was missing her legs, but it was never easy.

"It's a long story, but the doctors had to amputate her legs to save her life," his voice got choked up as he said the last part. "But they saved her, and I'm grateful every day."

Turning back towards Jack, he continued talking without giving them a chance to respond. "I'm not sure you realize how much your brother helped me out. Between the real estate commission, the renovation, and the quick turnaround time, I made enough money to make some changes to my house to help Sally be more independent and to get her one of those power wheelchairs. Please tell him how much I appreciate it."

Much to Jack's credit, he didn't correct Walter on the fact that it was *his* money and not Robert's that had made all that possible. Instead, he nodded, and said, "I will. He'll be happy to hear it."

"I'd better go help Kacie out. Good meeting all of you."

Jack watched as Kacie gently lowered Sally, who was already dressed in a bright blue bikini, onto a large boulder near the water. Perched like that, the little girl really did look like a mermaid.

Kacie stripped off her t-shirt and shorts to reveal a basic black bikini and stepped into the water. She turned to Sally, gently picked up the little girl, and carried her in.

The sound of Sally's delight and Kacie's obvious attachment to the child brought on an unexpected wave of emotion in Jack. *This*, he thought, was shaping up to be one of the best Sunday afternoons in a very long time.

"We brought sunscreen, right?" Jack asked, reluctantly turning his attention back to his companions.

"By 'we,' I'm assuming you mean me because the royal 'we' that you are referring to doesn't often do things for himself. And, yes, to answer your question. *I* brought the sunscreen." Ellie dug out the bottle and threw it at him.

"Are you planning on going in the water?" Laura asked skeptically.

"Yes. And you're *both* coming with me." His tone let them know he wouldn't broach any disagreement on the matter.

∞∞∞∞

"I could get used to living here," Jack said as he stretched out on the sofa after dinner that night.

Laura and Ellie looked at each other, neither wanting to ruin Jack's mood by reminding him that he'd have to go back to his life in the spotlight at some point.

"I can sense you two looking at each other, and I know what you're thinking. But for now, I'm going to pretend like we never have to leave. I'm going to go swim in that pond with Sally the Mermaid every weekend if I want to."

And that's just what he did.

∞∞∞∞

After more than a month in Sycamore Ridge, Jack had finally started getting used to the idea that no one recognized him. And, if on the off chance someone did, they really didn't seem to care.

The unexpected part of all of it was that being unrec-

119

ognizable didn't bruise his ego at all. If he was being honest, he barely recognized himself. The ridiculous blonde highlights he used to have had completely faded away to reveal his natural brown hair color, and his face was always clean shaven. He had put on weight and had Laura to thank for the fact that all the extra pounds had been parlayed into muscle. He swam every day in their pool and met Kacie, Sally, and Walter at the meadow every weekend after that first time. He was fit, sun-kissed, relaxed, and happier than he had been in a very long time.

The thought of leaving Sycamore Ridge and his new friends brought on a hollow feeling in his chest, and he pushed it away anytime it tried to rear its ugly head.

# PART 2

# CHAPTER 12

## *An Afternoon in Paris*

It was a beautiful early summer afternoon in Paris, and Sarah felt like celebrating her small victory. She was seated outdoors at a bistro table at her favorite café just off the Champs Elysée. It wasn't the most famous or the trendiest, but it was the one she most preferred for its excellent food and attentive service, and her server had just placed *"un café et un pain au chocolat"* on her table.

*"Merci."*

*"Bon appétit."*

Sarah couldn't wait to bite into the flaky, golden viennoiserie with the warm chocolate ganache at the center. One bite followed by a small sip of the dark, bitter café was absolute perfection. And she wasn't going to deny herself anything today. In fact, on her way back to her hotel, she was going to stop by the Ladurée shop and pick up a dozen of the best macarons money could buy.

As with every other visit, Sarah was enjoying her stay in Paris. The service at the Four Seasons Hotel George V just around the corner was superlative as expected, and the incredible restaurants she frequently ordered from didn't disappoint in serving the rich, undeniably delicious food she so enjoyed. Of course, it didn't hurt that she was on an all-expenses paid trip to the capital city and had an unlimited supply of diet pills to shed any unwanted pounds. On this particular trip, Sarah had even roused herself to visit several of the city's world-renowned museums for appearance's sake. Art just wasn't her scene, but the last few times she had visited Paris, several of her colleagues had looked askance at her when she told them she hadn't seen any of the tourist attractions.

And one thing Sarah hated was drawing attention to herself. So, on this trip, she had gone just to tick off the "must-see" items at the Musée du Louvre, the Musée d'Orsay, and her least favorite, the Musée d'art Moderne de Paris. She had even braved the throngs of tourists at the Tour d'Eiffel and paid to have one of the street artists sketch a picture of her standing in front of the famous tower.

As she sat enjoying the last bites of her *pain au chocolat*, she watched the seemingly non-stop hustle and bustle of people going about their business. Trendy millennials, old moneyed women out for a day of shopping, businessmen, and the ever-present tourists filled the sidewalks with constant motion. But no one noticed Sarah because she was completely unremarkable in every way. She wore her medium length, medium brown hair loose. She had brown eyes, a button nose, and clear skin with a few freckles. She was of average height and build. She was neither beautiful nor unattractive. She was just unremarkable, at least in physical appearance.

There were, however, two ways in which she was very remarkable. Exceptional even.

∞∞∞∞

At an early age, Sarah had realized she had a knack for computers. She had been taking an introduction to programming class during her senior year of high school, and while the other students around her struggled with writing basic programs, coding had come easily to Sarah. Within a few short months, she had become bored with the lessons being taught in class and started challenging herself with more complex programming. She had consciously chosen not to reveal this quickly developing skill to her teacher or any of the students in her class. She was already a bit of an outcast for reasons she never fully understood and being a "computer nerd" wouldn't have done anything to help her image.

Until one day when she overheard one of the popular girls at school lamenting her poor grades. It was a comment Sarah heard often, and one that always annoyed her. Didn't "those girls" realize how easy it would be to just hack into the school's new online grading system and change their grades? And that's when it had hit her. They didn't even know that changing their grades was a possibility.

Sarah had lain awake in bed late into that night thinking about how she could leverage this information. Should she offer to change the girl Piper's grades in exchange for a chance at friendship? Her highly analytical mind ran through a series of scenarios, and she quickly realized that the resulting friendship, if any, would be fake and easily cast aside. Maybe, Sarah thought, she could change the grade in exchange for a small fee. It would be a simple transaction that would be difficult to trace, and it was in both of their best interests to keep the deal a secret. Piper would get what she wanted, and Sarah would make a little money.

Deciding that this would be the ideal solution, Sarah had stalked Piper the next day, waiting for a chance to get her alone. She finally got her opportunity when she saw the girl walk into one of the school bathrooms without her ever-present gaggle of friends. Following her in, Sarah had waited by the sinks practicing what she would say. But as soon as Piper stepped out of the stall, Sarah's mouth went dry, and she couldn't remember her words.

Piper gave her a derogatory once over and snapped, "What are you staring at?"

"I, ummmm, I can help you," Sarah fumbled nervously.

"Help me with what? Washing my hands? Gross."

"With your grades. You know, your math grade."

That seemed to get Piper's attention, but she played it cool. Washing her hands, she looked at Sarah out of the corner of her eye, and asked, "Oh yeah? What makes you think I need help?"

"I heard you talking the other day."

"So, you were eavesdropping?"

"You were talking loudly."

Piper squinted her eyes at Sarah but took the bait anyway. "Okay, so let's say I do need help. How exactly can *you* help me?"

"I know how to get into the school grading system," Sarah blurted out artlessly. "But it'll cost you."

"Oh, really? How much?"

"Fifty bucks."

"How do I know you're telling the truth?"

"You'll just have to trust me."

"Well, I don't."

"Fine, then I guess you can kiss that Ivy League university goodbye." Not knowing if her next statement was even true, Sarah added, "Daddy's not going to be very happy with you, is he?"

A flicker of concern crossed the girl's face for only a

moment, but it lasted long enough for Sarah to recognize that she had hit the mark. Feeling an odd sense of excitement at having this newfound power over the most popular girl in school, Sarah turned to leave.

"Wait, wait a second. Come back. How much did you say it would cost?" The concern about what her daddy would think translated into a hint of desperation in Piper's normally confident voice.

Sarah stopped and without turning back to face Piper, said boldly, "A hundred bucks."

"I thought you said fifty before." The slight hint of desperation was amplified as Piper realized everything she wanted – a chance to get into her dream school and her daddy's approval – might slip through her fingers.

Sarah faced the girl and took pleasure in the worried look on her face. "The price just went up," she said calmly, and again, she felt a warm pulsing sensation coursing through her body.

"Can you really do it?"

Sarah stared coldly at Piper and didn't answer. She watched as Piper bit her lower lip and wrung her hands, weighing her limited options. With each passing second, Sarah grew more confident that her offer would be accepted.

"Ok, how about fifty now and fifty after it's done?"

Again, Sarah calmly looked at the girl without responding. She could almost imagine herself as a hunter with her little prey caught in a corner, and the thought excited her.

"Fine. A hundred dollars," Piper acquiesced, feeling a combination of resentment and relief.

∞∞∞

From that first misguided offer to change Piper's grade for a hundred dollars, Sarah had made her initial foray into the world of professional computer hacking. As it turned out, though, Piper hadn't kept the deal a secret. As soon as her grade had been changed and she had proof that Sarah could do what she claimed, Piper had turned the tables on her and followed *her* into one of the school's bathrooms.

She had nervously broached a subject which Sarah had never even considered. The girl had offered to be a middleman between Sarah and other students who needed their grades changed.

"I've been talking to my friends, not just at this school, but some of the other schools, too. Including the private schools. I know there are a lot of kids out there who would be willing to pay big money to have their grades changed."

"You told people about me?" Sarah seethed.

"No, no, relax. I'm not that stupid. I posed it as a hypothetical question. Just to see if people would be willing to take the risk and how much they'd be willing to pay. I'm telling you, we could make a lot of money."

"*We?*"

"Yes. We. I find the kids who want their grades changed and get their money. Once they've paid me, you change the grades. We split the amount. Fifty-fifty."

At first, Sarah had bristled at the notion. "Why would I split the money with you? I'm the one with all the skills and the one bearing all the risk of getting caught."

"And I'm the one with all the connections. Just think about it. People hand me the money, but I don't actually *do* anything wrong. And you? You get to remain completely anonymous. No one even knows that it's you changing the grades. And, let's face it, who'd ever think that there was any connection between someone like me and my friends and someone like you. It's a win-win situation for both of us."

∞∞∞∞

Piper had been right. Within a few short months, she and Sarah had built up a considerably sized side hustle. Sarah had been shocked by how much money high school and college kids were willing to spend to change their grades. Piper seemed to know exactly how much each student would pay based on what school they attended, what cars their parents drove, and what street they lived on. Sarah never meddled in that side of the business. Piper supplied her with a seemingly endless list of students needing their GPA improved, and Sarah quickly learned to hack into a variety of grading systems to make those changes. Thankfully, she and Piper had agreed early on that they would only change one grade per student per term and never by more than a few points. Small changes, they assumed correctly, would go overlooked. And for many students, it was a matter of changing scores just enough to make the difference between a C+ and a B-.

Things had run smoothly for the first year and a half, and Sarah was making more money than she knew what to do with. Although she had slowly grown confident in Piper's impeccable discretion and her own burgeoning hacking abilities, she was also well aware of the increasing software security being employed by companies. She would have been happy and carefree had it not been for the constant paranoia of stepping into some new security trap and triggering a virtual alarm. Which is exactly what ended up happening when she was trying to hack into the

128

online grading system of an elite Ivy League university.

Sarah had been intently focused on one particular line of code when a message from an unfamiliar sender had popped into her email inbox. The subject line of the email was just one word: "Impressive." But there was something about it that made the hair on the back of Sarah's neck stand up. Double clicking on the email, she opened it and read the one line it contained. At that moment, she knew she had been caught.

∞∞∞

"So, what do you think," the man had asked her, delicately placing his napkin across his lap.

Sarah stared at the one-page offer letter and looked up at the handsome gentleman sitting across from her. They were seated at a prime table inside one of the nicest restaurants in town. A place Sarah had never stepped foot inside of but from which she treated herself to decadent takeout meals on an almost weekly basis. While she had felt awkward and out of place in the room full of well-dressed patrons, her companion managed to stand out. Dressed in a perfectly tailored, expensive navy-blue suit and a crisp white shirt, Gerard turned quite a few heads as they were escorted to their table.

The whole experience was surreal, and Sarah pinched herself on the thigh for the tenth time. She knew she would be covered in little bruises in the morning, but she didn't care. When Sarah had first read Gerard's email, she had been terrified. The single sentence had made her blood run cold and her imagination run wild: "We should discuss your naughty behavior over dinner at the Waterside Grill at eight o'clock sharp." For the next several hours, Sarah had tried every trick she knew to figure out who had sent the email. Tried and failed. As the hour to meet drew closer, her panic had intensified. Was the sender going to turn her in to the police? Would he or she try to blackmail her?

By the time she had arrived at the restaurant, Sarah was a nervous wreck. She had spent so much time at her computer that she hadn't had time to change her clothes. Her jeans were too tight, and her oversized black t-shirt was faded and dingy. Her palms were sweating, and she could feel her heart pounding in her chest. Worst of all, she could smell the foul odor of her own sweat begin to permeate the air around her. Unsure of what to do, she stood in the shadows outside the restaurant watching as people came and went.

At exactly eight o'clock, a fancy and expensive looking black car pulled up to the valet, and a tall, elegant man stepped out of the driver's side door. Handing his keys to the valet, he looked around and stopped when his eyes landed on Sarah. She tried to move further into the shadows, but he continued to stare. Even from a distance, Sarah could tell he was the type of man who would normally never even look at a person like her. She considered walking away, but his steady gaze rooted her to the spot.

Slowly approaching her, he smiled and said warmly, "Ahhh, you must be Sarah."

Barely nodding her head in acknowledgement, Sarah stared at his shiny leather shoes.

"Well then, it's a pleasure to meet you, Sarah. I'm Gerard Wang. Shall we?" He had asked as he held the door open for her.

ꝏꝏꝏ

"I promise you won't get a better offer from anyone

else."

Sarah was certain he was speaking the truth. Looking back down at the offer letter, she pinched herself again as she read the salary terms.

"I'm not sure what to think. I'm not even done with college yet, Mr. Wang. Why would you offer me so much money?"

Gerard chuckled and was about to reply when the server had come to get their order. And without missing a beat, he had proceeded to order all her favorites.

"You're not the only hacker on the planet, you know," was his reply to her barely contained surprise.

"Anyone can figure out what I order from here just by going through my garbage," Sarah retorted, feeling defensive.

"Is that the kind of man you think I am?" Gerard asked calmly. "The kind who goes digging through garbage?" He picked an invisible piece of lint off his suit jacket and adjusted his cuff links in what looked like an often-practiced maneuver. There was something about him, with his slicked back dark hair and dark eyes, that reminded Sarah of a black jaguar about to pounce.

But Sarah wasn't quite ready to back down yet. Grasping at straws, she insulted him further. "You could have figured out what I like by slipping the delivery guy a couple of bucks."

"Look at the number on that offer again Sarah. And think." Fixing his dark eyes on Sarah's, Gerard sighed. "Very well, we'll do this the hard way." He reached into the inside pocket of his suit jacket and took out an envelope. Removing the papers from it, he slowly unfolded them and placed them on the table in front of her.

Sarah flipped through the pages with mounting disbelief as she saw her entire life laid out in front of her. Her social security number, her high school transcripts, her bank account information, her last set of credit card statements, her previous addresses, her utility bills, a list of shows she binge watched, the restaurants she frequented and what she ordered. Everything which she believed to be protected, personal information was all right there in front of her.

"This is illegal," she whispered.

"And so is this," Gerard reached into his pocket once again and pulled out one last sheet of paper. Sarah glanced down and read the first two rows of small print. The evidence was damning, she didn't have to read the row after row of names of every student whose grades she had changed to know that she was sitting across from a master.

"I'm offering you a chance to do what you're so good at on the *right* side of the law. Hear me out."

Unable to detect any malice or disingenuousness in his voice, Sarah had nodded and then listened with rapt attention as Gerard had told her about the software security company he owned. Multinational companies, he said, hired his firm to discreetly hack into their software systems to identify any shortcomings. Then, they paid him again to help fix those deficiencies. From the looks of her offer, it was a very lucrative business.

"Why me?" Sarah had asked quietly over dessert.

"Because my clients expect me to hire the best. I've been watching you this past year. The way you hack into multiple systems? Get access control, tiptoe around firewalls, and cover your tracks? It's like watching a dancer."

"You've been watching me? How did you even know I existed?"

"You'll learn very quickly, Sarah, that there isn't much in the hacking world that I don't know about." Gerard took a sip of his after-dinner coffee and placed the cup back in the saucer. Without taking his eyes off Sarah, he reached into his pocket, took out a pen and held it out to her.

∞∞∞

That had been over a decade ago. Since then, Gerard had invested hundreds of hours in training her and rewarded her growing list of accomplishments with the choicest software security and development projects all over the world. In due time, Sarah had developed a specialty in digital security for high end hotel chains and wealth management firms. She regularly stayed at five-star luxury hotels and ate at the finest restaurants.

Not a bad life for an otherwise outwardly unremarkable woman, Sarah thought as she took another bite of her *pain au chocolat* and smiled to herself. Her hacking abilities had once again served her well today. And she knew her other skill would serve her well over the next few months.

Besides being a master computer hacker, Sarah was also remarkable in that she had a second-degree black belt in Tae Kwon Do and could bring a man twice her size to his knees within seconds. She often spent her lonely evenings in the hotel rooms practicing her punches and kicks over and over until she was dripping in sweat. She was determined to keep her skill razor sharp, no matter where in the world she was.

For now, she knew she was one step closer to her love, and she was content with that.

# CHAPTER 13

## *That Night in Dubai*

Sarah could remember every detail from the moment she and her love had first met just over a year ago. She had been working on a software and internet security project for Jumeirah Hotels and had been staying at the Burj Al Arab in Dubai. The hotel was supposed to be spectacular, but, apart from her short stop in the opulent main lobby at check-in, Sarah hadn't seen any of it. In fact, she hadn't left her suite in almost four days. She had asked housekeeping not to disturb her and, as requested, all of her in-room dining meals were left at the door and announced with a subtle knock.

Sitting at a desk for hours at a time and treating herself to one extravagant meal after another had done nothing for her weight loss goals, but Sarah hadn't cared. She hadn't cared how she looked either. She couldn't remember the last time she had bathed or bothered to change her clothes. All she had cared about was getting the job done, and she had hit a brick wall.

Frustrated at her lack of progress late one night, Sarah had decided that maybe she needed to take a break and clear her mind. Although it was almost two a.m., she had called housekeeping and asked them to clean her room. This would be almost unheard of in most hotels, but she had known the Burj Al Arab staff wouldn't think twice about fulfilling her wish. Her suite would be spotless when she returned.

Sarah had dug through her still fully packed suitcase and put on a clean, oversized, t-shirt and a pair of loose-fitting pants. Grabbing her room key, she had taken the elevator down to the main lobby and had been surprised to see that it was still abuzz with activity. Several small groups of people had been scattered about talking and laughing. No one had even noticed her as she made her way outside following the signs to the pool. There had been people in the water, too. Mostly couples, huddled together and whispering quietly to each other.

Sarah had strolled slowly past them, looking on longingly at their intimacy. The dimmed lights around the pool area and soft music playing on discreet speakers had created a romantic, sensual mood. Sarah had tried to focus on where she was walking, but her eyes had been drawn again and again to the intertwined couples in the pool. She had wondered what it would feel like to have a man look at her and caress her as if she was the only person in the world. She had been so wrapped up in her daydreams she hadn't noticed the lounge chair in her path. She had stumbled and fallen onto all fours with a loud grunt. The impact with the surface of the pool deck had knocked the breath out of her and brought tears to her eyes.

But before she had been able to pull herself up, she had heard a man's voice and felt his hands around her waist.

"Whoa, are you okay?"

Startled by his unexpected appearance, she had been immediately on her guard and ready to defend herself if necessary. But his hands and voice had been gentle as he helped her stand back up.

"I tried to warn you about the chair, but I guess you didn't hear me. Come on, sit down over here and let's take a look to make sure you're all right." He had straightened out the chair she had stumbled over and helped ease her into it.

Her knees and palms had been stinging from the impact, and she had felt a small trickle of blood slowly dripping down her left leg. Without asking, the stranger had taken her palms in his hands and said, "Your hands look okay. Just a little friction burn on them. Let's check your knees."

The stranger had looked at her and smiled kindly. Although the dimmed light had made it difficult to make out his features, there had been something familiar about him. Something about his long hair, the structure of his face, and his smile. Dim light or not, there was no denying how good looking he was.

Sarah's heart had fluttered, and a warmth had started to flow through her body. "I'll be okay. I should watch where I'm going. Stupid me," she had managed to blurt out.

The thought of this man looking at her legs had made Sarah acutely aware of her physical appearance – something that normally never occurred to her. She hadn't showered in days, and she hadn't bothered to shave her legs in ages. She could just imagine what he was thinking and how she appeared to him. Overweight, unkempt, likely malodorous, and with a poor attempt at bleach blonde hair that was slowly fading back to her natural mousy brown color. She had wanted to run away, but his gentleness had rooted her to the chair.

And again, without waiting for her permission, he had

slowly rolled up her pant legs. "That doesn't look so good. We should probably get it cleaned and bandaged."

∞∞∞

One of the lifeguards on duty had also seen Sarah fall and had rushed over with a first aid kit. Sarah had been annoyed by the lifeguard's sudden appearance, worried that the handsome stranger would use it as an excuse to leave. But much to her pleasure, he had sat next to her on the chair while the lifeguard cleaned and bandaged both her knees.

Sarah had been so focused on the warmth from the stranger's closeness, that she hadn't noticed the lifeguards ill-concealed distaste for her appearance.

"I think you will be okay, madame. Please call the front desk if you should require further assistance," he said in a thick accent.

As the lifeguard started packing up his first aid kit, the stranger had stood up and held out his hand to Sarah to help her stand up. She placed her slightly clammy hand in his cool, soft, strong hand and looked up at him, and her breath caught in her throat. One of the few lights off to the side had framed his head in a soft halo and highlighted his beautiful face. Sarah's heart began pounding in her chest and the warmth that had been flowing through her body intensified. As he heaved her up, she felt an awareness of his strength, which made her weak in the knees.

Sarah knew she should say something, thank him, but her mouth had gone completely dry, and she didn't trust her voice. The stranger didn't seem at all surprised or discomfited by her reaction. In fact, he looked rather accustomed to it.

"There you are!" A loud male voice broke the tranquility of the surroundings, and Sarah and the stranger turned simultaneously towards the sound.

The stranger smiled as the man walked over to them. "You found me."

"You'll be happy to know that your suite is finally empty. We should probably get you up to bed. It's really late." As he had been saying all this, the man had looked at Sarah. And although he had been better than the lifeguard at concealing his reaction to her, she had nonetheless noticed the slight crinkling of his nose as he caught a whiff of her scent.

"Thanks. Listen, do me a favor, make sure this young lady gets up to her room okay." Turning to Sarah, the stranger gave her another one of his heart-stopping smiles and added, "Take care. Good night."

That was how Sarah had first met the man of her dreams. She had fallen twice that night. Once over a chair and once head over heels in love.

∞∞∞

By the time she had gotten back to her room, Sarah had started thinking of ways to find her handsome stranger. Their brief interaction had awoken feelings in her which she had never felt before, and she wanted desperately to see him again. But not looking the way she did. She had forced herself to take a long, hot shower and shave her legs. The soap and scalding water temperature combined to sting her newly wounded skin, but she felt an odd sort of pleasure in the pain.

All the while, Sarah had fantasized about seeing him again. Closing her eyes and imagining the strength with which he had lifted her off the ground mixed with the gentleness with which he had tended to her wounds had made her body pulse with yearning. She imagined going to his room to say thank you, and him pulling her inside, into his arms. Looking at her in the same, intimate way the men in the pool had looked at their partners. He would lift her off her feet without a word and take her to his bed. Thinking about all the things he would do to her after that was more than she could bare. The heat from the water beating down on her blended with the heat from her body and made her lightheaded. She had finally turned off the water.

Grabbing the unused plush bathrobe from the closet and wrapping it around herself, she had sat down in front of her laptop and started punching search queries into the hotel's database. When her first few searches didn't yield any immediate answers, Sarah had begun to get frustrated. Switching gears, she began sorting through the online copies of passport photos that the hotel was required to keep for all international guests. That's when she finally found the information she had been searching for. The name of the strong, gorgeous man who had come to her rescue. The only man who had ever made her feel that throbbing desire. The only man, she was quickly and unreasonably becoming convinced, who would ever be able to make her feel that way. The only man she would ever want to be with.

His name was Jett Vanders. For a brief moment, Sarah had been ecstatic at finally learning his identity. She had practiced saying his name out loud a few times, enjoying the feel of it rolling off her tongue. She said his name with a flirtatious tone, a sexy tone, an angry tone. All of them excited her.

"This is my husband, Jett Vanders," Sarah said looking

at herself in the mirror, imagining him standing behind her with his arms wrapped around her waist. And that's when she realized her dreams would never come true. That's when she realized where she had seen him before and why his name had sounded vaguely familiar. He was a world-famous musician. A rock star. An idol.

Her growing desire for him would be thwarted by his celebrity status. There was no doubt about it. What chance did a girl like her have with a man like him?

∞∞∞

In those first few weeks after she had left Dubai, Sarah had tried to forget about Jett. She had tried to focus on her work and put him out of her mind. But at night, thoughts of him came roaring back into her dreams. She would wake up drenched in sweat, her body still responding to the things she imagined him doing to her. At first, she had tried taking cold showers to clear her mind, but after a while, even that stopped working.

One night, she decided to attempt to allay her longing by looking at photos of him with other women, of which there were plenty online. But all that had served to accomplish was to add jealousy to her rising desire for him. After that, it was as if floodgates had been opened and she couldn't get enough of looking at his online photos and videos. She had quickly and increasingly become infatuated with him.

Putting aside her work at every opportunity, Sarah had spent hours fantasizing about Jett. She printed out every photo she found of him and placed them neatly, almost lovingly into a folder. A folder she took with her wherever she went.

And as time went by, the line between reality and her

often steamy fantasies about Jett began to blur in an unhealthy way. She would find herself talking out loud to him when she was alone in her hotel room. Several times, she pretended he was travelling with her and went so far as to purchase an airline ticket for him.

Her growing obsession with Jett had often made her miss work deadlines. On several occasions, she got the feeling her co-workers were happy that "Gerard's little pet" was failing.

There was one particularly close call during a project meeting with a French client that had made her realize she needed to be more careful. She had just managed to finish an extensive report on the client's software security deficiencies and had printed the final copy moments before a crucial meeting. Grabbing all the papers on the printer and stapling them together, she had inadvertently included a sheet that had two photos of Jett on it. During the meeting, as the client was flipping through the report, he had stopped at that page and stared. After an awkward pause, Gerard had asked if there was a problem, and the client had held up the page for everyone to see.

The blood had rushed to Sarah's face as she realized her mistake. Several people had chuckled uncomfortably, and Gerard, unaccustomed to any mistakes by Sarah, had simply cleared his throat and stared at her waiting for an explanation.

"*Je suis désolé.*" Sarah had mumbled. "I'm sorry. I'm a big fan."

"So is my fifteen-year-old daughter," one of the men on the other side of the table had said. Fortunately, this had broken the awkward tension in the room, and everyone had a good laugh at Sarah's expense. More importantly, everyone seemed to believe the photos had been just a silly mistake, and not a warning sign of Sarah's fixation.

The client had ripped the page out and handed it across the table. "A gift for your daughter." Everyone laughed again as Sarah raged silently at how foolish she must have appeared.

From that moment on, Sarah had pledged herself to being completely discreet about her feelings for Jett. After the meeting, she had gone back to her hotel room and destroyed any physical evidence of her obsession.

It hadn't really mattered, though, because by that time, she truly believed she knew everything there was to know about him. And besides, she had stored digital copies of everything she had just torn up on the cloud.

∞∞∞

*"Mademoiselle? Mademoiselle? Voulez-vous un autre café?"* The sound of her server's voice roused her from her frequent reverie, and Sarah forced herself back to reality. A reality that she believed would soon include Jett.

# CHAPTER 14

## *Semper Gratus*

A chauffeur driven black Mercedes slowly pulled into the driveway of the house on Willow Avenue and parked near the front walkway. Without waiting for the driver to open the door, a woman stepped out of the back seat into the late afternoon sunshine. Jana had been looking forward to her trip to Sycamore Ridge for months, and now that she was finally here, she couldn't contain her anticipation. All she wanted to do was see her baby brother in person. As if on cue, the front door opened and Jack quickly strode towards her, reflecting the same level of eagerness as she felt.

"Jackie?" she exclaimed, not believing her own eyes that the handsome, healthy, happy looking man now standing in front of her was her brother.

Jack wrapped his big sister in a bear hug and lifted her off her feet, fighting back tears as he said, "I'm so happy to see you."

Jana had been like a mother to him for over a decade, and he loved her more than words could express. Jack wished he could take her with him wherever he was, but a job she loved as the principal of a small private school kept her from traveling to see him when he was on tour internationally. And while they always made time to have video calls, it was never the same as being in the same room as him.

Anyone who saw the two of them together couldn't help but notice their family resemblance. She was considerably shorter than he was, and almost ten years older, but she had the same beautiful eyes, skin tone, and hair color as him. They looked so similar as babies they often couldn't tell which one of them was pictured in a photograph. When their parents had announced, almost embarrassedly, the surprise third pregnancy, Robert and Jana had been thrilled. From the moment they saw the chubby, squirming newborn, both of them had fallen in love with Jack. And that feeling continued to this day.

"Put me down! I want to look at you!"

Jack obeyed and placed her gently on her feet. Jana reached up and cupped his face in her hands and fought back tears of her own. "Jackie...you look so wonderful. Oh, I'm so happy to see you like this." Pulling him towards her, she planted a big kiss on his forehead.

"Welcome to Sycamore Ridge! What do you think of my new home?" Without waiting for an answer, Jack added, "You're going to love it here. Come on, let me show you around the house and then we can spend the rest of the evening catching up."

∞∞∞

"Soooo, Jackie, tell me about some of the people you've met here."

Jack was stretched out on a lounge chair by the pool, feeling relaxed and happy to be enjoying an evening under the stars, this time with his sister next to him. While he had been expecting a question like this, he hadn't expected it quite so soon. "Which 'people' do you want to hear about?"

Jana looked up at Ellie, who made a gesture with her hand as if prompting her to keep asking more questions.

"I don't know. What about Kacie?" Jana tried to keep her tone conversational. "I've heard her name mentioned a few times."

"Have you now? I don't remember mentioning her to you."

"Not from you. I think Ellie or Robert may have mentioned her." Jana's curiosity had been aroused by the frequent stories she had heard about Jack's budding friendship, but she had been frustrated by the lack of details anyone could share. She had been designated, under pressure by Robert, Laura, and Ellie, as the person who would most likely be able to get some answers.

"Is that right? There's not much to tell really. Anyway, you'll meet her yourself tomorrow. I told her you were coming out for a visit, and she's looking forward to meeting you."

"You want me to meet her?" Jana asked nonchalantly.

The subtle change in the phrasing of what he had said put Jack on his guard.

"That's not what I said. I said she's looking forward to meeting you."

"You said you told her about me. That means you want me to meet her."

Feeling defensive now, Jack swung his legs off the lounge chair and put his feet on the ground so that he was in a sitting position. He looked from Ellie to Laura, and then his eyes settled on his sister. "What's with the inquisition?"

"No inquisition. Just asking a simple question." Jana decided to go for broke. "I've been hearing a lot about her from Robert. And while you were in the shower earlier, Laura and Ellie told me about how much time you've been spending with her. I just want to know what's going on."

Jack glared at Ellie and Laura, both of whom calmly stared back at him, emboldened by his sister's presence.

"Have they now? I didn't realize you had nothing better to talk about than me. For your information, there is nothing going on," Jack snapped. He hadn't meant to sound quite so defensive, but he couldn't help it.

"Why are you getting so upset?"

"Look, it has been years...*years*...since I've met someone who I enjoy spending time with and who wants absolutely nothing from me. Kacie is easy to talk to and she's funny."

"And she's easy on the eyes," Ellie chimed in.

"So I've heard."

Laura nodded in agreement. "Don't tell me you haven't noticed. I saw you checking her out in her cute bathing suit the other day."

Jack rolled his eyes. "Whatever."

"Don't tell me you don't think she's pretty."

"I do think she's pretty. But you've seen the kind of women I've been with. They're all pretty. So what? What has that ever gotten me? A couple of relationships that ended badly and a lot of sex. And I'm not looking for any of those things right now. I haven't been this happy in a long time. I mean look at me. When was the last time you saw me like this? Being out of the public eye and in Sycamore Ridge is doing wonders for me."

Jana was tempted to point out that maybe it wasn't just the time out of the spotlight that was making him so happy. Maybe it was the time he was spending with Kacie.

"You do look gorgeous," Laura laughed, partly to break

the tension.

Jana followed Laura's lead. She would hold her tongue for now but would definitely keep a close eye on how her brother acted when they met Kacie the next day. Changing the subject, she asked, "Do we have any ice cream?"

∞∞∞

"I can see why you're all so taken with Sycamore Ridge and especially with Kacie," Jana said to Ellie as they sat by the pool watching Jack swimming laps the next day. Earlier that morning, Jack had taken Jana for a tour of Fountain Walk. The ease with which he was able to move around the picturesque cobblestone street warmed Jana's heart. No one seemed to pay Jack much attention, apart from an occasional look from the opposite sex which lasted just a tad longer than was polite because of how good looking he was.

The tour had culminated in an almost hour long visit to Kacie's shop.

"Some more than others," Ellie said pointedly.

"Agreed. But I'm not bringing it up to him again. It'll be good to spend some more time with her this evening. I can't believe he invited her over for dinner even though we already saw her today. How often does she come to the house?"

"Only when you or Robert are in town. Otherwise, he usually sees her during the daytime. He goes to her shop a couple of times a week."

"A couple times a week?"

"Yup." The two women exchanged knowing glances.

"What do you think of her? Robert has told me his opinion, but I'd like your take."

"There's not much to tell, really. From what I've

gathered, with Kacie, what you see is what you get. And I think that's one of the best things about her. She's always friendly and welcoming, makes time for anyone who walks through her front door. She's smart, funny. And she treats Jack like a normal human being. I haven't seen that from anyone outside of us and his family in a very long time."

"For someone whose job it is to always be suspicious of people, it sounds to me like she's earned your seal of approval."

"I don't think it's my seal of approval that he wants."

"When he goes to see her at her shop, how long does he usually stay there?"

"Couple of hours. He's always coming home and raving about some new project she's working on or some new tool she taught him how to use."

"And you're sure that's all they're doing?"

"When have you ever known Jack to be discreet about being involved with a woman? Trust me, if there was something going on, he would have told us. Or he would have that stupid grin on his face. You know? The one he gets every time he gets...."

Jana, knowing full well what Ellie was going to say, cut her off before she could finish. "So, he sees her during the weekdays and only when Robert or I are in town?" She was almost disappointed. Although they had only spent a short time with Kacie that morning, Jana had been drawn to her open and friendly nature. At one point, she had teased Jack mercilessly because he couldn't remember where the power button was on one of the tools he was trying to show his sister. Jack had burst into laughter and the sound of it had reminded Jana of how happy her little brother used to be.

"And we go to the meadow to swim every weekend with some other friends he's made."

"He had mentioned something about that to me. I'm surprised you let him go swimming in public. His tattoo is pretty recognizable."

"He doesn't listen to a single thing I say anymore," Ellie laughed. "But, in all seriousness, there are very few people out there. It's apparently some highly guarded secret location that the locals don't tell anyone about. Plus, we're all spread out, so I doubt anyone would even be able to see the tattoo clearly."

Jack chose that moment to hoist himself out of the pool. He sat at the edge looking out over the yard with the water slowly dripping down over the Latin words "semper gratus" tattooed across the lower left side of his back. As if sensing that they were talking about him, Jack turned his head towards them and flashed them one of his megawatt smiles.

Jana smiled back and sighed. "I love that kid."

"He's not exactly a kid anymore, Jana. I know how protective you feel towards him, but I don't think there is anything for you to worry about."

"Maybe you're right. But there's no harm in trying to get to know her a little better tonight."

∞∞∞∞

"I wasn't sure if Laura would let you eat dessert after you brought those morning buns over this morning," Kacie teased as she watched Jack take a second helping of her peach cobbler.

"Laura doesn't have a say over anything anymore," Laura laughed, referring to herself in the third person. "Jack does whatever Jack wants."

"Not true," Jack said between mouthfuls. "I know you're going to make me pay for this tomorrow with a brutal abs and thighs workout." He took another bite and added for good measure. "Which is why you're the best personal trainer on the planet."

"Where'd you learn to bake, Kacie?" Jana asked.

"Chef Google."

Jana laughed. "The world at our fingertips, right?"

Dinner was almost over, and despite Jana's earlier determination to learn more about Kacie, she had gotten swept up in the pleasant conversation and easy banter. Her first impressions of Kacie were only reinforced, and she liked her even more now. Reminding herself there was no time like the present, Jana decided to take the plunge.

"You're the mayor, you own your own business, and you make a mean peach cobbler. You're quite a catch. Guys must be lining up at your door. Are you seeing anyone?" Jana had meant to keep her tone light and friendly, and yet the last question ended up sounding like an accusation.

A tense and expectant hush fell over the table as everyone except Jack looked down at their peach cobbler as if it may hold the answer to Jana's question.

Jack glared at his sister. But a part of him, he realized suddenly, wanted to know the answer. On the other hand, he was also dreading hearing something he didn't want to know. He was about to tell Jana to mind her own business when Kacie's answer took him by surprise.

"I am, actually." Kacie hadn't planned on telling any of her new friends about the relationship, but she wasn't going to lie about it either. "Jerome set me up with a new assistant professor at the university a couple of weeks ago. We've only been out together twice, but he seems like a nice guy."

"That's fantastic, Kacie," Jack said a little too loudly.

"More cobbler anyone?" Laura asked to break the tension.

∞∞∞

"That was a bold move." Ellie took a sip of her wine and looked over at Jana. Everyone else had gone to bed and the two women were sitting on the back porch enjoying the cool night air.

"I've never seen people eat cobbler that fast. I don't know what got into me. Did you see his reaction?"

"Definitely a more-than-friends reaction. But maybe he was just taken by surprise."

"Maybe. We'll see how he behaves over the next few days. If he stops going over to see her, than we know for sure that he has feelings for her. If things continue as they are, then I'll believe it when he says he just wants to be friends with her."

# CHAPTER 15

## *Three-Date Limit*

"Hey Jack, great day for a swim. Where's your sister? I was looking forward to meeting her."

Jack joined Walter at the edge of the pond where he was watching Kacie and Sally swimming and playing in the water. "She should be here in a few minutes. She and Laura were in the middle of some new yoga workout, so I walked over here with Ellie."

"Kacie said she really enjoyed meeting her. I heard you had her over for dinner the other day, and she made her peach cobbler. Did Laura let you have any?"

"Contrary to what you all might believe, Laura is not the boss of me." Walter's look of disbelief brought a smile to Jack's face. "Well, maybe she is. But just a little."

"What kind of projects does Kacie have you working on these days? You know, for all the work you do for her, she should start paying you."

"With Jana being in town, I haven't had a chance to go over there these past few days. I wasn't even sure we'd come swimming today, but Jana really wanted to see this place." Jack tried to keep his voice casual as he added, "I figured Kacie was busy with her new boyfriend, anyway. Have you met him yet?"

"Nope. No point really. He's not her boyfriend any-more." Walter shot a quick side glance at Jack to gauge his reaction.

It took a moment for that to sink in, and Jack could feel a little of the tension he had been carrying around release. He hoped Walter wouldn't notice his sense of relief.

"Really? That was quick."

"Yup, that's Kacie for you. I think she has a three-date limit. She goes out on the first date to make whoever is trying to set her up happy. The second date because she feels bad for the person who took her out. And the third date to end it. It's a pattern."

"I'm sure that'll change when she meets the right person. Come on, let's go join the girls."

Walter had to pinch himself to keep from laughing at his newfound friend's obvious joy in Kacie's doomed relationship.

∞∞∞

"Hello? Kacie?" A rock ballad was blaring from the back of the shop and Jack smiled as he realized it was one of his songs. He had always been amazed that his least rock rock song had become one of his greatest hits. Apparently, his female fans couldn't get enough of it.

But the smile was immediately wiped off his face at the next sound he heard.

"We've got this one liiiiiiffffe, and we must choose to be gratefullllll."

Jack gritted his teeth and hoped the singer wouldn't try to hit the next high note, but he hoped in vain.

"Alllllwayyyyys grrrraaaaatefulllll."

He forced himself not to cover his ears or go running out of the front door. Instead, he walked into the shop and switched off the radio.

Kacie, whose back had been turned as she applied a

153

second coat of mineral oil to an antique dresser turned abruptly towards him.

"Wow, you weren't kidding," he joked. "You really can't sing."

Taking the teasing in her stride, Kacie shot back, "I warned you! Maybe that'll teach you not to sneak up on me."

"I promise I'll never do it again."

Kacie smiled, happy to see him in her shop again after what felt like a prolonged absence. She realized she had missed having her 'apprentice' around. "Where's Jana?"

"Shopping at Min-seo's. I just wanted to stop in to say hello. Haven't been to the shop in a while."

"I figured you would be busy with your sister. But don't worry," Kacie added with a smile on her face, "I've managed to hold down the fort without my trusted apprentice."

Jack returned her smile, grateful once again for her easygoing attitude. He had worried she would be upset or aloof after not having seen him at the shop since the dinner. And he would be lying to himself if he didn't admit he had avoided visiting her ever since finding out she was seeing someone. It would be an even bigger lie to say that he hadn't felt considerable relief when Walter told him that Kacie was once again single. The only thing Jack wasn't ready to be honest with himself about was why he felt that way.

"I'd stay longer, but we're driving up to the university as soon as Jana's done shopping. Apparently, an old friend of her husband works there now, and she wants to see him."

"I didn't know she was married," Kacie said surprised.

"Emphasis on 'was.' Cancer. They had been married for

more than fifteen years. He was a great guy, too. It really left her, and the rest of our family, devastated."

Jack thought he noticed his own sadness reflected in Kacie's eyes.

"I'm so sorry to hear that." Kacie cleared her throat and continued, "I'm sure any connection to her husband will make her feel just that much closer to him. It'll be good for her to see his old friend."

Jack had been hesitant when Jana first said she wanted to go meet her husband's friend, but hearing the way Kacie put it, he thought maybe it wasn't such a bad idea.

∞∞∞∞

"That was such a bad idea. I am so sorry to have exposed you like that, Jackie."

"It's not your fault. It was bound to happen sometime."

"It's my fault. I'm the one who's responsible for your security," Ellie broke in. "What kind of fool am I to let you go to a university of all places? A place that's literally crawling with your fan base." Ellie's panic was worsened by her sense of guilt for having slowly let her guard down ever since moving to Sycamore Ridge. Switching gears into problem solving mode, she added, "We need to come up with a game plan. Maybe move somewhere else. I think we should call Robert."

"And I think we should all calm down." Jack said in a voice that did not invite argument. "Those girls were far away, they did not manage to take a picture, and if they say they saw me, it'll just be another one of those rumors that are always surrounding me."

"I don't know, Jack. I'm worried. I agree with Ellie. If Jana hadn't seen them get all excited, they would have gotten the photo."

"But she did see them. And they didn't get the photo. Look, call Robert if you want. But I'm not moving. Period."

The three women looked at each other, unsure of what to do.

"Listen to me," Jack continued quickly, taking advantage of their hesitation. "Instead of panicking and uprooting my life, let's think this through. What can we do to discredit any rumors that start?"

Laura was the first to answer. "We can always ask Lindsay to leak old photos of you in some other location. Make it look like you're on a vacation somewhere."

"That's not a bad idea," Jack agreed, hopeful to get the other two on board. "We have tons of photos of me from some vacation or another where I'm by myself on the beach. She can blur them up a little and leak them to the press. No one will know the difference. And once it's in the tabloids, everyone will believe it." Feeling his blood pressure rising at the thought of the paparazzi, Jack forced himself to take a deep breath, and then burst into laughter.

"Are you kidding me? What is so funny right now? This is serious."

"Think about it for a second. The last two times we've interacted with the press has been to manipulate them into creating rumors to protect me instead of expose me."

"I guess." Ellie, still feeling disappointed in herself for not having thought things through, added, "But I think we need to do more. We've all gotten too comfortable since we've moved here. It's one thing to let our guard down at home and around Sycamore Ridge, but we were stupid to come out here and think none of these co-eds would recognize you."

"What do you mean 'do more'? I'm not walking around

with bodyguards, and I'm not going to be a prisoner in my own home."

"Fine. Then we need to do something to make you less recognizable."

Both Laura and Jana sucked in their breath. They knew exactly what Ellie was getting at, and they were prepared for Jack to throw a tantrum. His response, however, was completely unexpected.

# CHAPTER 16

## *Just Friends*

The weather in Sycamore Ridge had taken a definitive turn towards the dog days of summer, and Asha and Shelby congratulated themselves on having the foresight to arrive at Fountain Walk just before the lunch rush began in earnest. They had managed to snag an outdoor table with an umbrella cover, and they were looking forward to enjoying their weekly lunch while being able to people watch to their hearts' content.

The tables were starting to fill up fast, mostly with locals who knew how hard it would be to secure an outdoor table in warm weather.

"You know," Asha said between mouthfuls of her sandwich, "we could use some new faces around here. I recognize almost everyone."

"Give it another few minutes. As soon as it's really hot and there are no tables left, all the tourists and foodies will be out in droves hovering over us to grab our table as soon as we take our last bites."

"Eat slowly then. I don't want to go back to work until we absolutely...," Asha abruptly cut herself off mid-sentence, and Shelby looked up from her salad, surprised to see her friend sitting with her mouth wide open and full of food.

"What's wrong? Asha!"

Swallowing with a noticeable gulp, Asha tilted her head in the direction just over Shelby's shoulder. Taking this as a signal to turn around, Shelby did just that and immediately understood Asha's reaction. Walking towards them was a man they had never seen before. An incredibly gorgeous one. Tall, tanned, with long brown hair and dressed in a pair of jeans and a grey t-shirt.

As he got closer to their table, he noticed both of them unabashedly staring at him, and for a moment, his heart rate sped up out of fear they would recognize him. When neither of them reached for their cell phones to take photos, though, Jack reminded himself he was in Sycamore Ridge and there was nothing for him to worry about here. This was his home, and he could continue walking around without fear. These were just two young women who found him attractive.

Judging from their homemade lunches, he pegged them for locals and decided he would do the neighborly thing. As he walked past, he turned towards them, nodded his head, and smiled at them briefly.

They followed him with their eyes until he went into a shop, and then turned towards each other with their eyebrows raised.

"Wow! Who was that?"

"I have never seen him before."

"He was gorgeous. And did you see his...."

"Shhhh, someone will hear us, Asha."

Asha lowered her voice and said, "I know one thing for certain. He does *not* have his own library card. Because if that man had ever walked into my library, I would remember." She wiggled her eyebrows up and down, and Shelby giggled while nodding her agreement.

"Let's be serious for a minute. We live in a small town, we should be able to figure this out."

"You're right. We've only had two new families move to the area in the past couple of months that I know of. That young couple who moved out here from California and...."

Shelby interjected, "I met them the other day at the hardware store. Kacie introduced me to them. She and I were there buying that spray thing to keep the front door of the library from creaking every time it opens and closes, and they were there buying the same thing. Isn't it a small world?"

"Shelby! Get to the point!"

"Oh, right. Well, it's definitely not that guy. The one I met was shorter and had dark hair and glasses."

"The only other new person who has purchased property here is Robert."

Shelby snapped her fingers, "I know who it is! That *has* to be Robert's brother. Remember when we were in line at Rebekah's a while back standing behind the Randalls? It was raining and Erica had on that gorgeous outfit, and I was so worried it was going to get ruined. And then I realized Mr. Randall was carrying an umbrella and their office...."

"Shelby! Get to the point!"

"Oh, right. Anyway, while you were trying to decide what to order, I overheard them having a conversation about how they hoped Robert's brother had the same design style as him. And I remember thinking, 'hmmmm, why would it matter if Robert's brother liked the design of the house?' See?"

"So you think Robert spent all his money to buy a house and renovate it and now his brother is living there?"

"That's the only thing I can think of. Maybe he's house sitting until Robert can move out here?"

"Yeah, that might be it. He did look a bit like Robert... especially his...."

"Asha!"

Another round of giggling followed, and the two friends spent what was left of their lunch hour trading theories on who Robert's brother was, what he did for a living, and most importantly, how they could meet him.

"I bet you Kacie knows about him. She knows everything that goes on in this town."

Asha packed up her lunch container and stood up, "Yeah, but you know her. She's all about respecting people's privacy. There's no way she would tell us anything. I wonder if Suzanne knows something. Do you think we could get her to talk?"

When Shelby didn't answer, Asha followed her gaze in the direction the handsome stranger had gone, eagerly anticipating a chance to catch sight of him again. But they weren't prepared for what they saw or what happened as he walked past.

"Hello ladies. Have a great day," Jack flashed them one of his signature megawatt smiles and went on his way.

Neither one of them managed to respond.

∞∞∞∞

Kacie and Erica were waiting to be seated for lunch at one of Remy's outdoor tables when they saw Shelby and Asha half-running, half-walking towards them.

"Bet you a morning bun they just saw a hot guy."

"No way I'd take that bet. You'd win every time."

"Kacie! You are not going to believe this," Shelby said

161

breathlessly. "Asha and I were having lunch at one of the covered tables over by the Sandwich Shop. You know the ones? Not the ones across from the Sandwich Shop, but the ones right in front of it. We managed to grab a table with an umbrella before the lunch rush started. How lucky was that? I had my salad that I brought from home and Asha was having...."

"Get to the point, Shelby!"

Asha, impatient to tell Kacie who they had seen, jumped in at this point. "We saw this gorgeous man who we've never seen before. I mean, gorgeous, with a capital G. He had long hair and a great..."

"Asha!"

"Right, right. He had this incredibly sexy long hair."

Shelby picked up the thread as Asha stopped to fan herself with her hand. "We saw him walk into a store, but we couldn't tell which store because of where we were sitting. We ate as slowly as we could hoping we would be able to see him again."

"And then he came out of the store, and we almost didn't recognize him. But then he got closer, and we realized it was him and as he walked past, we realized we must be right about him. He must be Robert's brother because they both have the same great...."

"Asha!"

Kacie, feeling relieved that the ladies hadn't recognized Jack, added as nonchalantly as she could, "You must mean Jack. He's been staying at Robert's new house."

"Hello again, ladies."

All four of them turned towards the voice, but only Kacie recognized it right away. What she almost didn't recognize was the breath-taking man standing in front of her.

Jack's hair had been cut and styled so that he looked like a completely different person. The sides were shaved very close, and all the old blonde highlights had been cut away, leaving only his natural dark brown hair. The top was a little longer than the sides and had been spiked up a bit, giving him a sexy, edgy look. The dramatic change also had a marked impact on his face. His chiseled jawline was more pronounced, and his eyes and mouth somehow became even more appealing than before.

Kacie's heart was pounding a little faster than normal and she was trying not to stare. Fortunately, all the time she had been spending with Jack had helped her become slightly more immune to his good looks than the others, and she was able to save them all from looking too foolish.

"I almost didn't recognize you! I'm surprised Laura let you do it."

"She doesn't know yet, but it needed to be done. Change is good, right?"

"You're a brave man." Kacie knew how much Laura loved his hair and was glad she would not be around when Laura saw him for the first time.

Jack smiled, "Are you going to introduce me to your friends?"

Kacie, despite being worried one of her friends might pass out with excitement, did as he asked and hoped for the best.

∞∞∞

"I took Sally to the library yesterday."

"Did you? I bet she loved that." Kacie had a feeling she knew what was coming, but she didn't take the bait.

"When we were checking out our books, I got to talking

163

with Asha and Shelby. Those girls can talk."

"They sure can."

"They were telling me all about how they met Jack."

"I introduced them."

"They had a lot of, shall we say, 'observations' to share with me."

"Is that right?"

Realizing Kacie wasn't going to make this easy for him, Walter put his coffee down on Kacie's desk and sat staring at his friend as she typed away on her laptop.

"I know you're not typing anything important."

"How can you know that? I'm a successful business owner and the mayor of a town. I have lots of important things to type."

"Don't you want to know what the only observation that Asha and Shelby could agree on was?"

Without waiting for an answer and without taking his eyes off her, Walter continued. "They said the sparks were flying between you and Jack."

Kacie could feel a blush creep up her face. She had been expecting something like this because of the way Erica, Asha, and Shelby had been scrutinizing her and Jack outside of Remy's. She knew they saw things that Walter would never have noticed.

Walter may not have been the most observant man, but he was no fool. "You two seem to be spending a lot of time together."

"We enjoy each other's company. We've become good friends." Kacie had tried not to sound defensive. Tried and failed.

"Do you really think that's all it is?"

Kacie sighed. There was no denying she found Jack physically attractive. And the more time she spent with him, especially in the company of his family, the more she was drawn to him. He was warm and funny, smart and honest. She was hard pressed to find something about him she didn't like. When she was with him, she was happier. And when they weren't together, she often found herself thinking about him. More than often.

But she knew she would never make a move on him. It would only bring her heartache. He had told her in passing the other day that he had started writing music again and was back in touch with his bandmates. And to Kacie, that meant it was just a matter of time before he left Sycamore Ridge and went back to his previous life. If she started a relationship with him now, what would happen when he left? She was unwilling to leave her life behind to live his nomadic lifestyle. And, anyway, she was getting ahead of herself. For all she knew, he just thought of her as a friend. A friend who offered him a brief respite from his fame.

"For me, Walter, that's all it is."

# CHAPTER 17

## *Three Sounds*

"Good morning, Jackie. Happy birthday!"

"Thanks," Jack replied, giving his sister a big bear hug.

"What time is everyone coming over?"

"Around eleven. I can't believe I'm having a pool party for my birthday. What am I? Eight?"

Jana laughed. "Hey, it was your idea."

"Is anyone else up yet?"

Jana shook her head. "Who's invited today?"

"Just a small group. The Randalls, Walter and Sally, and Kacie. But when you throw in the two of us, Laura and Ellie, Lindsay, and Robert and Lorraine and my three constantly growing nephews, it'll be a pretty big crowd."

Laughing, Jana teased, "This from the man who can fill a stadium."

"Fair enough. Let me restate that. It'll be the *perfect* sized crowd."

"Speaking of crowds, I heard you up late last night video conferencing with the band."

"Yeah, I've talked to each of them on the phone, but Lindsay thought it would be a good idea for us to 'see' each other again. And you know how she is. Once she thinks something is a good idea, she's going to make it happen."

"She's usually right."

"Don't tell her that. But yes, she was right. It was great to reconnect. We started talking about working on a new album."

This was the opening Jana had been waiting for. She had been wanting to talk to Jack about his plans for the future, and now she had an opening. And she knew she had to take advantage of it. She also knew she had to navigate the conversation carefully. "A new album? I wasn't expecting you to say that. It usually means months in a recording studio and then a tour. Are you thinking about leaving Sycamore Ridge?"

Jack didn't know how to respond. It seemed lately, each time he picked up his guitar or even talked about music, the same question stirred in the back of his mind. He was completely torn and hated to think of his future as a choice between two options. Stay and give up making music with his band or go and give up the happiness he had found in his new life.

When he had moved to Sycamore Ridge, he had been convinced that he wanted to leave his old life behind. He didn't need the money, and the fame had taken a dramatic toll on his well-being. He never thought he would make another album, let alone go on tour. But as the weeks went by, he realized music was like air to him. It was not something he would ever be able to give up. At first, he satisfied his needs by picking up his guitar and playing some of his old music. This slowly turned into feeling the urge to write new material. Once he started doing that, he found himself wanting to talk about it with his bandmates. They had been together for so long, and the idea of making new music was inseparable from the other musicians. The conversations he had had with Derek and Lola had been just like old times and flowed as smoothly as the music once had. They both sounded as happy and relaxed as he felt. Thankfully, no one seemed in any real rush to jump into the recording studio.

"I don't know," Jack sighed. "I love it here. You see how happy I am. Each time I start thinking about what comes next, I freeze up. I can't imagine leaving this house, the freedom I have, the friends I've made."

"Maybe some friends more than others?" Jana asked gently.

Jack looked at his sister and knew exactly what she was trying to ask him. He had been expecting it. "I know you're asking about Kacie. But we're just friends, Jana. There's nothing more. I don't want to do anything to hurt her. She is one of the most amazing people I've met in a long time, and she just lets me be me. She never wants anything from me other than my company. Spending time with her is easy. And fun."

Jana wondered if Jack realized that he was literally describing what it means to care for someone. "Do you really think that's all it is?"

"Yes. And I intend to keep it that way."

∞∞∞∞

As he was getting ready for bed later that day, Jack knew he would never forget this birthday. It had turned out to be an idyllic day, one of those days when the weather and the food and the people all collide to make for an unforgettable afternoon.

He had been worried his conversation with Jana in the morning would weigh heavily on him, but once his friends and family had arrived, the weight had lifted, and he had thoroughly enjoyed himself. He couldn't remember which one of his nephews had convinced him to play his guitar, but he had ended up playing one of the new pieces he was working on. To be sitting at his house, surrounded by family and friends, and playing his music had almost moved him to tears.

There was one other moment which he knew he would never forget. The image had been burned into his memory, and it kept coming to him unbidden. Sally had managed to swim the width of the pool without anyone's help, and Kacie had been clapping and cheering her on. She had been sitting on the edge of the pool smiling from ear to ear, her wet hair pulled back and the water glistening off her beautiful skin. Jack couldn't remember what her bathing suit looked like, but he knew he would always remember how radiant she had looked.

And then he remembered what she had given him as his birthday present and laughed out loud: his very own, personal, handheld sander.

∞∞∞

"Have you seen this?"

It was the day after Jack's party and while everyone else was sleeping in, Robert and Ellie had gotten up early trying to get some work done before his flight out later that day. Ellie was sorting through email while Robert had been going through the paper mail when a postcard caught his attention. He held it up as Ellie looked up from her laptop.

"No, Laura usually goes through the mail, but I don't think she's done it the past few days. What is it?"

"It's a blank postcard. It looks like it was mailed from Charles de Gaulle airport. Or at least, purchased from there."

"Strange." Her tone was even, but her heart was beating faster and the hairs on her arms were standing.

"Look at the mailing address." He handed the postcard to Ellie, who flipped it over to see an unfamiliar handwriting.

"This is the address we have up on the band's website for fan mail. But that's supposed to be sorted by someone on Lindsay's team. Only the stuff that needs our attention gets forwarded here."

Robert ran his fingers through his hair. "Maybe it slipped through the cracks? At least it wasn't sent to the Willow Avenue address."

"Small consolation." Ellie paused to gather her thoughts. "It's strange that the one postcard with nothing written on it got forwarded here. I don't like it."

"Yeah, neither do I," Robert agreed. "Have you been using the security system?"

"Religiously. We turn it on every night before going to bed and anytime we're all out of the house."

"Good. Make sure you keep doing that."

"And what about Jack? Should we tell him?"

"No. No way. Did you see him yesterday? I don't think we should take that happiness away from him." Robert paused and then continued, "At least, not yet."

∞∞∞

"I had a great time with everyone, but I'm glad to have some time to ourselves. I think this is my favorite day of the week."

"Tuesday? Really? We need to get out more."

"You know what I mean." Laura rolled onto her stomach and looked at Ellie stretched out next to her. "Jack is busy doing his 'apprenticeship' at Kacie's, and we get to come out here and have our picnic."

Ellie laughed aloud. "Can you believe he actually calls himself her 'apprentice?'"

Laura shook her head, "I love them both to pieces, but they are moving at a glacially slow pace."

"Remember, he wants to be 'just friends' with her." Ellie rolled her eyes, placed one corner of their picnic blanket over her face to block out the sun, and settled in for a little nap.

"Who is that?" Laura asked. "I've never seen anyone on this trail before."

Without opening her eyes, Ellie replied, "It's public property. Anyone can hike here."

"She looks lost. Let me see if I can help her."

Ellie smiled to herself. Her sweet Laura wasn't happy unless she was being helpful to someone. The soft sound of Laura's footsteps walking across the wild grass towards the lost hiker and the distant mumble of voices were lulling her off to sleep. Until she heard three sounds that made her blood run cold: an electrical buzzing, a dull thud, and the grating sound of metal against metal as a gun was cocked.

# CHAPTER 18

## *Oblivion*

Sarah watched as the woman, who had just moments before been resting peacefully on the picnic blanket, suddenly rolled onto all fours, ready to jump into action. The way she moved reminded Sarah of someone with military experience or maybe a former police officer, but it didn't matter. Sarah was well prepared. She kept her gun pointed at the prone figure at her feet and her eyes on the suddenly alert woman. She noticed her cast a quick sideways glance at a backpack laying nearby and wondered if she was packing a gun in there.

"Don't even think about it and don't make a single sound. You should know that I won't hesitate to shoot her. She's still alive right now. Don't blow your chance to save her." Sarah couldn't believe she was saying these words. Hearing them come out of her own mouth only added to the adrenaline already surging through her body.

Ellie stayed as still as she could, not wanting to spook the hiker. Staring steadily at the woman, she took the time to consider her options. The hiker didn't look particularly strong. She was of average height and build. Other than that, there was nothing at all about her that stood out with the exception of her outfit, which looked like it came directly out of the pages of an advertisement for hiking gear. It was almost comical.

"Stand up slowly and walk towards me," Sarah said.

There was nothing comical about her voice, though. It was cold and calculating, and almost as scary as the gun she was pointing at Laura.

Ellie stood up slowly and began walking. She considered bending forward and charging the woman like a bull when she got closer to throw her off balance. Ellie was confident she could easily overpower the stranger. But when she had covered half the distance between them, the woman commanded her to stop. Without taking her eyes off Ellie, she reached into her pocket with her free hand, pulled something out, and threw it at Ellie.

"Pick those up. You know what they are and how to use them. Put them on. Tightly."

Ellie took a couple of small steps to where the item was, reached down, and took a deep breath. They were heavy duty zip tie handcuffs. The kind used by the police. She wracked her brain for an alternative, but not seeing any, she picked up the zip ties, put her hands through the loops, and pulled them tight with her teeth. Maybe, she thought, when she got close enough, she could kick the gun out of the woman's hands.

"Now, get down on your knees and come the rest of the way."

Moving forward on her knees with her hands tied in front of her was not easy. Small pieces of gravel scratched at her knees and shins, and she could feel the warmth of fresh blood being drawn, but Ellie kept moving until she finally made it to Laura's side.

Laura was laying on her back, unconscious. One side of her face and her hair were matted with blood, but she was still breathing. And that was all that mattered.

Stifling a sob, Ellie looked up at the hiker and her sob turned into a guttural growl. No longer able to control her rage, she tried to stand up and pounce at the woman, but again, the stranger was one step ahead of Ellie. She hit Ellie with a jolt of electricity that almost knocked her to the ground and finished the job with an unexpectedly powerful kick to the side of her stomach.

Sarah, feeling proud of herself for having the foresight to bring multiple tasers, found it almost funny to see the two women, who had been picnicking nearby just moments earlier, both lying on the ground, one bleeding and unconscious and the other writhing in pain. It had been almost too easy.

Even though it was highly unlikely someone would come down the trail, Sarah reminded herself to finish up quickly. She bent at the knees and dropped the discharged taser she had been holding into her open backpack. Reaching into the pocket of her shorts, she pulled out the taser she had used on Laura and placed it inside her backpack as well, all while keeping one eye on Ellie and her gun pointed at Laura.

Then, carefully reaching into a separate cargo pocket in her shorts, she pulled out two small syringes filled with a clear liquid.

Ellie's blood ran cold as she tried frantically to think of a way out. "What do you want? Whatever it is, I can help you get it. Please...." Her voice was desperate, pitiful.

It had no impact on Sarah whatsoever. "Shut up," she said as if she was talking to an annoying dog who was barking too much.

Ellie, unable to control her tears or her panic, pleaded, "Listen to me, someone will be here any minute. This trail is crawling with people. If you run now, no one will even know you were here. They'll never be able to find you. I promise we won't go to the police. Please, just let us go."

"Nice try, but you and I both know that no one hardly ever uses this trail on a weekday."

Fear was clouding Ellie's judgement, and she couldn't think straight. She wondered if she should scream. Or maybe try to rush the woman again. But the gun in the hiker's hand pointed right at Laura's head rendered every option an impossibility.

"Some bodyguard you are," Sarah mumbled as she pulled off the cap of the first syringe with her teeth. Looking at Ellie, Sarah was pleased to see her comment had hit its mark. Fear now mixed with confusion about how much the stranger seemed to know about her.

"You didn't really think I was here for you, did you?" Sarah laughed. Without waiting for an answer, she bent over Laura's prone figure and injected the contents of the syringe into her limp, unresisting arm.

As Ellie watched the unknown liquid flow into Laura's arm, her thoughts drifted to Jack. The man she was paid to protect. The man she had failed over and over again. Whatever happened to him, whatever this woman did, was all Ellie's fault. As this realization dawned, all the fight began to drain out of her. She didn't even have the strength to struggle as she watched the hiker pull the cap off the second syringe and inject it into her arm.

Her eyes fluttered to a close a few seconds later, and Ellie almost welcomed the sense of oblivion.

∞∞∞

Standing over the two women, Sarah marveled at how easy it had been. A little planning and preparation were all it took to dispose of two of her biggest obstacles. Now, she just had to make the whole scene look as idyllic as it had a few moments earlier just in case some person did happen to walk along this trail on a weekday afternoon.

Grunting with the effort, she dragged both limp bodies back to their picnic blanket and arranged them to look as if they were enjoying an afternoon nap. Then she went back over the area where she had dragged the bodies and kicked as much dirt, gravel, and grass around as she could to cover her tracks.

Sarah stepped back and surveyed her handiwork. It wouldn't stand up to extreme scrutiny, but there was no reason to think anyone out on a leisurely nature walk would have any cause to examine the scene.

Grabbing her backpack, she reassumed her role of hiker and continued down the trail. Emboldened by her triumph over Laura and Ellie, Sarah smiled as she went. From the moment she had first stepped foot on American soil, every step in her well laid out plan had fallen into place perfectly, starting with her move to the university town just a short drive from Sycamore Ridge.

∞∞∞

"You're a graduate student at the university?" The elderly woman had asked as she showed Sarah the dingy, fully furnished off-campus rental apartment.

Sarah had been prepared for some level of questioning and she had her lie ready. It flowed surprisingly easily from her lips. "Not a full-time student. I'm just here for the semester to take some classes in ancient Greek and Roman history that aren't offered at my school."

The woman had stared at her blankly. Sarah knew a quick call to the university's registrar's office would expose her lie, but she was confident the woman would never bother making that call.

"I got a stipend from my school to cover the rent, so I can pay for all four months up front," Sarah had added innocently, just to grease the wheels a bit, "If that's okay with you?"

The statement had had exactly the effect she had hoped, and the apartment was hers. She had handed the woman her security deposit and rent money in cash, and the woman had practically run out the door with the wad of bills clutched tightly in her hand. Sarah knew she'd never see or hear from her again. Which is exactly what she wanted.

Taking off the non-prescription glasses she had been wearing as part of her "grad student" disguise, Sarah had looked around the dark and musty-smelling apartment with her nose crinkled. It was a far cry from the five-star hotels she was used to staying in, but she would deal with it because it would provide her with the perfect cover and home base for the next step in her plan.

∞∞∞

Reaching the end of the trail just on the outer edge of the beautiful property she had been scoping out for the past few weeks, Sarah hid in the trees and took a minute to calm herself. Between the jolt of adrenaline from overpowering the two women and her quick pace to arrive at her destination, she was breathing heavily, her heart was beating rapidly, and a thin layer of sweat had formed on her upper lip and along her hairline.

Sarah knew it would be foolish to let her excitement interfere with her plans. She had to remain calm. She forced herself to close her eyes and practice her deep breathing strategy. Deep breath in until the count of five. Hold. Exhale slowly to the count of ten. She was doing fine until her third deep inhale, when a picture of Jett walking shirtless on a beach suddenly invaded her thoughts.

Mentally inserting herself into the picture, she imagined sitting provocatively in the sand as he approached. Imagined how he would drop down onto his knees before her and all the things he would do. Her breathing became erratic once again, and she almost moaned aloud. The thought of being physically closer to him than she'd been since that first time they met made a warmth explode inside her. All her months of preparation had finally led her to this moment. To Jett. Her Jett.

# CHAPTER 19

## *A Toxic Mix*

The sound of his name had always aroused her, from the moment she had learned his identity that night in Dubai. And until that embarrassing experience during the meeting when her client exposed her juvenile obsession, Sarah had been content with collecting photos and videos of Jett and using them to fuel her fantasies. But when those figments of her imagination ceased to be enough, she had been compelled to find other means.

Not a fan of loud, crowded spaces, she had nonetheless forced herself to attend a few of his concerts, especially on the occasions when her job and his tour dates had them staying in the same European city. Sarah had convinced herself that if only they could meet again, he would feel the same way she was certain he had the first time they had met. She had tried desperately to get backstage passes so she could see him face to face. But after a security threat earlier on in the tour, backstage access to the band had been practically eliminated.

In the end, the only thing the concerts accomplished was to add another layer of frustration and jealousy to the dangerous cocktail of feelings that were brewing inside Sarah. She hated seeing all the screaming fans go wild each time Jett took the stage. She was disgusted by the things she overheard many of the women saying about the man she loved. Sarah didn't even like the music his band played. It was loud and obnoxious and nonsensical in her view. When they were together, she knew he would give it up for her the moment she asked.

Sarah was only too happy to stop going to his concerts, but she had been desperate to find other ways to get close to him. Unsure of what to do, she had begun sending letters and post cards to his fan club telling him how much she loved him and reminding him that he felt the same way. She'd wait weeks for a response, but the only thing she ever got for her efforts was four copies of the same autographed photo of him.

The toxic mix of disappointment, frustration, desire, and loneliness had continued to eat away at her. Feeling helpless to make her dreams come true, she laid awake in bed night after night thinking of ways to get close to Jett. Until one night when an idea from an old movie she had watched years earlier popped into her head. Instead of sending letters to his fan club, she decided to take what she hoped would be a more attention-grabbing approach. She had cut out letters from different magazines she had laying around, glued them to a sheet of paper and sent a message she believed would illicit a response: "If I can't be with you, no one can."

Less than two weeks later, she read a tabloid magazine article about a fan who was stalking Jett Vanders. The article said that out of concern for his safety, his management team would be reviewing their safety protocols. Sarah felt a rush of power knowing that a short message from her could have such an impact on so many people.

ooooo

From that moment on, Sarah couldn't get enough. She began sending the same kind of threatening messages from wherever she happened to be in the world. Then she'd wait with growing anticipation to see herself mentioned in the news. Whenever the paparazzi asked Jett about it, he always gave the same, canned answer, "Sorry, guys, no comment." But Sarah was certain she could see the fear in his eyes. Thinking about having the power to disrupt his perfect life by doing something so small as sending a letter sent that now familiar, heady rush surging through her body.

But like every addiction, the rush slowly became harder to come by. When sending the letters failed to satisfy her, Sarah searched for another way to get to Jett. Late one night, while forcing herself to focus on a project for a boutique European hotel chain, an idea had come into Sarah's mind. Knowing Jett's tour dates and locations by heart, she knew he was scheduled to perform the following night in Frankfurt. She did a quick internet search for high end hotels in Frankfurt and was able to narrow down the list to just three hotels because, by that time, she had a pretty good idea of the types of places the band preferred.

It had taken her longer than she had expected to hack into the hotel's reservations system, and she knew that meant she wouldn't make her work deadline. But Sarah hadn't cared. All she could think about was Jett. Once she had gotten into the system, it had been fairly simple to find which room he was staying in. Unfortunately, when she called the hotel and asked to be connected to his room, they absolutely refused, and Sarah was forced to find another solution.

Thinking creatively, she checked the incoming and

outgoing phone records for that room and found only one number, a number with a U.S. area code. Sarah took a deep breath and dialed the number, hoping someone would answer. She hadn't expected that someone to be a woman.

"Who is this?" the woman had demanded, seeing a blocked caller on her screen.

"I want to talk to Jett."

"Is this the person who has been sending letters to Jett? We can help you. Turn yourself into the police, and we'll get you the help you need." The response had seemed calm and almost rehearsed, but Sarah thought she detected a hint of fear.

"Why would I turn myself in? I haven't done anything wrong." Sarah paused and then added, "At least not yet."

"What do you want?" The fear began to intensify, and Sarah could feel the rush begin to hum through her body. The feeling was almost euphoric.

"You know what I want. And I won't stop until I get him."

The woman had hung up the phone, but for Sarah, it had been enough. Her craving had been satisfied.

ooooo

Sarah had been trying to ignore the incessant ringing of the phone, but when it became clear that the caller wouldn't stop, she answered with a groggy and rude, "Hello?"

"Do you have any idea what time it is?"

"No."

"It's two in the afternoon, Sarah. Do you know what that means?"

"Gerard, I was up late last night, I'm not in the mood.

What do you want?"

"You were up late last night? Doing what? Because you clearly couldn't have been working."

"What do you want," Sarah had repeated.

"You missed the meeting this morning, Sarah. You lost me a client I've been trying to land for months now. What is the matter with you?" Gerard, who prided himself on never losing his cool, was as close to yelling as he would ever get. "You have missed one deadline after another these past few months."

Sarah could tell Gerard was expecting her to apologize, maybe even grovel a little and promise to never let it happen again. But she didn't care. "So what? I'm still the best person you have working for you."

"You're wrong about that," Gerard had seethed, furious at the way she was treating him. "The best person I have working for me is me."

Tauntingly, Sarah had asked, "What are you going to do, Gerard, fire me?"

"Consider it done."

Sarah had stared blankly at the phone in her hands for a few moments and then slowly put it down. For most of her adult life, her sense of identity had almost been entirely defined by her job. She had grown accustomed to Gerard telling her where to go and what to work on. And even though she hadn't been as focused recently as she had been in the past, losing her job had never been part of the plan.

Laying back down on her bed, Sarah let her highly analytical mind do what it did best.

Financially, she knew she had nothing to worry about. Gerard had always paid her well, and, having almost no social life, she had barely spent any of the money she had earned. She had also banked tens of thousands of hotel points and frequent flyer miles from all her travels. Sarah felt confident she could continue staying in the hotels she preferred and living the lifestyle to which she had become accustomed for the foreseeable future.

"Maybe this is for the best," Sarah had said aloud to the empty hotel room. "Now I'll have more time for Jett."

∞∞∞

"Does this woman have nothing better to do with her time?" Ellie had been flipping through a dossier she kept filled with every encounter they had with Jett's stalker. Every letter they had gotten, a record of every phone call that had been made, including a rough transcript of the conversation. She was desperately searching for a clue, anything that would help them find this woman and make her stop.

They had woefully little to go on, apart from what they had been told by a criminal behavior expert they had consulted with. He had been very confident that the stalker was a woman, likely in her late twenties or early thirties and definitely a loner. Someone who was isolated and obsessive, possibly prone to violence or violent fantasies. His best guess was that all the letters and phone calls were from the same woman.

"They've gotten more frequent these past few weeks," Robert said.

"I just don't understand how she's able to figure out our room numbers. I mean, it's one thing for her to narrow down which hotel we're staying at, but every hotel manager I've spoken with has assured me over and over again that they don't allow any phone calls to be connected directly from the main switchboard to a guest's room. They always take a message. How is she dialing us directly? And how on earth did she find my cell phone number?"

At precisely that moment, as if on cue, the phone rang.

"Hello?" Ellie answered tersely.

"When are you going to let me talk to Jett?"

"Never."

"You know you can't stop me, right?"

"Can't stop you from what?"

"I'm so close right now, I can almost smell him."

Ellie looked up at Robert and mouthed, "Has she ever said anything like that before?"

Robert shook his head, and that's when Ellie heard an ambulance going past outside the hotel room. But that wasn't the only place she heard it. She could also hear it faintly in the background of her phone call. Hanging up the phone, she had screamed, "She's here, somewhere close!"

∞∞∞∞∞

As soon as Sarah had heard the ambulance, she had known she had made a terrible mistake, taken a foolish risk which could expose her. Forcing herself to remain calm, she had walked quickly out of the thankfully busy lobby of the hotel where Jett was staying and across the street to a crowded café. She found a small table near a window facing the street from which she had a clear view of the hotel and watched in panic as Ellie had come running out of the front doors, followed by an unfamiliar man. They looked around for a minute before exchanging a few words and running back inside.

Relief washed over Sarah, and she almost laughed aloud. What had they been expecting? That she'd be standing outside the hotel with an "it's me" sign hanging around her neck? Her initial fear quickly dissipated, and she lingered at the café watching as the police arrived and hotel guests and employees were interviewed before being allowed to enter or leave the building.

Again, she saw the unfamiliar man she had seen earlier exit the hotel and have a lengthy conversation with a police officer. She watched him closely, wondering who he was. His body language indicated that he was someone important, but Sarah couldn't remember ever seeing him photographed with Jett or reading about him in connection with Jett. Her curiosity had been peaked, and Sarah committed his appearance to memory. She would go straight back to her hotel as soon as the chaos outside settled down and do some research. She couldn't be certain, but she had a strange feeling that finding out who this man was would be crucial to finding a way to bring her and Jett together.

As it turned out, the strange feeling she had, had been correct.

∞∞∞

Once she knew what she was looking for, it had only taken Sarah a couple of hours to find photos of the man in her extensive collection of online files. He was always in the background, but he was in quite a few of them. Between getting a sense of how important he was outside of the hotel room and the frequency with which he appeared in the photos, Sarah felt certain he was someone intimately connected to Jett.

Feeling a quickening of her heartbeat, Sarah used professional photo enhancing software to zoom in on his face and sharpen the image. When she realized what she had been missing, Sarah gasped aloud. The man in the photo looked incredibly similar to Jett; similar enough, in fact, to be related to him.

Sarah's heart was now pounding in her chest, and her hands were clammy and unsteady. She hacked into the hotel's reservation system, thinking she would be able to find an online copy of his passport, but oddly enough, there were no photos of anyone resembling the man. Frustrated, Sarah scoured the internet for the next several hours until she finally found what she had been looking for. In an article that was several years old, she found a brief mention of a man running Jett's management agency. A man named Robert Wilkens. Once she had this piece of information, it only took a few moments to find out his basic personal information: married, father, rich. Apart from that, the information was quite scant, unlike most people who laid out their entire lives on social media. This man Robert seemed to keep an uncommonly low profile.

And that's when it had occurred to her. Maybe Robert played a much bigger role in Jett's career and life than he wanted people to know. Maybe, if she could find Robert, she would find Jett.

∞∞∞

Sarah's phone vibrated in her pocket and caused her heartbeat to speed up despite her best efforts. Standing at the edge of Jett's beautiful property, she looked down at the screen and smiled. Her love was home.

# CHAPTER 20

## At Last

Jack unlocked the door and was surprised to hear the alarm start beeping. It took him a moment to realize that it was Tuesday afternoon and Ellie and Laura were enjoying a quiet picnic together. He quickly punched in the code for the security system. The loud beeping grated on his nerves, but he knew arguing about it with anyone would fall on deaf ears. Robert had been smart and had the system installed during the renovation. *Before* Jack could weigh in on whether he wanted to have one or not. All things considered, though, Jack would take an annoying security system over being surrounded by security guards any day. He loved his life in Sycamore Ridge, and he knew he owed so much of it to Robert.

And he'd be lying if he didn't admit to himself that he also owed so much of it to Kacie. They seemed to be spending more and more time together, mostly from his doing. There was no denying how much he enjoyed being around her. On the days when he didn't have plans to see her, he found himself thinking about her again and again. He looked forward to seeing her and found excuses to go into town just so he could stop by her shop and talk. He loved hearing about all the projects she was working on and found himself talking about anything that popped into his mind.

And, then of course, there was the food. He had never met a woman who loved talking about food as much as Kacie did. Whenever he was telling her about a country he had visited on tour, the conversation invariably turned to food. Kacie would grill him on which restaurants he'd eaten at and what his favorite dishes were. Sometimes he wouldn't be able to give her the level of detail she needed to satisfy her gastronomic curiosity, and she would get angry at him for not paying attention to the food he was putting in his body. Every so often, she'd find recipes for some of the dishes he said he'd really enjoyed and cook them. She'd drop by the house and watch with anticipation as he tasted what she'd made. Her reaction, when he invariably said that the dish was delicious, was pure joy.

Jack could literally spend hours with Kacie and not even notice the passing of time. But the thing that made her happiest, the thing that would put a smile on her face every single time, was when he brought her a morning bun and a steaming hot cup of coffee from Rebekah's. Like he had earlier that day.

ooooooo

"You're going to make me have to buy new jeans, you know that?" Kacie had asked as she reached out to take the paper bag Jack was holding.

He loved how she *didn't* say, "you're going to make me fat." Her biggest concern was having to buy a new pair of jeans. Which would be a travesty because the ones she had on today made her legs look a mile long.

"Oh? You don't want it? Great! Then I'll eat both." Jack took the bag and walked over to the small table at the front of the shop.

"I didn't say that!"

"No, you didn't. But I'm just trying to be a good friend. I wouldn't want you to have to buy new clothes just because I brought you a warm, fresh out of the oven, flaky, buttery, delicious morning bun with this perfect cup of coffee with two shots of full fat cream and one sugar."

His detailed description had the intended effect.

"If you don't give me that, I'll tell Laura that you ate them and that you're starting to get fat!"

Jack laughed and handed over the bag.

"What are we working on today?" he asked between sips of his coffee.

Kacie finished chewing her first huge mouthful and said, "I have a treat for you today."

A small flake of food stuck to her lower lip, and Jack suddenly found himself having to fight the impulse to gently lick it off. The sharp urge caught him off guard, but it wasn't the first time he had felt that sensation. He wondered what her mouth would feel like against his. He imagined her lips would be soft and moist and would yield under just the right amount of pressure from him.

"Jack? Jack!"

"Sorry, what?"

"I said I had a treat for you today. Don't you want to know what it is?"

Jack nodded and took a sip of the scalding coffee to refocus his attention.

"I'm going to teach you how to use a lathe to turn some table legs." When she still didn't get a response, Kacie took a closer look at Jack's face. His cheeks were unusually flushed, and his eyes looked a little out of focus. "Are you feeling okay? You don't look so good." She got up and walked over to him, putting the back of her hand against his forehead. "You don't feel feverish."

Her unexpected closeness unnerved him further. Jack could feel the warmth coming off her body and could smell a fragrance he hadn't even realized he thought of as being distinctly hers. It was a combination of something flowery and woodsy. He looked up at her concerned face and right into her eyes. The gaze lasted just a split second longer than was necessary. Just long enough for him to feel a slight shift in the air. He knew from the slow blush that appeared on her cheeks that she had felt it, too.

∞∞∞

Kacie could feel her face getting warm and desperately wanted to look away. But she couldn't. Jack's expression had her rooted to the spot. He was looking at her in a way she hadn't seen before. The potent mix of desire and vulnerability she could see in his eyes made her want to kiss him softly. She fought desperately against her sudden urge to give in to the desire she had been suppressing for weeks. Her gaze drifted down to his perfect, beautiful mouth for a brief moment, but as always, the fear of ruining their friendship stopped her.

That and the ringing of the bell on the front door.

"Hey you two! Just the people I was looking for!" Jerome walked in with a big smile on his face. Fortunately, he didn't notice the tension in the air and continued talking.

"How's my chess board coming along?" he asked Kacie. And, turning to Jack, asked, "And when does my chess partner get here?"

Happy to have an excuse to walk away and compose herself, Kacie led Jerome into the shop to show him her progress on the custom chess board she was making for him.

Using the interruption to pull himself together, Jack had reminded himself for what felt like the hundredth time that he would be a fool to let his physical desire ruin one of the best friendships he'd ever had.

∞∞∞∞

Jack took his shoes off and walked towards the kitchen. He knew he should take a shower to wash off all the fine saw dust that was stuck to his clothes, but he needed a cold drink first. Pouring himself a tall glass of the freshly squeezed orange juice Laura always made sure was in the fridge for him, he leaned back on the kitchen counter and guzzled half of it.

Thankfully, by the time Jerome had left the store, he and Kacie had gotten themselves back on familiar ground. And despite the unexpectedly charged start to their afternoon, they had enjoyed the rest of their time together in the same easy, effortless way that he had come to cherish. To Jack, it was just another sign of how much each of them valued their friendship. Kacie had patiently taught him how to use the lathe, and he had turned out four relatively symmetrical table legs. As usual, the hours had slipped by, and it wasn't until her phone buzzed to remind her of a town board meeting she had to attend that they had finally gone their separate ways.

As he stared out the kitchen windows, the sun sparkled off the pool and lured him into forgoing his shower in favor of a late afternoon swim.

∞∞∞∞

Sarah watched with heightening anticipation as the

patio doors opened, and Jett stepped into full view. Every nerve in her body was on high alert and throbbing. Pulsating to the rhythm of her heartbeat. As quietly as she could, she pulled her binoculars out of her backpack and focused them on Jett. She rested her gaze on his face first, the face she loved more than anything else in the world. She moaned quietly as she imagined kissing his beautiful mouth and making him beg her for more.

She watched with eager expectation as he pulled his t-shirt off over his head to reveal his toned body and imagined running her hands over his smooth skin. Kissing his tattoo. Running her tongue over his stomach. Her body swayed with the desire, and she almost lost her balance. Sarah pinched herself hard and repeatedly to force herself to focus on the task at hand. She couldn't afford to make any mistakes. Not now that she was so close to him.

∞∞∞

Jack did a clean dive into the cool, refreshing water and easily swam twenty laps. Laura would be pleased, he thought as he pulled himself into a sitting position on the edge of the pool and looked out towards his backyard. The sun was just beginning to set, but it was still warm, and he sat letting the water slowly roll off his body. Again, his mind wandered back to what had happened earlier that day with Kacie. Again, he thought about the small crumb stuck to her lower lip and felt the rush of desire.

Angry with himself for going down that path again, Jack knew he needed to get his feelings for Kacie sorted out once and for all. There was no doubt in his mind that her friendship meant more to him than almost any other relationship he had, apart from his family. But the question he really needed to answer was: was he falling in love with her?

He would be lying to himself if he didn't admit he found her attractive. If he was being truly honest, he would say that he found her downright sexy. The more time he spent with her, the more he got to know her personality quirks, the sexier he found her. Like her obsession with morning buns. Just thinking about her eating one aroused him again. He stifled a moan as he closed his eyes and pictured her mouth with those full lips and overlapping two front teeth. He wondered how she would feel if he ran his tongue lightly over her teeth?

Shaking his head to clear the picture out of his mind, Jack opened his eyes and suddenly realized there was a woman standing in his backyard watching him.

∞∞∞

Sarah had waited patiently while Jett was swimming, but once he had pulled his glorious body out of the water, being patient had become harder and harder. He was like a magnet to her, pulling her towards him. She watched him through the binoculars as he closed his eyes and let his head fall back, exposing his long neck and chiseled jawline. Her heart was beating wildly, and she knew she had to make a move to appease her desire before it forced her to run headfirst towards him. Pinching herself again, she quietly put the binoculars in her backpack and picked it up. As she started walking towards the edge of the tree line, she took out her water bottle. Pouring a little water into her hand, she wet her hair to make it appear she was sweating and then poured the rest of the water onto the ground.

Taking a deep breath, she left the cover of the shade and stepped into the setting sunlight. She was still staring at him when he suddenly shook his head, opened his eyes, and looked right at her.

Waving her arm at him, she called out "Hi, I hope I didn't startle you. I'm a little lost and my phone isn't getting a signal out here. Can you please help me?"

∞∞∞

For a brief instant when Jack first saw the woman, he had felt a tinge of fear. But hearing her call out to him for help, he reminded himself of where he was. There was nothing for him to be afraid of. Not in Sycamore Ridge.

"Sure. Let me grab my towel. Come on over."

He wrapped his towel around his waist and watched as she walked towards him and almost laughed at himself for being afraid. The woman walking towards him was of medium height and build and looked like she couldn't hurt a fly. Her almost comical outfit made her look like she had dressed for the part of a hiker in a low budget movie.

"I'm so sorry to bother you," she said. "I feel like I've been walking in circles for the past half hour. I don't know where I took a wrong turn."

"No bother. Where are you trying to get to?" Jack tried to meet her eyes, but she seemed a little shy and averted his gaze. As she pulled a crumpled trail map out of her pocket, Jack got a slight whiff of the scent of her sweat. There was something strangely familiar about it, but he couldn't quite put his finger on it.

∞∞∞

Sarah had been confident Jett wouldn't recognize her from their brief meeting in Dubai. After all, she had lost almost 20 pounds and had stopped dying her hair. But now that she was standing so close to him and he was staring at her, she began to worry. Thinking quickly, she said, "I just moved in with my mom about six months ago, and I've heard a lot of people talking about a pretty little place where you can go for a swim. I had the day off today so I thought I would try to find it. Stupid me."

The hairs on the back of Jack's neck stood as he listened to her. There was something so familiar about this woman's mannerisms and voice, but he couldn't figure out where he knew her from. And the odor coming off her body, the cloying mixture of sweat and muskiness, made him once again uncomfortable.

Reminding himself again to be reasonable and calm, Jack reasoned with himself that it was entirely possible he had seen her around town. Deciding it was best to just give her directions and send her on her way, he pointed towards the trail she had come from. "Head back down that trail towards the right. When you come to the creek, just follow it for about a half mile and you'll be at the watering hole."

"Great. Thank you!" She started walking away, and Jack felt an immediate sense of relief. But it was short lived because she stopped and turned towards him again.

"Actually, do you mind if I refill my water bottle? I guess I didn't bring enough." She shook her water bottle as if to prove to him that it was empty.

Again, Jack hesitated. His gut was sending off all kinds of warning signals that there was something that felt off about this whole encounter.

"I really am sorry to bother you. But it's just so hot, and I've been wandering around for much longer than I had expected." Sarah knew she had to find a way to get closer to his house. She could drag him from where they were standing, but it would take a lot of effort, and she still had so much to do. If she could just get him closer to the back door, things would be a lot easier.

"I can wait outside while you fill it for me. Would that be okay?"

Jack reluctantly took the water bottle from her out-stretched hand. As he started walking towards the house, he realized she was walking along just a step behind him, babbling on about how beautiful the area was and how happy she was to have moved in with her mom. When they stepped onto the patio, Jack finally decided to listen to his instincts. And besides, he thought, it wouldn't be rude to ask a stranger to wait outside. He turned towards her and said, "Wait here. I'll be right back."

That's when he noticed the small black device she was holding in her hand.

"I can't do that, Jett. I've been searching for you for over a year, and now we can finally be together."

Those were the last words he heard before a sharp pain knocked him to his hands and knees. The next thing he felt was a pin prick against the side of his neck followed by a stinging sensation. And then everything went black.

ooooooo

Feeling disoriented and in pain, Jack slowly opened his eyes. He had to blink several times to bring his eyes into focus so that he could get his bearings. Terrified that he would find himself in an unfamiliar place, Jack was re-lieved to realize he was seated on one of his dining table chairs inside his own kitchen. The still-stinging sensa-tion on the side of his neck made him wonder what had caused it, but when he tried to move his hands to touch his neck, he realized they were tied firmly behind his back. His feet, too, had been tied together in front of him. He tried to pull himself free, but the tough plastic binding cut into his wrists and ankles, causing him more pain.

"Stop it. You know it won't work. Besides, I don't want you to start bleeding right now and have scars later."

Jack turned abruptly towards the sound, almost toppling over the chair to which he was tied. The woman who had attacked him was walking towards him from the hallway which led to his garage. Walking as if she owned the place. As she passed his kitchen island, his attention was drawn to two items that were completely out of place: her backpack and a gun. Jack's blood began to run cold, and he started fighting against the sturdy zip ties again.

"Please don't struggle, my love," she said in a voice which was both overly sweet and had a threatening tone to it. "And don't be afraid. Once you realize that we were meant to be together, you'll be so much happier."

Jack got the distinct impression that she thought she sounded sexy. Nothing was further from the truth.

"Who are you?" Trying to hide the fear in his voice, Jack asked, "What do you want?"

"What do I want? What do I want?" She tilted her head back and laughed. "What I want is you. Ever since the night you helped me. When I fell down by the pool. In Dubai."

Jack tried to clear the fog from his brain, and suddenly the memory of that strange encounter came crashing down on him.

∞∞∞

He remembered that he had been hosting a party in his luxurious hotel suite at the Burj Al Arab, a party that had started to get a little too rowdy for his taste, and he had snuck out to get some fresh air. Thankfully no one had noticed him leaving, and he had made his way down to the beautiful outdoor pool. Stretching out on a lounge chair away from prying eyes, he breathed in the cool night air and was wondering what would happen if he never went back to his room when he noticed a woman stumble and fall. Feeling sorry for her, he had walked over to see if she needed help. The poor thing had looked so pathetic that he had sat with her until the hotel medical staff tended to her wounds. Then he had gone back to his room. As far as he could recall, they had barely spoken to one another.

He did vaguely remember that the girl had poorly dyed blonde hair and was quite heavyset. It had been difficult for him to help lift her into a seat after she had fallen. But she looked nothing like this woman standing in front of him.

But as Sarah got closer to him, he caught another whiff of her scent and knew for certain it was the same girl. He remembered being put off by the smell of her that night in Dubai. There had been something pungent and cloying about her, and it was the same now.

Seeing the changing expression on his face, Sarah smiled with delight. "You do remember me! I had hoped you would, my love!" Feeling overwhelmed with happiness and desire, she straddled him in his seat and grinded herself against him like she'd seen women do in movies. "I wish I could make love to you right now." She put her hands on either side of his face and leaned towards him for a kiss.

Disgusted by her smell and her movements, Jack struggled to turn his face away from her. But she was stronger than he had expected. Gripping his face so that her nails dug into his skin, she forced his head still and kissed him on the lips, trying to pry them apart with her tongue. He managed to keep his teeth clenched firmly together, and she abruptly stood up.

Letting out a guttural yell, she abruptly backhanded Jack across the cheek, almost knocking him over backwards in his chair. Watching his expression go from disgust to fear only served to arouse her even further. She watched as a small trickle of blood dripped down from his lip.

Jack knew he had to find a way to take control of the situation. There was no doubt in his mind that the woman standing in front of him was completely unhinged.

"Listen to me. I have money. I can pay you."

Laughing, Sarah replied, "I have money. I don't need yours. And if you think I'm here for your money, you're a fool. I'm here for you, my love."

"My friends will be home soon. And then what will you do? Will you shoot us all?"

"Your friends? You mean the two women who were out on a romantic picnic today? Ellie and Laura, is it?" Sarah watched with pleasure as the news sank in. "Yeah, I don't think they'll be here any time soon."

Feeling rage welling up inside of him, Jack shouted out, "If you hurt them, I swear I'll...." Before he could finish, she slapped him again.

"You'll what?" Sarah smiled sweetly, and went on as if nothing had happened, "Don't worry, my love. No one will interrupt us. I made sure of it." Sarah glanced over at her gun knowingly, eagerly awaiting his reaction. And he didn't disappoint.

Struggling wildly to remove the restraints, Jack lunged towards her with his full body weight. But Sarah was ready. She deftly moved aside and watched him fall to the floor, still tied to the chair.

# CHAPTER 21

## *Eyes in the Dark*

With barely any sunlight left, Kacie decided to let Cooper off his leash and let him run ahead of her on the trail. The air was warm and balmy. It was a perfect evening for a stroll. A great way to wind down after a day that had thrown her off balance.

"Oh, Jack," she said to no one. "Why did you have to look at me like that?"

Cooper, hearing her mumbling, came running back to her side. Kacie smiled and bent down to pet him. "It's alright, boy. I'm just talking to myself." Hearing the reassurance in her voice, Cooper ran ahead again, and Kacie stood and started to follow him down the familiar path. They walked this portion of the trail almost every evening, and it was almost always deserted. Which is why the sudden, low, warning grumble coming from Cooper stopped Kacie short. Squinting in the dimming light, she could tell from Cooper's posture that something was very, very wrong.

Grabbing her phone and turning it to flashlight mode, she slowly made her way towards the dog. Scanning the area where he was looking, she noticed what appeared to be a couple laying on a blanket. But when Cooper's low growl turned into a loud bark, Kacie was surprised that there was no movement or response at all. Taking Cooper by the collar, she slowly advanced towards the blanket, her heart pounding with a strange combination of fear and concern.

As she took another step closer, the light from her phone reflected off a pair of eyes staring straight at her, and Kacie screamed.

∞∞∞

Grunting and sweating with the effort, Sarah finally managed to drag Jett, who was still tied to the chair, past the kitchen and down the long hallway to the garage. Luckily, it hadn't been as hard as dragging his limp body inside after she had tased him. When his chair had fallen, he had landed on a small area rug near the patio doors. That had given Sarah the idea of dragging the rug with him. It would be a lot easier than dragging the chair across the floor. She had been partly right and hadn't had to expend as much energy as she had originally been fearing.

Her next obstacle was going to be getting him into the car. Of course, she was prepared to do anything to make that happen. She would tase him again if she had to. But it would be so much easier on both of them if he just got into the car on his own.

"My love, I need you to get into the car. I can tase you again and drag you in, but that'll be hard on both of us."

Jack didn't respond. He couldn't. His entire body was shaking with rage and fear. Rage for what she may have done to Laura and Ellie; fear for what she was going to do to him. One thing was certain, he would fight with every ounce of strength to stay out of that car. If she untied him, he was certain he could overpower her. As long as she didn't tase him. He knew from watching her that she kept that taser in the left side pocket of her shorts and that she was left-handed. He had to play along until she loosened his ties. He had never hit a woman in his life, but he didn't think of this person in front of him as a woman. No, she was a monster, and he would do whatever was needed to subdue her.

Mastering control of his emotions, he demanded, "Where are you taking me?"

"Far away from all of this. To a place where you and I can be alone together. Forever."

The way she said "forever" sent a shiver down Jack's spine.

"If I loosen your zip ties, will you promise to cooperate and get into the car?"

Jack debated what his answer should be. If he said yes, she might suspect he was bluffing. If he said no, she would hurt him again. He decided his best bet would be to keep talking. Maybe someone would stop by the house and realize something was wrong. Maybe Laura and Ellie were fine, and this woman had been lying. But he knew that was just wishful thinking on his part.

"Fine, we'll do things the hard way." Sarah reached into her pocket for the taser.

"No, wait! You don't have to do that. I'll cooperate. I promise."

Sarah squinted her eyes at him. He was lying. There was no doubt about that. He was just waiting for the right moment to attack her. She had seen the anger in his eyes when he thought she had hurt Laura and Ellie. His love and protective instinct for his friends was much stronger than she had anticipated. Grasping how powerful his feelings were, Sarah had an idea that might help her. If he felt that strongly about his friends, he must feel even more strongly about his family.

"Don't lie to me."

"I'm not lying. Please, just don't tase me again. I promise I'll get in the car."

Sarah stood up and gently placed her hiking boot on Jack's bare chest. "I said, don't lie to me."

She slowly started applying more pressure with her foot and could see the expression of pain Jack was trying to hide.

"I want you to listen very carefully to what I'm about to say."

Jack tried to keep from squirming under her. The coarseness of the boot's sole against his chest hurt. But what hurt even more was the pain caused by the pressure. The harder she pushed down on him, the more stress his own body weight applied to his shoulders and arms, which were still tied behind his back and under the chair.

"Are you listening?" Sarah eased up the pressure just a little. Enough to get a nod of acknowledgement. "Good. If you don't do what I say, Laura and Ellie won't be my only victims."

Jack stopped squirming.

Knowing she had his full attention, Sarah continued. "I'm going to help you stand up and then I'm going to loosen the ties around your feet. You're going to walk to the back door of the car. Once you're there, I'll pull the chair loose and you'll get in the back seat. If you don't do this exactly as I've just explained to you, more people you love will pay the price."

Despite the searing pain in his shoulders, chest, and arms, Jack remained completely still, looking into her cold, calculating eyes.

Her next words made his blood run cold, and he knew

he would do exactly what she said.

∞∞∞

It took a split second for Kacie to recognize the eyes staring at her in the dusk. She stopped screaming and stood absolutely still, wondering if anyone was hiding nearby wanting to hurt her. After a couple of seconds that felt like hours, Kacie sensed there was no one else there. Maybe Cooper's barking and her scream had scared them away. At least she hoped they had.

Running towards Ellie, she pointed her phone light down towards her feet so she wouldn't trip on anything. She wouldn't be of help to anyone if she ended up getting hurt. Once she got close enough to the picnic blanket, she shined her light towards the two women lying there and gasped in horror. Ellie looked terrible. She was sunburned and her lips were raw and cracked. Fear was written all over her face.

But Laura looked much, much worse. Blood had dried and caked up in her hair and on her face. She wasn't moving at all, and Kacie bent towards her first. Fortunately, she knew enough first aid to check Laura's pulse. It was steady, but a little weak. Still, Kacie thought, or at least hoped, that her injuries, while serious, were probably not life threatening.

"She's okay, Ellie. There's just a lot of blood from this head wound. But she's breathing fine."

Realizing that Ellie was trying to say something, Kacie moved closer to her.

"Water. Bag. Please."

Holding up her phone, Kacie quickly found a backpack with water bottles in it and helped Ellie drink some.

"I need to call for help. Do you know who did this to

206

you?"

"Hiker. Help Jack. Hurry," Ellie managed to croak out through her parched throat.

"A hiker? He's gone to the house?" Kacie tried to keep her voice calm, but it was no use. "I'm calling the Sheriff."

"Not a man. A woman. Please hurry."

# CHAPTER 22

## No Words of Comfort

Frank was watching an episode of his favorite nature show, and this one happened to be a fascinating one about the mating habits of penguins. Which is why he was annoyed when his phone rang. Never far from his reach, he grabbed it on the first ring and barked, "This is Frank."

"Frank, it's Kacie. Something's happened."

Although Kacie's voice was quiet, Frank immediately sensed the fear and urgency in it. Sitting up, he turned off the tv and grabbed his pen and notepad from the coffee table.

"Okay. I'm going to help you. First, calmly tell me if you're okay." His stern, professional words belied the worry he felt for the woman he thought of as his own daughter.

"I'm fine. I was out walking with Cooper, and I found Laura and Ellie. They were tied up. Laura is injured." Kacie's sentences were coming out in short, staccato bursts as she made sure she was giving Frank all the information he needed. "She has some kind of head wound. They've been lying in the sun for hours. Both have sunburn and are dehydrated. Hold on a sec," Kacie turned towards Ellie, who was trying to tell her something. She nodded and got back on the phone.

"Frank, they were tased and injected with some sort of sedative. They need an ambulance. We're on the trail that runs along the creek up by Creekview Lane. I think we're close behind the Jackson residence. Do you know what I'm talking about?"

"Yes. Emma's already on the phone with the hospital and they're dispatching the ambulance. I'm on my way, too."

"No! Wait. Listen to me. Ellie says it was a woman who attacked them – medium build, brown hair, dressed like a hiker. She's here for Jack. She went to his house. They think she's the same woman who's been stalking him." Any semblance of control started slipping away from Kacie as the next sentence came out of her mouth. "Ellie thinks she's planning on kidnapping him!" Kacie stifled a sob. "Frank, Ellie's phone still has power, and I've turned it to strobe light mode. The paramedics will be able to find them. I'm heading over to Jack's now."

"Kacie! Listen to me! Do not go over there! It is too dangerous! Kacie! Kacie?" But it was too late, Kacie had already hung up and was running down the trail with Cooper by her side.

Grabbing his gun, Frank barked orders at Emma and ran out the front door. He just hoped he wasn't too late.

∞∞∞∞

Kacie was out of breath by the time she neared the end of the path that opened onto Jack's backyard. Bending down with her hands on her knees, she took deep breaths to calm herself. Cooper, also panting from the effort, was sitting at attention by her side, listening for any sounds of danger.

Unsure of what to do, Kacie slowly made her way to the backyard, terrified of what she would find.

The patio doors were wide open, and all the lights were on inside. But an eerie silence proclaimed that no one was home.

Her panic was palpable, and her hands were shaking violently as she tried to turn off her phone light so that she could approach the house without being seen. Not wanting to expose herself by walking across the open backyard, Kacie decided to make her way along the tree line towards the side of the house where the garage was. The unexpected, low rumble of a car engine from inside the garage stopped her in her tracks.

Grabbing Cooper by his collar, she stepped further back into the shadow of the trees and watched with dread as the garage door opened and an unfamiliar car slowly pulled out.

The light from the garage briefly illuminated the inside of the car, and Kacie thought she could make out a woman sitting in the driver's seat.

With fear pounding in her chest, she took a few steps forward. Should she jump out and try to stop the car? What if the woman was armed? What if Jack was inside the house? Injured? Or worse.

Kacie had no idea what to do, and there was no one around to help her. The unanticipated vibration of her phone in her back pocket made her jump. Grabbing it, she was about to answer when she realized what she had to do.

She set her phone to night mode and focused the camera on the license plate and took about a dozen photos as the car made a turn to face the street and started rolling forward. She managed to take a blurry photo of the driver's profile before the car turned left out of the driveway and drove away.

Kacie waited, still hidden, until countless seconds had passed. Frightened of standing outside and doing nothing and even more frightened of what she might find inside, Kacie gathered up her courage and stepped onto the driveway.

Her phone vibrated again in her hand, and this time she answered it. "Frank?"

"Where are you?" Frank's voice was clipped and professional, but she knew he must be worried sick about her.

"I'm at the house. Standing on the driveway. I got here just in time to see a woman pull out of the garage and drive off. I managed to take a few photos."

"Good. Now, I want you to listen to me. Do not, I repeat, do not go inside that house by yourself. Do you understand me? It's likely a crime scene. I'm only five minutes away. You stay on that driveway where I can see you when I pull in. Is Cooper with you?"

"Yes."

"Okay, both of you stay put. Text me the photos you took. Which way did the driver head?"

"Left, out of the driveway."

"She couldn't have gotten that far, but it's going to be tough finding her. You stay put. I need to make some calls. I'm on my way."

∞∞∞

Kacie opened the door as quietly as she could and peeked inside.

Laura was lying in the hospital bed with her head partially covered by a bandage and a nasty bruise slowly spreading across the right side of her face. Other than that, she appeared to be sleeping peacefully.

"I'm so glad she's going to be okay."

Kacie's head whipped towards the sound of the voice, and she saw Ellie sitting on a window bench inside Laura's hospital room. "Ellie! What are you doing in here?" she whispered. "They told me you were sleeping in the next room."

"I couldn't be that far away from her." As if the fear and stress of the day had finally caught up with her, Ellie's posture crumbled, and she began to cry with her head in her hands.

Walking quickly to her friend's side, Kacie sat down and put her arm around Ellie's shoulders without saying a word.

"I have never been so scared in my whole life. I thought we were going to die out there. There was a moment when I thought Laura was already dead." The last words caught in her throat and brought on a fresh wave of tears.

Kacie rubbed Ellie's back and tried to comfort her. "It's okay. She's okay. I spoke with Emma, and she said Laura's injuries aren't serious. She just needs to be here overnight for observation. You're both going to be just fine."

"We might be fine, but what about Jack?"

This time, Kacie had no words of comfort to offer.

# CHAPTER 23

## *Driving in Circles*

After driving down the freeway for almost two hours, Sarah felt confident enough to pull over at a gas station to use the restroom and pick up some coffee. She looked over her seat to make sure Jett was still sleeping.

Getting him into the car had been much easier than she had expected. As soon as she had mentioned the names of each member of Robert's family, Jett's body had gone completely limp, and the fight had left him. Sarah had loosened the zip ties around his feet and helped him to stand up, but she had kept her taser at the ready just in case. In the end, though, she didn't have anything to worry about because he followed every order she gave him.

"Let's go," she said as she nodded towards the unfamiliar car parked in Jett's garage. "Isn't technology great?"

He stared at her with a blank expression, waiting for his next set of instructions like an obedient little boy.

"I bought an old used car off the internet two days ago and had the driver deliver it here an hour ago while you were sleeping. I paid him online, and voila, we have our getaway car." Her excitement and joy were in stark contrast to Jack's abject fear and sense of defeat.

"I'm going to shimmy this chair out from behind you

213

and then help you get into the car. I don't want any trouble, got it?" What she didn't tell him was that she was going to inject him again with the same sedative she had used earlier. The look of surprise on his face made her smile as she pushed him into the backseat of the car.

Jack had slept soundly the entire car drive and would probably stay asleep for at least another hour. But by then she'd be at the secluded cabin she had bought, online and sight unseen, with an all-cash offer less than a month earlier.

Pulling into a dingy looking gas station, Sarah parked her car in front of one of the pumps. She slipped her taser and her gun into her pocket for safe keeping and stepped out of the car. The lighting was dim and one of the fluorescent bulbs was flickering on and off. Seeing the signs for the restrooms, Sarah followed the arrows to the back of the convenience store building. It was even darker behind the building, and Sarah felt no fear.

Looking around, she noticed a couple of men sitting on the curb next to a dumpster. The flame of a lighter came to life followed by the haze of smoke. The men looked harmless enough, even though the neighborhood she was in didn't look all that safe, but it didn't bother her. She'd just finish her business, grab her coffee, and drive on to her new life.

∞∞∞∞∞

"So, you're really going to retire, huh?"

"Yup. Time to turn in my badge."

"It's not going to be the same without you, man. We've been partners for what? Four years now?"

"Four of the longest years of my life! Why do you think I'm retiring?"

"Ha. Ha." Emilia knew Mitch was joking and that was one of the reasons she was going to miss him so much. A thirty-year police veteran, Mitch was a legend and known to most of his fellow officers as a gentle giant. He used his massive height and size to dominate a situation but was incredibly gentle when it came to dealing with victims. He was always quick with a joke and had an uncanny way of diffusing a situation.

Emilia, on the other hand, had been known as the serious one. Always following the rules to make sure the bad guy didn't get off on any procedural technicalities. About half the size of Mitch's body weight, she was a compact, no-nonsense woman and an accomplished sharpshooter.

"I need to use the facilities. Let's pull into that gas station."

Emilia rolled her eyes. "It's a good thing you're retiring. No one else would put up with your declining bladder health."

"That's age discrimination, you know."

"Yeah, yeah, make it quick, will ya?"

Emilia pulled up to the front of the little gas station convenience store and turned off the car. "I'm going to run in and grab some snacks. You want anything?" she called out as Mitch opened his door.

"I'm good. Watching my weight. You know you shouldn't...." Mitch was halfway out of the car when he stopped mid-sentence.

Immediately on alert to his sudden change in demeanor, Emilia asked him what was wrong.

"Check out the car in the rearview. The little grey hybrid with the red racing stripe. Didn't we get a BOLO on it?"

Emilia looked in the rearview mirror, and sure enough,

a car fitting that description was parked at one of the pumps. Typing into the squad car's computer, she looked up the BOLO and read out the license plate number and added, "It says the female driver is a suspect in a kidnapping and is armed and dangerous."

"Doesn't look like anyone is in the car. I'm going to go take a look around. Maybe they decided to ditch the car and get a different one."

While Mitch kept his eyes on the car and stood in front of the building with his back up against the wall, Emilia got out of the driver's side and crouch-walked her way to the front door. Peaking inside the glass door, she saw a bored looking older man sitting behind the register reading a magazine.

"All clear," she said. "Be careful."

"You know it."

Mitch sidestepped to the corner of the building and quickly looked around the side. Seeing no signs of anyone around, he ran to the front of the car with his gun drawn but lowered. The license plate was a match. Looking up towards Emilia, who was now standing with her back up against the corner of the building where Mitch had been just seconds earlier, he nodded his head once signaling to her that it was the car in the BOLO alert.

Crouching down, he made his way to the passenger side. The front seat had a backpack on it but was otherwise empty. The rear window was dirty and hard to see through. He cupped his hand over his eyes and pressed his face up against the glass. He was expecting the car to be empty. Abandoned. Before he could get over his shock of seeing a person lying on the back seat, he heard someone screaming like a banshee. Then he heard a loud pop and felt a sharp, searing pain in his left shoulder.

Falling to the ground, he barely registered the three other gunshots that followed.

∞∞∞

When investigators asked Emilia for details after the shooting, all she could say was, "It all happened so fast. I heard this crazy screaming and then a gunshot. Saw Mitch hit the ground and a woman running towards him. I yelled for her to freeze, and she turned towards me and got off a shot. After that, I didn't wait. I shot her. I killed her."

The security cameras mounted around the gas station captured the whole scene on video, confirming, without a shadow of doubt, the validity of Emilia's story.

# CHAPTER 24

## *Milk and Honey*

Kacie stepped out of Laura's hospital room and rolled her head on her shoulders. She had managed to convince one of the nurses to set up a small cot in the room so that Ellie could stay with Laura and still get some much-needed rest.

"You want me to find someone to drive you home?" Emma asked gently. She wasn't officially on duty tonight, but there was no way anyone could have kept her from Kacie's side.

"No. I need to be here. Have you heard anything from Frank?"

As if on cue, Frank walked off the elevator towards the nurses' station with an unreadable expression on his face.

"What? Have they found Jack? Is he okay?" Kacie demanded, the fear obvious in her voice.

Before answering, Frank wrapped one arm around Emma, knowing his next bit of news would bring on difficult memories for her. He simultaneously reached out his other hand and held one of Kacie's hands gently. "There was a shooting, sweetheart. One police officer was injured, but Jack's fine."

At hearing those last words, Kacie's exhaustion gave way to tears of relief. Emma gave her husband's hand a squeeze before moving out of his embrace to take Kacie into her arms.

"The officer I spoke with said Jack's giving the paramedics a hard time about driving home instead of to the local hospital closer to where he is. Said Jack offered to pay everyone's salary for a month if they'd drive him back to Sycamore Ridge." Frank shook his head and chuckled as if to emphasize the fact that everything was just fine. He pulled a handkerchief out of his pocket and handed it to Kacie. "Take it easy, Kacie. He'll be here in less than an hour. I guess someone took him up on his offer. Turns out, that woman had been driving in circles in some strange attempt at not being caught. She never got more than 40 miles outside Sycamore Ridge."

"Is she in custody?"

"No. No. She had a gun, and apparently, when she saw a cop near the car where she had left Jack, she kind of just lost her mind. Started screaming. Pulled out her gun and got off a couple of shots. She hit one police officer in the arm and fired shots at the other one who had no choice but to return fire. The woman died on the scene."

Taking a moment to digest the information, Kacie asked, "Was Jack hurt?"

"The officer I spoke with said he's pretty banged up, but nothing some ice, a couple Advil and a good night's sleep won't take care of. I think, right now, what's hurting him the most is what happened to Laura and Ellie."

"We should tell them, but first, I need to call Robert and Jana and let them know Jack's okay."

"I imagine they'll be coming?"

"Yeah...they're worried sick. Last I spoke to them, they were trying to get on the first flight out. They should be here sometime tomorrow morning." Kacie looked down at her watch and grimaced. "I guess it would be more accurate to say, sometime later today."

"It's been a long day for you. Why don't I get someone to drive you home?"

"No way. I'm not leaving until Jack gets here."

Frank and Emma had expected no less and stayed with Kacie just long enough to see for themselves that Jack was okay.

∞∞∞∞

When Jack finally stepped out of the elevator almost an hour later, they were all shocked by his appearance. He was wearing a hospital gown on top, what appeared to be swim shorts on the bottom, and he was barefoot. His hair was tousled, and his eyes had dark circles around them. He looked exhausted and frantic all at once.

"Where are they?" He demanded as he walked towards the nurses' station where Frank and Emma were standing, talking quietly to each other.

Before they could answer, Jack spotted Kacie sitting in the adjoining waiting room. He was unprepared to see her and incredibly surprised that she was even there.

"What are you doing here?"

"It's a long story." She walked to him and said gently, "Come on, I'll take you to see Laura and Ellie." As she got closer, he noticed that she, too, looked very tired and as if she'd been crying.

"Why are you crying? Oh no...," fearing the worst, Jack grabbed Kacie's arms and almost screamed in desperation, "Are they okay?"

Frank stepped towards Jack and placed a warning hand firmly on his arm. "Jack, take your hands off of her."

Realizing that he was squeezing Kacie's arms, Jack immediately dropped his hands to his sides. "Can someone please tell me what's going on?"

Frank interjected before Kacie could answer. "Laura and Ellie are okay, Jack. But only because Kacie found them. And you're okay only because of Kacie."

"What? What does Kacie have to do with it?" Jack looked from Frank to Kacie, who avoided meeting his eyes.

"Please, let's not talk about that right now. Let me take you to see Laura and Ellie. They've been so worried about you," Kacie said, her voice soft and gentle.

Acquiescing reluctantly, Jack followed Kacie until she stopped at one of the private hospital room doors.

"You go on inside."

"And where will you go? I need to talk to you. I need to know what happened."

"I'll be right here when you come out. Don't stay in there for too long. They both need their rest."

∞∞∞

When Jack came out a short time later, the frantic look in his eyes had gone. Now, he just looked completely drained. His eyes searched the nurse's station and then the waiting room, where he was relieved to see Kacie waiting for him.

"You waited."

"I told you I would."

"Where's Frank?"

"He took Emma home. She wasn't even on duty tonight, but she stayed the whole time."

He nodded with appreciation. "I need to get home."

"Emma left me the keys to her car. I can drive you."

After thanking the nurses and getting their assurances

that they'd call if anything changed in Laura or Ellie's condition, Kacie and Jack walked towards the elevators together. Neither one of them seemed to know what to say, and an awkward silence fell between them as they made their way to Emma's car and then drove the short distance to Jack's house.

As she pulled into the driveway, Kacie decided not to cut the engine, thinking that maybe Jack wanted to be alone.

She was wrong.

"You're not going to make me go in there by myself, are you?" Jack asked, looking out the window towards the house.

Kacie turned off the car and gently said, "No. I'll come in with you."

They got out of the car together and walked towards the front door before Jack realized he didn't have the keys.

"There were some people here earlier collecting evidence. Maybe they left one of the doors unlocked? I wonder if we're even allowed to go inside."

Jack looked at her blankly. It hadn't occurred to him until she mentioned it that his home, the place where he had felt safest, was now a crime scene. It rattled him to his core, and he had to remind himself that *she* was dead.

"I'm not waiting for permission to enter my own home. Come on, let's go see if one of the other doors is open." As it turned out, no one had remembered to lock the patio doors.

"So much for protecting the crime scene," Jack said as he opened the door and stepped inside. His momentary relief at being able to get inside quickly vanished and was replaced by an intense wave of emotions that he hadn't been prepared for. His home, his beloved home, had been violated by a complete stranger. Rage filled him as he looked around and imagined *her* standing in his space, moving around in his kitchen, saying and doing things that made his blood crawl.

Kacie, too, felt the odd sensation that she was in an unfamiliar place. As she looked around the kitchen, it was difficult to imagine that it was normally a place filled with love and laughter, friends and family. Everything looked exactly the same, and, with the exception of one chair that was missing from the dining table, nothing was out of place. But the knowledge that someone had been in the space with the intention of hurting Jack made her feel like she had never been there before.

"Maybe coming here wasn't such a good idea," she said as she watched the changing expression on Jack's face which seemed to mirror her own thoughts.

Jack shook his head as if trying to physically shake the thought of what had happened out of his mind. "No. No," he repeated with a rueful determination. "This is my home. *My* home," he pointed at his chest as if trying to convince himself of the fact. "And I will not allow what she did to ruin the sanctity of this place."

His voice broke as he said the last words, and Kacie worried he'd have an emotional breakdown after all the stress he had been through.

"Listen, why don't we find you a hotel room for a couple of days? Or at least until Jana and Robert get here?"

Jack took a deep breath and gazed steadily into Kacie's eyes. Her suggestion only served to strengthen his resolve. He was unable, or unwilling, to accept the fact that *that woman* could force him out of his own home. Mastering his emotions, he said, barely above a whisper, "I'm going to go take a shower. Please don't leave. I don't think

I can be alone tonight."

Without waiting for her response, Jack walked away towards his bedroom and left Kacie standing there alone and unsure of what to do. She looked around trying unsuccessfully to keep her imagination at bay. Not knowing the details of what had happened to him only served to make her mind go to the darkest, most frightening places.

And then, suddenly, unexpectedly, her stomach growled. Loudly. Kacie almost laughed aloud at the relative normalcy of something like hunger pulling her thoughts away from the terrifying scenes she had imagined taking place only hours earlier. But the reminder that she hadn't eaten since lunch brought her back to reality. This, she reminded herself, was the kitchen she had sat in many a time. The kitchen in which she had heated her popular cobblers and laughed with her newfound friends. The kitchen in which Jack was at his happiest and most relaxed.

"She's gone." Kacie said out loud. "She can't hurt us anymore." And with those words, she set about to make a snack. Assuming that Jack hadn't eaten in some time either, she decided to warm up some milk and make toast with honey, a comforting treat her mom used to give her when she couldn't sleep.

She was lost in her own thoughts as she spread the honey on the warm toast and didn't notice Jack standing near the kitchen watching her.

"Hey," he said gently.

She turned to see him looking considerably more relaxed and refreshed. He was clean shaven and had changed into his pajamas.

"Feel better?"

"You have no idea." He came and stood next to her as

she finished spreading the honey on the toast. "Kacie."

The way he said her name made her stomach turn somersaults. Unsure of what to do, but suddenly and absolutely certain of what was to come, Kacie slowly put down the knife and waited. Jack reached his hand out and tenderly tucked a stray piece of hair behind her ear.

"Look at me."

Taking a deep breath, she turned towards him and tilted her head back so she could look into his eyes. "I know you want to know what happened. But I don't think this is the best time to talk about it," she said.

"I don't want to talk about anything right now. I just want to be with you. But I need to know that you want the same thing."

Not realizing she had been holding her breath, Kacie let it out slowly. She closed her eyes and gave an almost imperceptible nod. It was all he needed to see. Holding her gently in his arms, he bent and kissed her mouth. The fragrance of flowers and wood drifted off her and intoxicated him. And the moment her lips parted, and his tongue ran past her crooked teeth and into her mouth, he lost all self-control. Moaning, he picked her up, and she wrapped her legs tightly around him. He carried her all the way to his bed without ever breaking the connection between their mouths.

They never got around to drinking the milk or eating the toast with honey.

∞∞∞

A persistent, distant buzzing awoke Kacie. Disoriented, it took her a moment to realize where she was, and she blushed deeply remembering what had happened. Turning her head, she saw Jack lying on his stomach, fast asleep. He had reluctantly taken a prescription pain medication before going to sleep and he was still under its effects. His bare back with its smooth skin and taut muscles was like an invitation to Kacie to run her hands over his body. But she knew he needed to rest.

The buzzing started up again, and Kacie got out of bed as quietly as possible. Rifling through her clothes which were scattered all over the floor, she found her pants and dug her phone out of the back pocket. Her screen flashed on. It was just after eight o'clock, and she already had over a dozen missed calls and multiple text messages.

She answered the messages from her parents first, letting them know she had gotten home safely after dropping Jack off and apologizing for not letting them know sooner. It was a white lie, but she knew it would be better to tell them about what had happened in person.

There was also a message from Frank, which she answered with the same story.

The last text message was from Robert, letting her know he and Jana had landed and would be in Sycamore Ridge by eight thirty at the latest. It took her foggy brain a moment to process the fact that Jack's older brother and sister would be there any minute. She had no idea how Jack felt about them knowing what had happened between them, and it certainly wasn't her place to tell them.

Kacie hastily put on her clothes and ran her fingers through her hair. Then, she ran upstairs and grabbed a pillow and blanket from one of the upstairs bedrooms. She hurriedly threw them onto the sofa in the family room to make it appear as if she had slept on the couch the whole night. The story was thin, but Jana and Robert had no reason to suspect anything. After all, she and Jack had never been more than friends as far as they were concerned.

∞∞∞

"Do you think she realized her t-shirt was on backwards?" Jana asked Robert. The stress and worry of the previous night had almost fully dissipated once they had learned from Kacie that Jack, Ellie, and Laura were all okay. And the run-in with Kacie in the morning had eased the tension even further. A slow grin spread across Jana's face as she remembered Kacie's mad scramble to exit stage left as soon as they had arrived.

"I just don't get why she would feel the need to lie to us. Why the silly story about sleeping on the sofa so Jack wouldn't be alone in the house?"

"Seriously, Robert? After all this time, you don't know her any better than that?"

"What do you mean?"

"I'm not at all surprised she tried to cover up what happened. She wouldn't want to be the one to tell us. She would leave it up to Jack to do whatever he wants."

"Speak of the devil," Robert said as Jack came sauntering into the family room, looking surprisingly at ease for a man who had just been the victim of a violent kidnapping attempt.

Giving his siblings a big hug, Jack looked around and asked where Kacie was.

"We're fine, thanks for asking," Jana said with one eyebrow raised. "We flew all night to get here because we were worried sick about you, and that's the first question you have for us?"

For a brief moment, Jack worried that he had upset his sister, but a closer look at her face made him realize she was just teasing him. He gave her one of his megawatt

227

smiles and waited for an answer to his question.

"I guess we know where we stand now." Jana laughed. "For your information, Kacie hightailed it out of here as soon as we walked in the door, which was about three hours ago!"

"That medicine I took must have been stronger than I realized. I'm still feeling pretty groggy." Jack walked into the family room and sat down on the sofa. "What's with the pillow and blanket? Why didn't you just go upstairs and sleep in your rooms?"

"Oh, those weren't for us. They were here when we arrived. You know," Jana added sarcastically, "from when Kacie slept here."

Jack looked at this sister and burst out in laughter. "Of course, that's exactly what she'd do."

"Well, I'm glad to hear you laughing. You sound just like yourself. We were so worried about you last night after Kacie called us. We haven't even gone to see Laura and Ellie yet."

"Do you feel up to telling us what happened? We know bits and pieces from what Kacie and Frank have told us, but we want to hear everything from you."

"Coffee first? And I'm starving. How about I make some eggs while I tell you everything?"

Jack again flashed his signature smile at his brother and sister, and they knew, despite the ordeal he had been through, whatever had happened between him and Kacie had made him happier than he'd ever been.

# CHAPTER 25

## *The Important Question*

As soon as Robert and Jana had arrived at Jack's house, Kacie had practically sprinted out the front door. She had hated lying to them, but it certainly wasn't her place to tell them what had happened between her and Jack. Thinking about him sent her emotions into turmoil again, and Kacie knew the only way she could cope was to shut them down completely. She had done it once before, and she would do it now. Driving Emma's car to her own house without thinking, she ran inside and quickly threw some clothes and toiletries into a bag. The only thought in her mind was getting out of Sycamore Ridge as fast as she could.

She texted Frank and told him only that she was leaving Emma's car in her driveway. He would figure out the rest.

Grabbing her bags, she loaded them and Cooper into her own car and started driving. She kept the radio tuned to a news station and forced herself to concentrate on what was going on around the world. Focusing on what was going on anywhere but inside her heart and mind.

As she pulled into her parents' driveway almost two hours later, she could feel a lump forming in her throat and a stinging in her eyes. Turning off the car, she ran to the front door and rang the doorbell, hoping they were at home.

She managed to maintain her composure just long enough to see the surprised look on her mother's face when she answered the door. At that point, there was no reason to hold it together anymore. Kacie started crying before she even walked through the door.

∞∞∞

Kacie's parents, bewildered by her unexpected arrival and concerned by her uncharacteristic crying, let her get it out of her system without asking any questions. Her mother held her and stroked her hair while her father sat nearby holding her hand. As her wracking sobs finally began to subside, her father handed Kacie a box of tissues.

"Want to tell us what's going on?" he asked gently.

Wiping her tears, Kacie nodded, feeling like she had when she was a little girl and had come running to her parents any time she had gotten hurt.

"I'm not sure where to start."

"It's okay. Take your time."

"I guess I should start with what happened last night."

Kacie felt the weight slowly lifting off her shoulders as she told her parents every detail she could remember about the past twenty-four hours. With the exception of what had happened between her and Jack. In some ways, she was more traumatized by that than by the violence which had preceded it.

Her parents listened patiently in quiet horror as Kacie described the brutality with which the stalker had attacked her new friends, Laura and Ellie. But when she got to the part about running to Jack's place with just Cooper by her side, they became distraught fearing for what could have happened to their daughter.

"I didn't go inside."

"That's not the point! Frank told you to stay put with Laura and Ellie. What were you thinking?"

"Kacie, you could have been hurt or worse!" Tears had started to well up in her mom's eyes, but there was nothing Kacie could do about it. She had to finish telling them what had happened. So that she could finally tell them the real reason she had broken down in tears.

"I couldn't just stay there when I knew he needed help. I had to do whatever I could! That's how you raised me. And it's exactly what both of you would have done."

Sighing in defeat and putting his arm around his wife's shoulder, Kacie's dad nodded for her to keep going. By the time she told them about the shootout with the police, her mother was crying silently while her father shook his head in disbelief.

"All this for a man she had met for only a few minutes? What kind of woman does that?"

"Obviously, she was unstable. But what I can't believe is how someone like that can get their hands on tasers and guns. It's just incredible."

Kacie nodded and took a deep breath. "There's more," she said quietly.

The sudden change in her tone put her parents back on edge. "How can there be more if she was killed by that police officer?"

Taking a deep breath, Kacie continued. "After they brought Jack to the hospital to check on Laura and Ellie, I drove him home. And I spent the night there." Kacie knew she didn't have to explain any further. And just thinking about Jack brought on another fresh wave of tears.

"You know, sweetie, we're not surprised," her mother

said gently. "We've seen this coming for a long time."

"You have?"

"Do you have any idea how much you talk about him?"

"That's only because we spend a lot of time together."

"You spend a lot of time with a lot of people. But we haven't heard you talk about anyone like this before. Not since...." Kacie's father let the rest of his sentence go unspoken.

"Do I really talk about him that much?"

Kacie's mom nodded, "I can't remember the last time I spoke to you when the conversation didn't involve you talking about something the two of you worked on or ate or did together with his friends."

"Honestly, your mom and I were thinking about asking you about it when we came out for our next visit. Even though you talk about him all the time, there's so little we actually know about him."

"Well, apart from the fact that he seems to have a tight knit group of family and friends, enjoys eating almost as much as you do, and is your apprentice." As she said the word apprentice, Kacie's mom did a double quotation gesture with her hands as if she didn't quite believe the designation was appropriate.

Talking about the time she had spent with Jack instead of the events of the night before lightened Kacie's mood just a little. Wiping away her tears and letting her mom's comment slide, Kacie shrugged. "That's pretty much all there is to know about him."

"Really? I can think of a few other things I'd like to know."

Kacie sighed, knowing the direction this conversation was headed and worried about giving her parents an honest answer.

"You've never mentioned anything to us about what he does for a living. I mean, what kind of man has that much free time on his hands? He seems to spend hours a week at your workshop or going out to eat with you or hanging out at the watering hole. And I swear he's spent a small fortune on buying you morning buns every other day. How does he afford that? How does he afford his house? Does he even have a job?"

Her mother's voice, usually soft and gentle, seemed to be rising an octave with every question she asked. Kacie knew she had to tell them the truth. Whatever concern she had for Jack's privacy fell to the wayside in the face of her mother's worry. Besides, Kacie knew for certain that her parents would keep Jack's secret as safe as she had.

"You're not going to believe it," Kacie paused. "I can't believe I'm even saying this. You have to promise me you're not going to tell anyone."

Looking affronted that she'd even asked them, both her parents nodded.

"He's in a band."

"A band?"

"He's the lead singer."

"A singer?"

"A very famous singer."

"He's famous?"

"Why do you keep repeating everything I say?"

Her parents traded slightly amused looks with one another.

"You're falling in love with a singer?" Her father asked, trying to avoid the elephant in the room. "Interesting. Do we know any of his songs?"

Kacie's mom wasn't as subtle. "Wait a second, I don't think that's the important question here," she said. "I think the important question is: has he heard you sing?"

Her mother's attempt at lightening the mood hit its mark, and Kacie finally smiled. "He has."

∞∞∞

The inquisition that followed Kacie's revelation that Jack was Jett Vanders, the lead singer of Mirrors, was nothing short of intense. Her parents grilled her on every single aspect of his life. They, too, had heard the rumors about his wild lifestyle, and it took a lot of convincing for them to reconcile the rock star persona they had heard so much about with the man Kacie had told them so much about.

"And he doesn't drink or do drugs? At all? It's just really hard to believe."

At that moment, Kacie's phone rang, and she felt a momentary sense of relief at being saved by the proverbial bell. Until she saw who the incoming call was from. She briefly considered letting it go straight to voicemail, but she knew she should answer it.

"It's Jack. I'll be right back." With her heart pounding and her stomach in turmoil, Kacie answered the phone as she walked upstairs to her room.

"Hi Jack."

"Hey. You doing okay? I was going to call earlier, but I thought maybe you needed to get some rest."

"I'm okay. How about you? How are you feeling?"

"Sore. But Robert and Jana keep teasing me because I can't stop smiling. When can I see you again? Why don't you come on over, we can all have dinner together." Kacie could hear the happiness in his voice and imagined him smiling. She felt awful about having run away from him, but she hadn't known what else to do.

234

"Jack...I can't...I drove to my parents' house after I left your place this morning."

"You're not in Sycamore Ridge?"

"No, I...," unsure of what to say without hurting his feelings further, she added lamely, "I just needed someone to talk to."

There was an awkward silence as Jack seemed to be processing this unexpected piece of information.

"You could have talked to *me*."

"You know what I mean."

"What? That you needed someone who you could talk to *about* me?"

"Yes. And about everything that happened yesterday."

"And last night."

"Yes. I just needed to be with my parents."

"I understand," Jack said even though he didn't. After the night they had spent together, the only person he wanted to be around was Kacie, and it hurt him that she didn't feel the same. "When will you be back?"

"Maybe in a few days."

"A few days? Kacie, what is going on?"

"It's complicated."

"It's complicated? I think I deserve more of an explanation than that."

"You do. But I'm not ready to give you one right now. The past 24 hours have been really difficult for me. I need to rest and clear my head."

"They've been difficult for you? They haven't exactly been easy for me either."

Kacie didn't respond.

"Is it me? Is it because of what happened last night? I don't think running away from it is going to solve anything. You didn't strike me as the kind of woman who runs away from her problems."

That last comment struck its mark, and Kacie started crying. She had been running away from her problems for years, but now she was trying to face them. She just needed a few more days. She had to stand her ground.

"I need to go, Jack. Please try to understand."

Jack thought he could hear her crying softly, and he felt an unfamiliar hollowness in his stomach. How could he do or say anything to make this incredible woman he was falling in love with cry.

"Are you crying?" He asked in a considerably gentler tone.

"I need to go."

"Wait. Listen to me. I'm going to be here. If you feel like talking to me, I'll be here. And whenever you come back, I'll be here. Waiting for you. Do you understand?"

All the feelings she thought she had slowly gotten under control came rushing out again. Hanging up the phone, Kacie put her head in her hands, and sat on her bed crying softly.

∞∞∞∞

"Everything okay, Jack?" Robert asked as his brother came inside from the back patio. When Jack had stepped outside a few minutes earlier to make a phone call, Robert had assumed he was going to call Kacie. Jack had been relaxed and happy, but now he appeared crestfallen and dejected.

"I don't know. I don't understand what happened. She's not even in Sycamore Ridge right now. I guess when she left here this morning, she decided to drive to her parents' house."

"Kacie?"

Jack nodded and took a seat next to his brother. "I guess I expected her to be as happy about everything as I am."

"Why do you assume she's not happy? Or that that's why she left town?"

"Why else?"

"Gee Jack, I don't know. I'm just guessing here, but I think she went through a pretty rough ordeal last night, too. She was terrified when she found Laura and Ellie. She's the one who had to stay at the hospital worrying about what was happening to you while making sure Laura and Ellie were being cared for. She was the one who had to call me in the middle of the night to let me know what had happened. And, as if all of that wasn't enough, things happened between the two of you."

Jack felt his brother's reproof. "I thought she wanted the same thing."

"Maybe she did. But maybe she got scared of what it all means. Or maybe she just needed some time with her own family. A couple of days to recoup."

Jack laughed, but there was no joy in it. "You want to hear something crazy? I miss her. She's only been gone for a few hours, but I miss her already."

"Little brother, you got it bad."

Jack stretched out on the sofa and put his hands behind his head. "You're telling me."

# CHAPTER 26

## *Lemonade on the Patio*

Frank stepped out of his car and took a deep breath. He needed a moment to collect his thoughts and compose himself. Jack and his family had invited him over to give them an update on what the police investigation had uncovered, and Frank knew he needed to find the right balance between sharing information while not causing any additional stress. Under normal circumstances, he was confident in his ability to do this, but there was nothing even close to resembling "normal" about the circumstances of Jack's kidnapping.

He was about to start down the walkway towards the front door when Robert came around the side of the house and waved. "Frank. I thought I heard your car pull up. We're all sitting out on the patio enjoying the evening. If it's okay with you, can we talk out back?"

"Sure thing. Lead the way."

As they walked towards the backyard, Robert said, "Listen, Frank, I don't mind telling you I'm feeling very overprotective of my brother right now. So, please, whatever you can do to spare him any unnecessary details will be greatly appreciated."

Frank, not one to be set off course, replied, "I need to be up front and honest with him, Robert. You know that.

And, trust me, he will be better off for it."

Robert gave a curt nod and stepped onto the patio where the others were waiting.

Jack stood up and shook Frank's outstretched hand. "I appreciate you coming out here and talking to all of us together."

"Least I can do." While Frank had expected the traumatic experience would take a toll on Jack, he hadn't been expecting Jack to look almost like a different person. The handful of times he had seen him around town or at the watering hole, Jack had looked almost like a movie star. Handsome, healthy, and almost always smiling. Especially when Kacie was around. But today, there were dark circles around his eyes and a drawn expression on his face. He couldn't be sure, but Frank thought there was more to it than just the harrowing events of the previous week.

Frank sat down in the only available seat and took a tall glass of lemonade which a woman he hadn't met before held out to him. "I'm Jack's older sister Jana."

"Pleasure to meet you." Frank looked around at the small group gathered around the table. He hoped Jack knew what a lucky man he was to be surrounded by people who seemed to love him a great deal. "I see you got a lot of support around you, young man. A lot of people who care about you and want what's best for you. That tells me a great deal."

Jack looked down and sighed. "I don't know, Frank. It seems that the only thing caring about me did was put my family in harm's way."

"I want you to listen very closely to what I say." Frank waited patiently until Jack looked up and met his gaze. "This wasn't your fault. There was absolutely nothing you did wrong."

Out of the corner of his eye, Frank noticed Ellie about to object to his statement and cut her off. Turning towards her, he added firmly, "There was absolutely nothing *any* of you did wrong. Once you hear what we've already discovered, you'll understand."

"Before you start telling us about the investigation, how is the officer who was shot? I owe him and his partner my life."

"Good of you to ask, Jack. Mitch is doing well and should make a full recovery."

"We're glad to hear it," Robert added. "If there's anything the family needs, we're here to help."

Frank nodded his appreciation. "Tell me what you know so far about the investigation."

"We know how Kacie found Laura and Ellie and how the events at the gas station unfolded, but not much else," Robert answered for everyone.

"What do you know about this woman, Sarah Smith?"

"Was that her name?" Jack asked quietly, wondering how someone with such an innocuous sounding name could have caused him so much trauma.

"Sounds harmless, right? She was anything but."

"Did the investigator on the case tell you that I had met her once before? Almost a year ago in Dubai?"

"He did. And I can now confirm that she had been stalking you ever since you met."

Ellie and Robert exchanged knowing glances. "We guessed as much. How were you able to confirm it?"

Frank explained how as part of their background check on Sarah, they had come across employment records and contacted her former, and only, employer. "Apparently, he's some hotshot software security expert named Gerard

Wang, and she was his protégé, his star student. A prolific computer hacker who knew all the ins and outs of software development. Seems the two of them had a falling out a few months ago, and he was only too happy to tell us how she operated."

Frank didn't mention the "anonymous" files sent to the lead investigator which proved without a doubt what Sarah had done and had been planning to do. It was one thing to share the facts of the case with the victims, it was entirely another to reveal police procedural information about how the facts were discovered.

"If you'd like, I have a folder that I kept with copies of every letter she sent and detailed records of every phone call she made," Ellie added, wanting desperately to be of some help.

"That would be great, thanks."

"There is one thing I never quite understood, Frank. Maybe you can shed some light on it for us. A few months ago, just a short time before Jack moved to Sycamore Ridge, the letters and phone calls stopped. We thought we were out of the woods and then...this. Do you have any idea why?"

"I think I can make a well-educated guess." Frank flipped through a small notebook he pulled out of his shirt pocket and nodded almost to himself. "Ok, yes, here it is. That seems to coincide with our timeline of when she lost her job. We think that's when she figured out who Robert was."

Jack sat up in his chair. "What does Robert have to do with any of this?"

"We got access to all the files she kept in an online account. I can't get into the details of that, but right around then is when photos of Robert started getting saved in her account. We think that once she figured out who Robert was, she was able to hack into his personal records to find out about the home purchase in Sycamore Ridge."

"That's right! Robert, her letters and phone calls stopped right after the incident in Frankfurt," Ellie added. "We thought they had stopped because she got frightened of being caught. But, in fact, she stopped because she figured out how to get to Jack."

Robert shook his head. "I still don't get it."

"We know the phone call was made from inside the hotel or somewhere close by because we heard the ambulance siren. Think about it, Robert, you were in and out of the front door talking to the police and actively involved in the investigation. Maybe she was watching the whole time and got curious. If she was as good of a hacker as Frank says, then maybe she was able to put all the pieces together."

Frank nodded in agreement. "It makes sense. Fits the timeline. Plus, once she lost her job, she had all the time in the world to come up with her plan."

"But this?" Ellie questioned. "Stalking is one thing. We know a lot of celebs who've had problems with stalkers, but they usually stay in the shadows, preferring to remain anonymous. It's very rare to hear about a stalker taking things to the level that *she* did." Ellie still had trouble saying Sarah's name. "What I don't understand, though, is how she had so much information about our lives in Sycamore Ridge."

Frank paused to take a sip of his lemonade, knowing full well that the things he was about to tell them were a far worse violation of their privacy than anything he had shared so far.

"This is going to be difficult for you to hear, but it's important you know the facts." Taking a deep breath, Frank dove right in. "She rented an apartment less than an hour away from here and pretended for months to be a graduate student."

"She actually moved here?" Jana asked, shocked by how close this woman had come to her brother.

Frank nodded, "That's how she was able to collect so much information about all of you. Some of our traffic cameras picked up her car driving around town a few times."

"Robert," Ellie interrupted, "Remember that blank postcard we got right around Jack's birthday? We were so caught up in trying to figure out how it got to the home address, we completely overlooked the fact that it wasn't postmarked! I wonder if she actually dropped it in the mailbox herself." Ellie shook her head in frustration as more of the pieces began fitting together.

"I wouldn't be surprised," Frank said. "We saw her car a few times as close as the traffic light where Willow meets Main." Frank paused for a moment before continuing. "When the cops searched her apartment, they found some very sophisticated surveillance equipment, including a long-range drone, which they believe she used to surveil the property and your movements."

Ellie looked at Laura. "That's how she knew where we'd be that afternoon."

"That's not all. It seems she also managed to hack into your security system, which is no small feat. We have a computer forensics team digging into that right now. And of course, the security monitoring company has launched their own investigation."

Frank took another sip of his lemonade, thankful for the chance it gave him to collect his thoughts and continued. "We believe that's how she knew the minute you walked into the house. When you disabled your alarm, she got a notification on her phone. She watched you from that end of your property, which is where she had been waiting for you ever since she had attacked Laura and Ellie." Frank pointed out towards the tree line.

Jack shivered thinking about her staring at him while he was unaware. "I didn't think I could feel any worse than I did the night after it happened, but I was wrong. This is so disturbing."

Jana put her hand gently on Jack's shoulder. "Do you want to stop? Take a break?"

"No. I need to hear all of this."

"We all do." Laura, who had been quiet throughout the conversation, added firmly. She had been a victim of Sarah's, too, and she needed to hear everything.

"Once she got inside your house, she was almost in the clear. Her plan was meticulously laid out."

Jack shuddered. "Where was she planning on taking me?"

There was no easy way for Frank to answer this question, so he opted for complete honesty. "I wouldn't believe it if I hadn't seen the evidence with my own eyes, but this woman purchased a cabin a couple of hours away from where you were found. She bought it online with a full cash offer and a fake identity. The cabin was very remote and completely off the grid. The address was pinned on her phone's map. That's the only reason we know about it."

"How remote?" Jack asked, knowing he wasn't going to like the answer but needing to know anyway.

"Let me put it to you this way. If she had managed to get you there, it would have been the worst-case scenario."

A silence fell across the table as everyone absorbed that news.

"Well, let's all just be glad it didn't come to that," Robert said, trying to keep everyone's thoughts from going to that dark place.

"Those cops who found Jack are heroes," Ellie added.

Frank looked around at everyone, feeling a little frustrated. "I think it's only fair to give Kacie some credit, too."

"Absolutely. Without her, who knows what would have happened to Laura and me."

"And Jack. Who knows what would have happened to Jack?" Frank corrected.

Jack, who had been staring off in the direction of the trail, turned his head at the mention of Kacie's name and asked, "What do you mean?"

"She didn't tell you?"

"Tell me what?"

Frank shook his head and mumbled under his breath, "Why am I not surprised?"

"What's going on, Frank?"

"Jack, after Kacie found Laura and Ellie and called me, she ran to your house with Cooper. They hid in the trees over by your garage. She was there when that woman drove away with you in the backseat. She was the one who got photos of the car and license plate. Kacie's the reason we had a BOLO out on that car. The only reason. There is no way the cops would have stopped to check things out if it hadn't been for those photos. You all need to know just how much danger she put herself in to protect Jack."

# CHAPTER 27

## *Let Me Go*

Robert and Jana were deep in conversation when Jack joined them for breakfast the following morning. The abrupt silence as he entered the room would have normally roused his suspicion had he not still been processing all the information Frank had shared with them the day before. The extent of *that woman's* obsession with him had shaken him to his core. But it was the extent of Kacie's involvement in everything and the risks she had taken for him that had really been a shock to his system.

"Are you guys still talking about everything Frank told us?" Without waiting for an answer, Jack continued. "I can't stop thinking about it. I don't think I slept at all last night. I can't stop thinking about what could have happened to Kacie." Opening the refrigerator door, Jack stared inside blankly for a few moments before closing it again. "I can't even think straight."

Turning back towards his family, he finally noticed their grim expressions. "What?" he asked looking from Robert to Jana.

"Jack, sit down. We need to talk to you about something."

Doing as he was told, Jack sat down next to Jana and ran his hands through his already tousled hair. "Sounds serious. I don't know if I can handle any more serious conversations. Can I at least have some coffee first?"

Ignoring his request, Jana reached out, took his hands in hers, and said softly, "We got a call from the hospital today."

"Oh no...is Mitch okay? I thought Frank said he was doing well." Jack feared for the worst but was completely unprepared for what Jana said next.

"He's fine, Jackie. They'll be releasing him in the next day or two. That's not the hospital I'm talking about." Jana paused and looked at Robert for reassurance. His almost imperceptible nod confirmed that she should continue.

Taking a deep breath, Jana added meaningfully, "I'm talking about your hospital, Jack. The *family* contacted them. They'd like to meet you."

Although he hadn't been expecting this, it had been something he had wanted for a long time. He knew his answer with absolute certainty and replied without hesitation, "Tell them I'll do it."

Jana had known this would be his answer. And despite the fact that she knew in her heart that it was the right thing to do, she couldn't help but worry. Her baby brother had already been through so much emotional and physical trauma. "Jackie, are you sure? This is a very big deal. You've already been through so much in the past few days."

"It doesn't matter. You know I need to do this. And it has to be on their terms. Not mine. When do they want to meet?"

Robert looked steadily at his brother with a mixture of pride and concern. He, too, was both unsurprised by Jack's response and worried about the toll this would have on him. "The day after tomorrow."

"Fine. Tell Lindsay to arrange it."

∞∞∞

"I don't think Jack realizes how lucky he was."

"How do you mean?" Kacie stretched out on the family room sofa at her parents' house, put her legs up on the ottoman, and cradled her cell phone against her shoulder while flipping through the latest tabloid magazine. Thankfully, none of the press had picked up the story about what had happened to Jack. The police department had kept a very tight seal on what information was released, and apart from the fact that there had been an officer involved shooting, there was very little mention of Jack. What happened to Ellie and Laura hadn't even made it into the local papers.

"Kacie, that woman was certifiable."

"Did you find out more about her?"

"Are you still at your parents' house?" Frank asked, evading her question.

"Yeah."

"When are you coming back? You can't hide forever, you know."

"I'm not hiding. I'm just spending some time with my parents."

Frank was silent, not wanting to overstep by reminding her of her responsibilities in Sycamore Ridge. "Fair enough. What are your plans?"

"I have something I need to take care of tomorrow, and then I'll drive back to Sycamore Ridge this weekend. How is Emma?"

"She's good. She misses you. We *all* miss you."

Kacie thought she heard a particular emphasis in the way he said "all," but she couldn't worry about that right

now. She needed to focus on the meetings she had scheduled for tomorrow. Meetings that were long overdue.

∞∞∞

Hanging up the phone, Kacie went upstairs to say
goodnight to her parents.

"You doing okay, sweetie?" her mom asked with a ten-
derness that almost brought Kacie to tears.

"I think so. I need to do this. I can't keep pretending
that it didn't happen."

"You haven't been pretending. You've been coping.
There's a big difference." Kacie's mom held out her hand
and Kacie took it gratefully, sitting down on the edge of
her parents' bed.

"Maybe it's time to stop coping and start living." Kacie's
dad, who had put his nighttime reading aside when she
came in, added gently.

A tear slowly escaped Kacie's eyes, and she nodded.
"You're right. And that's why I finally agreed to do this."

"We'll be right there with you. It's going to be emotional, but we'll get through it. *You* will get through it."

Kacie smiled at her mother. She was the best cheer-
leader a girl could ask for. "There's something else I
wanted to tell you. I'm going to go back to Sycamore Ridge
in a couple of days. There are things I need to take care of."

"Things *and people*," reminded her mother, not at all
surprised by Kacie's announcement.

∞∞∞

Kacie lay in her bed accepting that sleep wouldn't
come easily tonight, as it hadn't in days. Snuggling down
deep in her favorite blanket, she thought back to how
much had changed in her life in the past few weeks

and wondered for the hundredth time, if Jack hadn't been attacked, would they have ended up spending the night together. Or would they have continued on as "just friends"? Would either one of them have made that first move?

Thinking about that first kiss and the tender way he had looked at her brought the sting of fresh tears to her eyes. She pictured herself standing in his kitchen with her arms, and then her legs, wrapped tightly around him. And then, unbidden, her thoughts wandered to how he had picked her up and carried her to his room. How he had touched her and the things they had done, and the sting of tears was slowly replaced by a warmth which flowed through her whole body. Jack had been the perfect mixture of gentle and rough, confident and needy. And his body. His body was absolute perfection with smooth skin stretched over taut muscles. Even the scar she discovered on the lower left side of his abdomen was sexy. Thinking about that scar, which she had never noticed before, made her think about his tattoo. And the thought of that tattoo and where it led brought another gush of heat. Kacie wanted nothing more than to be with him again.

Shaking her head to clear her mind, Kacie forced herself to focus. She needed to get her own feelings figured out before she involved someone else in them. Was she ready to open her heart up to someone? Was she ready to admit that she had been falling in love with Jack long before they had slept together? Was she ready to admit that falling in love with someone new meant that she was ready to let go of her past? To let go of Robert Patrick?

It had been more than six years since the first and only man she had ever loved in her life had been killed. She could remember it all like it had happened yesterday.

∞∞∞

"Hey babe."

"Hi, are you on your way home?"

"Yup, I should be there in another ten minutes."

"Any ideas on what to have for dinner?"

"Want to grill something? Eat out on the back patio, enjoy a glass of wine?"

"Mmmm, that sounds perfect."

"Great, I'll see you in a few. I love you, Katherine Claire."

"I love you, Robert Patrick."

Kacie had hung up the phone, not knowing then that it would be the last time she would ever hear his voice. It had taken about twenty minutes before she had started to worry. When he hadn't answered her repeated phone calls, she had started to get frantic. And when the doorbell had rung half an hour later, she had answered it with a sense of dread that her life was about to change forever.

∞∞∞

Kacie had spent almost a year staying with her parents after Robert's death, trying to pick up the pieces of a life she had never imagined. A life without her best friend. A life of shattered dreams.

But as time inevitably passed, Kacie had slowly begun to put one foot in front of the other with the support of her family and friends. Under her parents' gentle encouragement, she had gradually rebuilt her life. A life she was content with and which she was proud of. As the years passed, she opened her workshop and settled into a new home of her own. Her parents cheered for her every success and were thrilled when she had decided to run for mayor of Sycamore Ridge on a whim.

By all accounts, Kacie's career was beginning to thrive. But there was one obvious thing missing from her life. And despite wanting to see their daughter as happy and fulfilled as she had been with Robert, her parents had held off on suggesting she begin dating again. They knew that the decision to open her life up to someone had to come from within. And eventually, it did come. Kacie had started dating, but as everyone who knew her liked to tease, she had a strict three-date limit.

It wasn't until Kacie had met Jack, who she had *never* gone on a date with, that her parents had noticed a subtle change in her. A change they had hoped would bring her happiness.

Kacie finally drifted off to sleep, thinking in turns about Jack and Robert. But always, her thoughts returned to Robert. Her Robert. Her sweet, sexy, loving, loveable husband who was taken from her too soon. What would he have wanted for her?

∞∞∞∞

"Hi, are you on your way home?"

"Yup, I should be there in another ten minutes."

"Any ideas on what to have for dinner?"

"Want to grill something? Eat out on the back patio, enjoy a glass of wine?"

"Mmmm, that sounds perfect."

"Great, I'll see you in a few. I love you, Katherine Claire. You can let me go now. It's okay."

Kacie awoke with a start. Her t-shirt was drenched in sweat, and it took a moment for her to realize she had been dreaming. It had been the same dream she had had a million times before, but it had never ended like this. She could still hear Robert's voice, as if he had been lying right next to her.

"You can let me go now. It's okay."

Kacie sat up in bed, fighting back the uncontrollable emotions that were churning inside of her. Instinctively, desperately seeking comfort, she turned towards her nightstand where she kept a small pouch. A pouch she took with her wherever she went and that was never far from her reach. Tugging on the drawstrings, she opened it and emptied the contents into the palm of her hand. As she lovingly grasped the two objects, her breathing slowly began to steady.

Opening her hand, Kacie stifled a sob and looked down at what she was holding: her simple, gold wedding band and a small chunk of pink quartz in the shape of a heart which Robert had given her the day he had proposed. Tears began to flow steadily down her face.

"You can let me go now. It's okay."

Kacie knew it was finally time to do what she had begun to do years before. It was time to put one foot in front of the other.

Picking up the quartz heart, Kacie kissed it lightly and placed it back inside the pouch. Then she looked down at the wedding band waiting patiently in the palm of her hand. Choking back a sob, she lifted it to her lips.

"I love you, Robert Patrick."

"I love you, Katherine Claire. You can let me go now. It's okay."

Kacie placed the wedding band inside the pouch and closed it. Taking a deep breath, she put the pouch inside her nightstand drawer, and got back into bed. She let herself cry herself to sleep one last time for the man she had loved so much.

# CHAPTER 28

## *The Recipient*

Jack stood looking out the spotless windows of the newly built, modern hospital wing. The sun was shining, and the parking lot below was a bustle of activity as cars came and went, some dropping off patients and visitors and some picking them up. So much had changed since his last visit here, and yet, the movements of people flowing in and out remained the same. He wondered which car belonged to the family he was here to meet.

The exhaustion he felt from everything that had happened in the past few days battled against his anticipation at the upcoming meeting. He wanted desperately to be able to crawl back into bed and rest, but in equal parts, he wanted to make his best impression on this family. Thankfully, the soft sounds of conversation between Jana and Robert, who were seated on a small sofa in the comfortable waiting room to which they had all been escorted, offered him some much-needed solace.

The sounds abruptly stopped as the door opened, and a very perky blonde in dark blue scrubs came bustling in with a clipboard. "Hiii! My name is Ashley, and I'll be going over some do's and don'ts with you before your meeting! Which one of you is Mr. Jack Wilkens?"

Jack, who had turned from the window expectantly at

the sound of her voice, stepped forward. "I am."

Ashley looked at him and began to smile, but then did a double take and the smile quickly fell from her face. She stood dumbly staring at him with her mouth slightly agape. Robert, who had seen that look before many times, was immediately on guard. Clearing his throat rather loudly, he stood up quickly and walked towards Ashley. Placing himself between her and Jack to draw her attention, he introduced himself in a tone that commanded her notice. "I'm Jack's brother Robert, and this is his sister Jana."

"Oh, excuse me," Ashley said apologetically, forcing herself to look away from Jack for a brief moment, and then immediately turning back to look at him. Composing herself, she added, "I didn't mean to stare. It's just that, I'm sure you get this a lot, but you look just like the lead singer of Mirrors."

Neither Jack nor his siblings were surprised to hear her comparison. In the days since the attack, Jack had stopped taking care of himself, walking around the house unshaven and unkempt, refusing to eat properly despite everyone's efforts. And although he had made a valiant effort to look presentable today, there was no hiding the dark circles under his eyes and his weight loss. He looked very much like the man who had disappeared from the spotlight only a few months earlier.

But it wasn't just the physical violence that had been inflicted on him that was eating away at Jack. It was the excruciating guilt he felt about everything those closest to him had had to endure simply because they cared for him. He could only imagine the fear and helplessness Ellie must have felt when she thought Laura was dead. And each time he saw the scar and bruising on Laura's face, he felt a hollowness in his stomach that made him want to cry. Then there was Jana and Robert who had both once again dropped everything and come running to be by his side. Jack knew none of them would ever want him to feel guilty about everything that had happened, but he felt it all the same.

He felt that same intense sting of guilt each time he thought about Kacie and how much she had endangered her own safety to help him. She had put herself in harm's way by running to the house on her own that night, and she had taken a tremendous risk to get the photos of the driver and license plate. Without her, Jack knew his fate would have been sealed.

And then he had repaid everything she had done for him by sleeping with her. One small part of his mind kept trying to remind him that he had asked her if that was what she had wanted, and she had said yes. But the rest of him wondered if maybe she had been seeking out comfort from the trauma, she, too, had faced. Or worse, just trying to offer him comfort.

All he wanted at that moment was to talk to her. To be with her and tell her how he felt. He wanted desperately to hold her in his arms and hear her laughter.

But for now, he had to get through this meeting, and Ashley was staring at him expectantly.

"Yeah, I get that a lot. You were saying?"

"Right, let's see. Okay, here's how things will proceed. After I go over everything with you, I'm going to leave here to go get the family. It may take some time, so you'll have to be patient. Right now, they're with another family. As you can imagine, all of these meetings tend to be very emotional for everyone involved."

Ashley pulled a sheet of paper out of the folder she was

carrying and handed it to Jack. "All the information you need to know is written there, but I'll highlight the important items."

Jack tried to focus as Ashley ran through her list, but he couldn't stop thinking about Kacie.

"Do you have any questions?"

Noticing the distracted look on Jack's face, Robert interjected, "What are the names of the family members we'll be meeting?"

"I would love to tell you, but unfortunately, we're not allowed to. A few years ago, a family decided to back out of a meeting at the last minute, but we had already shared their names. It all just turned into a big mess. Now, we wait until you're all in the room together and then we do the introductions. In the meantime, is there anything I can get you?"

"No, thank you," Jana replied.

"Please don't leave the room unless you need to use the restrooms." And with that, she took one more sideways glance at Jack, smiled, and practically bounced out of the room.

∞∞∞∞

"What's taking so long?" Jack asked nervously, pacing between the door and the window. Pausing to look outside, he wondered again which car belonged to the family he was here to meet.

"Ashley said it could be a while."

"What if they change their minds?"

"Take it easy, Jackie. They're already here. It's just a matter of time now. It's like Ashley said, these are emotional meetings. They take time."

"I wonder what they're like." Jack asked pacing back to-

257

wards the door again.

"We'll know soon enough. Will you please stop pacing and come sit down?"

Jack turned towards his sister, who was gently patting the spot on the sofa next to her when he heard the door open. Ashley, whose tone was considerably more subdued than it had been earlier announced, "I'd like to introduce you to Katherine Claire Montgomery and her parents Gene and Maria."

As Ashley stepped aside to let the family in, Jana, the first one to see the woman walking through the door, stood up and covered her mouth with her hand. Robert stood next to her with a mixture of confusion and incredulity on his face. Wondering at their unexpected reactions, Jack turned towards the door.

Ashley, intent on following her introduction script word for word as she'd been trained, did not notice anything awry, and continued, "This is Jack Wilkens, the recipient of your late husband's kidney, his brother Robert, and his sister Jana."

Jack stood rooted to the spot with his eyes fixed on the woman standing in the doorway. He couldn't believe it. For a moment, time seemed to stand still as each person processed the revelation. No one moved until Ashley started shuffling through her papers in confusion, wondering if she had made a catastrophic mistake. Under normal circumstances, these introductions almost always ended with tears and an emotional reunion. She had never seen a donor family and a recipient family behave in this manner. Unsure of what to do, she continued flipping through the pages on her clipboard as if they might hold the answer.

Thankfully, someone in the room managed to recover

and saved Ashley from having to call a supervisor.

"Katherine Claire? Montgomery? I don't understand," Robert said softly.

Jack, grateful for his brother's presence and unable to take his eyes off the woman standing in front of him, waited for an answer. His heart was pounding so loudly that he barely heard the almost whispered response.

"K and C are my initials," Kacie managed. "Kacie is just a nickname," swallowing back a sob, she continued, unable to take her eyes off Jack's.

Kacie couldn't believe she was staring into the eyes of a man who had a piece of her late husband inside of him. Keeping him alive. The revelation was almost more than she could bear. So much had already happened. The past few days had rocked her once stable, predictable life to its core. The idyllic bubble she had helped to create in Sycamore Ridge had been marred by violence. The past she had finally managed to be at peace with had resurfaced, and all her feelings of sorrow over the loss of her husband had come roaring back.

"You were married?" Jack asked gently, struggling with his own emotions, which threatened to overwhelm him as he came to grips with the fact that Kacie's heartbreak had given him life.

Kacie nodded almost imperceptibly. "Montgomery is my married name. I never changed my name back after Robert was killed." The sob she had managed to suppress finally broke free, and Kacie was no longer able to control her emotions. Tears began flowing freely out of her eyes, already red and puffy from crying during her meetings with the other recipient families.

Jack wanted desperately to reach out to her. To pull her into his arms and wipe the tears from her eyes. But he was rooted to the spot, unsure of how she would feel about him now. The only thing he was certain of was that he was in love with her, that he loved her. He would never do anything to hurt her, and if she let him, he would spend his lifetime taking care of her and doing everything in his power to make her happy.

"This is why you can't drink. Because you have Robert Patrick's kidney," Kacie whispered, more a statement than a question. It was the one answer she hadn't been able to find in the tabloids.

"Oh, Kacie, I'm so sorry for your loss," Jack whispered gently. "I'm so very sorry."

Kacie looked up into Jack's eyes and saw the love he felt for her clearly reflected in them. And slowly, slowly, things began to make sense again. She had been falling in love with Jack from the day they first met. And maybe, just maybe, Robert Patrick had played a hand in it. A piece of the man she had loved was now inside of the man who she had been falling in love with for a very long time.

Sobbing, she threw herself into Jack's waiting arms and whispered in his ear, "He brought you here. He brought you to me."

# EPILOGUE

"I love you, Robert Patrick."

Kacie leaned over and kissed the little bundle on his forehead and quietly left the room. Although she knew he could sleep through just about anything, she tiptoed out of the room out of a habit she had developed when Layla, who, unlike her brother, was a very light sleeper even as a baby.

Reaching the bottom of the stairs, Kacie could hear Jack and Layla in the pool. She walked to the patio doors to join them for an afternoon swim and overheard them deep in conversation.

Jack was standing in the water in front of Layla, who was sitting on the edge of the pool chatting away in her sweet childish voice.

"Mommy taught me one of your songs, daddy."

"Oh really?" Jack asked dubiously. He knew he had to word his next question carefully. "How exactly did she teach you? Did she sing it for you?"

Layla giggled. "No way. Mommy is a terrible singer."

Jack had to stifle his laughter. "She's not that bad."

"Yes, she is. And she knows it. That's why she let me listen to it over and over on her phone. So I could learn it. I know the whole song now. Do you want to hear it?"

Taking a deep breath, Jack prepared himself to respond in an encouraging way regardless of how his sweet little girl sang. Saying a silent prayer that Layla sang nothing like her mother, he nodded. "I would love to hear it."

In a clear, beautiful, strong voice, his first born sang his biggest hit song.

"We've got this one liiiiiiffffe, and we must choose to be gratefullllll. Alllllwayyyys grrrraaaaatefulllll."

It was more than music to his ears. It was music to his soul. He felt intense pride mixed with a generous helping of relief that Layla had inherited his musicality. Beaming from ear to ear, he gently hummed along with her until the end.

"That was beautiful, Layla. You're my little rockstar."

And that's when he noticed his wife standing on the patio with her arms crossed and a slightly irritated expression on her face. "Try not to look so relieved."

Knowing full well that Kacie wasn't in the slightest bit angry, he smiled and teased her. "I'm not relieved, love. I'm overjoyed."

# ABOUT THE AUTHOR

## Shail Rajan

 Shail Rajan is the author of women's fiction and romantic suspense. Readers have described her books as feel-good reads with characters you'd want as friends and food you'd like to eat.

She was born in India, raised in beautiful Upstate NY, and is now soaking up the sun in California. When she's not lost in books, Shail loves spending time with her family, volunteering, cooking nonstop, tackling the occassional DIY project, and obsessing over her vegetable garden.

Shail loves connecting with her readers on social media. You can find her just about anywhere:
IG, Facebook and TikTok: @shailrajanauthor
Website: www.shailrajan.com

# BOOKS BY THIS AUTHOR

## The Summer Breeze: Bed & Breakfast

Will leaving behind big city success for small town living bring her happiness or heartache?

Callie Williams has finally traded in her high stress life in New York City for small town living. Taking on a a daunting renovation while navigating the complexities of small-town life, Callie forges lifelong friendships, eats more than her fair share of delicious food, and tries not to meddle in the lives of her guests. The only thing hindering her newfound happiness is the attraction she feels for Nick, a rough-around-the-edges construction worker who is determined to get under Callie's skin.

A late-night delivery will tear them apart, but a quintessential nor'easter snowstorm might just force them back together....

# LET'S BE SOCIAL

Instagram

Facebook

TikTok

To receive special offers, bonus content, and info on new releases, visit my website:

www.shailrajan.com

*Thank you for buying this book.*


*To receive special offers and giveaways,*
*bonus content, and info on new releases,*
*sign up for my newsletter.*


SIGN UP

Made in United States
Orlando, FL
27 April 2022

17234932R00164